OTHER TITLES IN THE SAS OPERATION SERIES

Behind Iraqi Lines
Mission to Argentina
Sniper Fire in Belfast
Desert Raiders
Embassy Siege
Guerrillas in the Jungle
Secret War in Arabia
Colombian Cocaine War
Invisible Enemy in Kazakhstan
Heroes of the South Atlantic
Counter-insurgency in Aden
Gambian Bluff
Bosnian Inferno
Night Fighters in France
Death on Gibraltar
Into Vietnam
For King and Country
Kashmir Rescue
Guatemala – Journey into Evil
Headhunters of Borneo
Kidnap the Emperor!
War on the Streets
Bandit Country
Days of the Dead

SAS
OPERATION

Samarkand Hijack

DAVID MONNERY

HARPER

This novel is entirely a work of fiction.
The names, characters and incidents portrayed in it are
the work of the author's imagination. Any resemblance to
actual persons, living or dead, events or localities is
entirely coincidental.

Harper
An imprint of HarperCollins*Publishers*
1 London Bridge Street,
London SE1 9GF
www.harpercollins.co.uk

This paperback edition 2016
1

First published by 22 Books/Bloomsbury Publishing plc 1995

Copyright © Bloomsbury Publishing plc 1995

David Monnery asserts the moral right to
be identified as the author of this work

A catalogue record for this book
is available from the British Library

ISBN: 978 0 00 815533 9

Set in Sabon by Born Group using Atomik ePublisher from Easypress

Printed and bound in Great Britain

MIX
Paper from
responsible sources
FSC

Prologue

Bradford, England, 14 March 1979
It was a Wednesday evening, and Martin could hear the *Coronation Street* theme music through the wall. His mother was in the back room ready to watch, but he had not been allowed to join her, allegedly because he had homework to finish. The real reason, though, was that there was a sex scandal going on; one of the characters was sleeping with another's wife, or something like that. His mother didn't like any of her children watching such things, and certainly not Martin, who at twelve was the youngest of the three.

He continued drawing the blue border around the coastline of England with the felt-tip pen. He liked drawing maps, and he was good at it, both as a copyist and from memory. England, though, was always something of a challenge: it was so easy to make the fat peninsulas too thin and vice versa.

The coastline was finished, and he stopped for a moment. It was dark outside now, so he walked over to draw the curtains across the front windows. The sound of raucous laughter floated down the street; it was probably the youths with the motor bikes who habitually gathered outside the fish and chip shop. Thinking about the latter made Martin feel hungry, even though he'd only had supper an hour or so earlier. His father, brother and sister would be getting chips on their way home from the game, like they always did, but by the time they came through the front door the only thing left would be the smell on their hands.

It was no fun being the youngest. Still, next season he would be able to go with them to the evening games. His father had promised.

Martin stood by the table for a moment, wondering whether to ask his mother again whether he could watch TV with her. But she would only say no, and anyway he didn't really want to – it was not being allowed that was so annoying.

He sat back down with his map, and started putting in red dots where all the First Division teams played. He had just put in the one for Norwich when there was a knock on the front door.

He hesitated in the doorway to the hall, but there was no sign of his mother coming out. It was probably only one of those political canvassers in any case, and Martin enjoyed telling them what he had once heard his father say: 'A secret ballot should be just that!'

He walked towards the door, noticing the shadow through the leaded glass, and pulled it open.

Almost immediately a foot pushed it back, and Martin himself was propelled backwards into the hall. He had a momentary glimpse of a helmeted figure silhouetted against the starry sky, before something flew over his head and exploded into flames in the hall behind him.

It all happened so fast. 'Burn, you Paki bastards!' The words seemed to echo down the street as the attacker scrambled back down the path and disappeared into the darkness. Martin turned to find a sheet of flame where his mother's wall hangings from home had been, and fire already spreading up the carpeted stairway. Then a sudden draught fanned the flames and he heard her scream.

He started forward, but the heat from the flames threw him back, the smell of singed hair in his nostrils. His mind told him his mother could get out of the window into the back garden, while his heart told him she needed him. But now the flames were forcing him back towards the front door, and he knew that to try to run through them would be suicide.

He backed into the front garden, and then spun round and raced next door, where he banged the polished iron knocker like a madman.

'What the blazes . . .?' Mr Castle said as he opened the door.

'There's a fire!' Martin screamed at him. 'Our house is on fire! Mum's inside!'

Mr Castle advanced two steps down the path and saw the light from the flames dancing in the porch. 'I'll ring 999,' he said, and disappeared back inside, leaving Martin in a paroxysm of indecision.

Then inspiration struck. He ran back out to the street, past their house and the other neighbour's, to where the passage ran through to the allotments. At the end of his own garden he clambered over the rickety fence and ran to the back of the burning house. The kitchen door was closed, and so was the back room window. Inside there was nothing but fire.

In later years, the rest of the evening would come to seem like a blurred sequence of images – the sirens of the fire engines, the people gathered in the street, his father, brother and sister coming home, the policemen with their bored expressions and stupid questions. But that moment alone in the darkened garden would never lose its sharpness, with the windows full of flames and the dreadful truth they told.

1

They were standing on a dry, broken slope. There were no fragments of masonry to be seen, no shards of tile or pottery, but the configuration of the land, the angular ditches and the flattened hillocks all suggested human occupation.

'This was the southern end of the original Afrasiab,' Nasruddin Salih told the tour party, 'which became Maracanda and eventually Samarkand. It was razed to the ground in 1220 by the army of Genghis Khan. Only a quarter of the population, about a hundred thousand people, survived. It was another one and a half centuries before Tamerlane revived the city and made it the centre of his empire. These buildings here' – Nasruddin indicated the line of domed mausoleums which gracefully climbed the desolate hillside – 'were probably the finest architectural achievement of Tamerlane's time.'

'Bloody incredible,' Mike Copley murmured, holding up his exposure meter.

It was, Jamie Docherty thought. The blue domes rose out of the yellow-brown hill like articles of faith, like offerings to God which the donors knew were too beautiful to be refused.

'"Shah-i-Zinda" means "The Living King",' Nasruddin was explaining. 'This complex was built by Tamerlane to honour

Qutham ibn Abbas, who was a cousin of the Prophet Muhammad, and one of the men most responsible for bringing Islam to this area. He was praying in a shady spot on this hill when a group of Zoroastrians attacked and beheaded him. Qutham finished his prayer' – Nasruddin acknowledged the laughter with a slight smile – 'picked up his head and jumped into a nearby well. He has lived there ever since, ready to defend Islam against its enemies.'

The guide smiled again, but there was something else in his expression, something which Docherty had noticed several times that morning. The British-born Pakistani had been with them since their departure from Heathrow six days before, and for the first few days of the tour had seemed all affability. But over the last twenty-four hours he had seemed increasingly under some sort of strain.

The tour party was moving away, down the path which led to the Shah-i-Zinda's entrance gate. As usual, Charles Ogley was talking to – or rather at – Nasruddin. Probably telling the guide he'd made yet another historical mistake, Docherty thought sourly. The lecturer from Leeds seemed unable to last an hour without correcting someone about something. His lecturer wife Elizabeth was the most frequent recipient of such helpfulness, but seemed to thrive on it, using it to feed some reservoir of bitterness within her soul. They were not an attractive couple, Docherty had decided before the tour's first day had ended. Fortunately they were the only two members of the party for whom he felt any dislike.

He banished the Ogleys from his mind, and focused his attention on the magical panorama laid out before him.

'I think you take photographs with your eyes,' his wife said, taking an arm and breaking into his reverie.

'Aye,' Docherty agreed. 'It saves on film.'

Isabel smiled at the idea, and for the hundredth time felt pleased that they had come on this trip. She was enjoying it enormously herself, particularly since phoning the children and setting her mind at rest the night before. And he was loving it.

They caught up with the rest of the party at the foot of the hill, and waited by the archway which marked the entrance to the complex of buildings while Nasruddin arranged their collective ticket with the man in the booth. Then, their guide in the lead, the party started climbing the thirty-six steps which led up past one double-domed mausoleum towards the entrance gate of another.

'This is called the "Stairway to Heaven",' Nasruddin said. 'Pilgrims count each step, and if they lose count they have to start again at the bottom. Otherwise they won't go to heaven.'

'I wonder if this is where Led Zeppelin got the song title from,' Mike Copley mused out loud.

'Idiot,' his wife Sharon said.

At the top of the stairway they passed through an archway and into the sunken alley which ran along between the mausoleums. Here the restoration work seemed to be only just beginning, and the domes were bare of tiles, the walls patchy, with swathes of mosaic giving way to expanses of underlying buff-coloured brick. At the end of the alley they gathered around the intricately carved elm door of Qutham's shrine, and Nasruddin pointed out where the craftsman had signed his name and written the year, 1405. Inside, the Muslim saint's multi-tiered cenotaph was a riot of floral and geometric design.

Docherty stood staring at it for several minutes, wondering why he always felt so moved by Islamic architecture. He had first fallen in love with the domes and mosaics in Oman, where he had served with the SAS during the latter years of the

6

Dhofar rebellion. A near-fluency in Arabic had been one legacy of that experience, and in succeeding years he had managed to visit Morocco and Egypt. His final mission for the SAS, undertaken in the first weeks of the previous year, had taken him to Bosnia, and the wanton destruction of the country's Islamic heritage had been one of several reasons offered by that war for giving up on the human race altogether.

Not to worry, he thought. After all, Qutham was down there in his well taking care of business.

He looked up to find that, once again, the tour party had left him behind. Docherty smiled to himself and walked back out into the shadowed courtyard, from where he could see the rest of the party strolling away down the sunken alley. Isabel, her black hair shining in the sun above the bright red dress, was talking to Sam Jennings. The silver-haired American didn't walk that gracefully, but at seventy-five his mind was as young as anyone's in the tour party. Both Docherty and Isabel had taken a liking to him and his wife Alice from the first day.

Their small bus was waiting for them outside the entrance. It had six double seats on one side, six single on the other, and a four-person seat at the back. Despite there being only fourteen in the party – fifteen counting Nasruddin – the four Bradford Pakistanis usually sat in a tightly bunched row on the rear seat, as if fearful of being contaminated by their infidel companions. This time though, one of the two boys – Imran, he thought – was sitting with Sarah Holcroft. Or Sarah Jones, to use the name she had adopted for this trip.

Docherty wondered if Imran had recognised her as the British Foreign Minister's daughter. He hadn't himself, though the girl had made no attempt to disguise her appearance, and her picture had been in the papers often enough. Isabel had, and so, if their behaviour was anything to go by, had both the Copleys and the Ogleys.

Brenda Walker, the social worker who usually sat with Sarah, was now sitting directly behind her. Docherty had his suspicions about Brenda, and very much doubted whether she was the social worker she claimed to be. He had come into fairly frequent contact with the intelligence services during his years in the army, and thought he knew an official minder when he saw one. But he hadn't said anything to anyone else, not even Isabel. He might be wrong, and in any case, why spoil the generally good atmosphere that existed within the touring party? He wasn't even sure whether Sarah herself was aware of her room-mate's real identity.

'Enjoying yourself?' Isabel asked, leaning forward from her seat directly behind his, and putting her chin on his shoulder.

'Never better,' he said. 'We seem to go from one wonder of the world to another.'

The driver started the bus, and they were soon driving back through the old city, up Tashkent Street and past the ruined Bibi Khanum mosque and the Registan assemblage of *madrasahs*, or Muslim colleges, both of which they had visited the previous afternoon. It was almost half-past twelve when they reached the cool lobby of the Hotel Samarkand. 'Lunch will be in five minutes,' Nasruddin told them, 'and we shall be leaving for Shakhrisabz at one-thirty.'

While Isabel went up to their room Docherty bought a stamp and postcard from the post office on the ground floor and then took another look at the Afghan carpets in the hotel shop. They weren't quite attractive enough to overcome his lifetime's hatred of having something to carry.

In the largely empty dining-room fourteen places had been set on either side of a single long table. The four Bradford

Pakistanis had already claimed the four seats at one end: as usual they were keeping as separate as civility allowed. The two older men flashed polite smiles at Docherty as he sat down in the middle of the other empty places.

On the first day he had made an effort to talk to them, and discovered that the two older men were brothers, the two younger ones their respective sons. Zahid was the family name, and the elder brother, Ali Zahid, was a priest, a mullah, attached to a mosque in Bradford. The younger brother, Nawaz, was a businessman of unspecified type, which perhaps accounted for the greater proportion of grey in his hair.

Ali's son Imran and Nawaz's son Javid were both about seventeen. Unlike their fathers they wore Western dress and spoke primarily in Yorkshire-accented English, at least with each other and the other members of the party. Both were strikingly good-looking, and the uneasy blend of respect and rebelliousness which characterized their relationship with their fathers reminded Docherty of his childhood in working-class Glasgow, way back in the fifties.

The two academics were the next to arrive, and took opposing seats at the other end of the table from the Zahids, without acknowledging either their or Docherty's presence. The Ogleys had really fallen on hard times, Docherty thought. They had probably expected a party full of fellow academics, or at the very least fellow-members of the middle class. Instead they had found four Pakistanis, a Glaswegian ex-soldier and his Argentinian wife, a builder and his wife, and a bluntly spoken female social worker with a northern accent. Their only class allies turned out to be a cabinet minister's daughter known for her sex and drug escapades, and elderly Americans who, it soon transpired, were veterans of the peace movement. The Ogleys, not surprisingly, had developed a bunker mentality by day two of the Central Asian Tours 'Blue Domes' package holiday.

Isabel came in next, now wearing a white T-shirt and baggy trousers. She was accompanied by Brenda Walker and Sarah Holcroft. The first had changed into a dress for the first time, and her attractively pugnacious face seemed somehow softened by the experience. The second had swept back her blonde hair, and fastened it with an elasticated circle of blue velvet at the nape of her neck. Even next to Isabel she looked lovely, Docherty thought. On grounds of political prejudice he had been more than ready to dislike a Tory cabinet minister's daughter, but instead had found himself grudgingly taking a liking to the girl. And with a father like hers, Docherty supposed, anyone would need a few years of letting off steam.

The two Americans arrived at the same time as the soup. Sam Jennings was a retired doctor from a college town in upstate New York, and his wife Alice had had her hands full for thirty-five years raising their eleven children. The couple now had twenty-six grandchildren, and a continuing hunger for life which Docherty found wonderful. He had met a lot of Americans over the years, but these were definitely the nicest: they seemed to reflect the America of the movies – warm, generous, idealistic – rather than the real thing.

As usual, the Copleys were the last to arrive. Sharon had changed into a green backless dress, but Mike was still wearing the long shorts and baseball hat which made him look like an American in search of a barbecue. With his designer stubble head, goatee beard, stud earrings and permanently attached camera, he had not immediately endeared himself to Docherty, but here too first impressions had proved a worthless guide. The builder might seem like an English yobbo who had strayed abroad by accident, but he had a smile and a kind word for everyone, and of all the party he was the most at ease when it came to talking with the locals, be they wizened women or street urchins. He had a wide-eyed approach to the world which was not that common among men in their late thirties. And he was funny too.

For most of the time his wife seemed content to exist in his shadow. Isabel had talked with her about their respective children, and thought her nice enough, but Sharon Copley, unlike her husband, had rarely volunteered any opinions in Docherty's hearing. The only thing he knew for certain about her was that she had brought three suitcases on the trip, which seemed more than a trifle excessive.

After announcing an hour's break for lunch, Nasruddin Salih had slipped back out of the hotel, turned left outside the doors and walked swiftly up the narrow street towards the roundabout which marked the northern end of Maxim Gorky Boulevard. A couple of hundred metres down the wide avenue, in the twenty-metre-wide strip of park which ran between its two lanes, he reached the bank of four public telephones.

The two at either end were in use, one by a blonde Russian woman in jeans and T-shirt, the other by an Uzbek man in a white shirt and a *tyubeteyka* embroidered skullcap. In the adjoining children's play area two Tajik children were contesting possession of a ball with their volume controls set on maximum.

Nasruddin walked a few more metres past the telephones and sat down on a convenient bench to wait. He was sweating profusely, he realized, and maybe not just from the heat. Still, it was hot, and more than once that morning he had envied Mike Copley his ridiculous shorts.

The Uzbek had finished his call. Nasruddin got up and walked swiftly across to the available phone. The Russian woman was telling someone about an experience the night before, alternating breathless revelations with peals of laughter. These people had no sense of shame, Nasruddin thought.

He dialled the first number.

Talib answered almost instantly. 'Yes?' the Uzbek asked.

'There are no problems,' Nasruddin told him.

'God be praised,' Talib said, and hung up.

Nasruddin heard footsteps behind him, and turned, slower than his nerves wished. It was only the Tajik boy's father, come to collect their ball, which had rolled to within a few feet of the telephones. Nasruddin smiled at him, waited until the man had retrieved the ball, and then turned back to dial the other number. The Russian woman was now facing in his direction, nipples pressing against the tight T-shirt, still absorbed in her conversation.

He dialled and turned away from her. This time the phone rang several times before it was picked up, each ring heightening Nasruddin's nervousness.

'Sayriddin?' he asked, struggling to keep the anger out of his voice.

'*Assalamu alaikam*, Nasruddin . . .'

'Yes, yes. You are ready? You know what to do?' Though if he didn't by this time, then God would surely abandon them . . .

'Of course. I deliver the message this evening, one hour after I hear from Talib. On Thursday morning I check *Voice of the People*. If there is nothing there I try again the next day. When I see it, then I call you at the number you gave me.'

'Good. God be with you.'

'And you, brother.'

Nasruddin hung up, and noticed that the Russian woman had gone. In her place was a young Uzbek, no more than seventeen by the look of him. He was wearing a sharp suit with three pens prominent in the top pocket. It sounded as if he was trying to sell someone a second-hand tractor.

Nasruddin looked at his watch. It was still only ten to one – time to get back to the hotel and have some lunch. But he didn't feel hungry. Nor did he fancy small talk with the members of the party.

He sat down again on the bench, and watched the world go by. The uneasy blend of Asian and European which was Samarkand still felt nothing like home to him, even though one side of his family had roots in the town which went back almost a century. A great-great-grandfather had origi-nally come as a trader, encouraged by the bloody peace the English had imposed on Afghanistan in the late nineteenth century. Nasruddin's side of the family had come to England instead, much later, in the mid 1950s. He himself had been born in Bradford in 1966, heard about his relatives in far-off Samarkand as a young adolescent, and had determined even then to visit them if ever the chance arose.

And here he was.

Two Uzbek women were walking towards him, both clothed head to foot in the Muslim *paranca*, eyes glinting behind the horsehair mesh which covered their faces. There was something so graceful about them, something so beau-tiful. Nasruddin turned his eyes away, and found himself remembering the pictures in *Playboy* which he and the others had studied so intently in the toilets at school. He watched the two women walking away, their bodies swaying in the loose black garments. When English friends had argued with him about such things he had never felt certain in his heart of the rightness of his views. But at this moment he did.

Not that it mattered. He had always been certain that the other way, the Western way, the obsession with sex, could never work. It had brought only grief in its wake – broken families, prostitution, rape, sexual abuse, AIDS . . . the list was endless. Whatever God expected of humanity, it was not that. In the words of one of his favourite songs as a teenager, that was the road to nowhere.

And whatever befell him and the others over the next few days, he had no doubt that they were on the right road.

He made his way slowly back to the hotel, arriving in time to supervise the boarding of the tour bus for the two-hour ride to Shakhrisabz. He watched with amusement as they all claimed the same places they had occupied that morning and the previous afternoon, and idly wondered what would happen to anyone daring enough to claim someone else's.

Now that the dice were cast he felt, somewhat to his surprise and much to his relief, rather less nervous than he had.

Docherty also registered the guide's change of mood, but let it slip from his mind as the views unfolding through the bus window claimed more and more of his attention. They were soon out of Samarkand, driving down a straight, metalled road between cherry orchards. Groups of men were gathered in the shade, often seated on the bed-like platforms called *kravats*.

'Do you think they're waiting for the cherries to ripen?' Docherty asked Isabel.

'I doubt it,' she said. 'The women probably do all the picking.'

'Aye, but someone has to supervise them,' Docherty argued. She pinched the back of his neck.

The orchards soon disappeared, giving way to parched fields of grain. As the road slowly rose towards the mountains they could see the valley of the Zerafshan behind them, a receding strip of vegetation running from east to west in a yellow-brown sea, the domes of Samarkand like blue map pins in the green swathe.

'What do you know about Shakhrisabz?' Isabel asked.

'Not a lot,' Docherty said. 'It was Tamerlane's home town – that's about all.'

'There's the ruins of his palace,' Mike Copley volunteered, open guide book in his lap. 'It says the only thing left is part of the entrance arch, but that that's awesome enough.'

'The son of a bitch didn't do anything by halves,' Sam Jennings commented. 'I was reading in this' – he held up the paperback biography – 'about his war with the Ottoman Turks. Do you want to hear the story?' he asked, with the boyish enthusiasm which seemed to make light of his years.

'Go on, educate us,' Copley told him.

'Well, the Ottoman Turks' leader Bayazid was just about to take Constantinople when a messenger from Tamerlane arrives on horseback. The message, basically, says that Tamerlane is the ruler of the world, and he wants Bayazid to recognize the fact. Bayazid has heard of Tamerlane, but thinks he's just another upstart warlord. His guys, on the other hand, are the military flavour of the month. The whole of Europe's wetting itself in anticipation, so he can hardly believe some desert bandit's going to give him any trouble. He sends back a message telling Tamerlane to go procreate himself.

'A few weeks later the news arrives that Tamerlane's army is halfway across Turkey. Bayazid's cheesed, but realizes he has to take time out to deal with the upstart, and he leads his two hundred thousand crack troops across Anatolia to meet Tamerlane. When the armies are a few miles apart the Turks get themselves in formation and wait. At which point Tamerlane's army hits them from every conceivable side. A

15

few hours later Bayazid is on his way to Samarkand in a cage. And the Turkish conquest of Constantinople gets put back fifty years, which probably saves the rest of Europe from Islam.'

The American smiled in pleasure at his story.

'I think it's a shame the way someone like Tamerlane gets glorified,' his wife said. 'In Samarkand he's becoming the new Lenin – there are statues everywhere. The man turned cities into mountains of skulls, for God's sake. He can't be the only hero the Uzbeks have in their past.'

'He wasn't an Uzbek,' Charles Ogley said, his irritable voice floating back from the front seat. 'None of the Uzbeks' heroes are. Nawaii, Naqshband, Avicenna. The Uzbeks didn't get here until the end of the fifteenth century.'

Docherty, Mike Copley and Sam Jennings exchanged glances.

'So who was here before them, Professor?' Copley asked.

'Mostly other Turkic peoples, some Mongols, probably a few Arabs, even some Chinese. A mixture.'

'Maybe countries should learn to do without heroes,' Sarah Holcroft said, almost defiantly.

'Sounds good to me,' Alice Jennings said.

Ogley's grunt didn't sound like agreement.

There were few signs of vegetation now, and fewer signs of farming. A lone donkey tied to a roadside fence brayed at them as they went past. The mountains rose like a wall in front of the bus.

The next hour offered a ride to remember, as the bus clambered up one side of the mountain range to the six-thousand-foot Tashtakaracha Pass, and then gingerly wound its way down the other. On their left were tantalizing glimpses of higher snow-capped ranges.

'China's on the other side of that lot,' Copley observed.

16

They arrived at Shakhrisabz soon after three-thirty. 'The name means "green city",' Nasruddin told them, and it did seem beautifully luxuriant after the desert and bare mountains. The bus deposited them in a car park, which turned out to occupy only a small part of the site of Tamerlane's intended home away from home, the Ak Saray Palace. It would have been bigger than Hampden Park, Docherty decided.

As Copley's book had said, all that remained of the edifice was a section of wall and archway. The latter, covered in blue, white and gold mosaics, loomed forty metres into the blue sky. Awesome was the word.

The other sights – another blue-domed mosque, a couple of mausoleums, a covered market – all paled in comparison. At around five-thirty, with the light beginning to take on a golden tinge, they stopped for a drink at the Ak Saray café. 'We'll leave for Samarkand in twenty minutes,' Nasruddin said, before disappearing back outside.

The tourists sipped their mint tea and watched the sun sliding down over the western desert horizon. As the jagged-edged tower of Tamerlane's gateway darkened against the yellow sky Docherty felt at peace with the world.

He smiled across the table at Isabel. Twelve years now, he thought, twelve years of the sort of happiness he hadn't expected to find anywhere, let alone behind enemy lines in Argentina during the Falklands War.

It was an incredible story. At the beginning of the war Isabel, an exiled opponent of the Junta living in London, had agreed to return home as a spy, her love of country outweighed by hatred of its political masters. Docherty had been the leader of one of the two SAS patrols dropped on the mainland to monitor take-offs from the Argentinian airfields, and the two of them had ended up escaping together across the Andes into Chile, already lovers and more than halfway to being in love. Since then they'd married and had two children, Ricardo and Marie, who were spending these ten days with Docherty's elder sister in Glasgow.

Isabel had made and mostly abandoned a career in compiling and writing travel guides, while Docherty had stayed on in the SAS until the early winter of 1992. Pulled out of retirement for the Bosnian mission a month later, his second goodbye to the Regiment in January 1993 had been final. Now, eighteen months later, the couple were preparing to move to Chile, where she had the offer of a job.

Chile, of course, was a long way from anywhere, and they had decided to undertake this Central Asian trip while they still could. It hadn't been cheap, but it wasn't that expensive either, considering the distances involved. The collapse of the Soviet Union had presumably opened the way for young entrepreneurs to compete in this market. Men like Nasruddin, Docherty thought, and idly wondered where their tour operator and guide had got to.

Nasruddin had crossed the road to the car park, and walked across to where two cars, a Volga and a rusting Soviet-made Fiat, were parked side by side under a large mulberry tree. There was no one in the cars, but behind them, in the circle of shade offered by the tree, six men were sitting cross-legged in a rough circle. Four of them were dressed modern Uzbek-style in cotton shirts, cotton trousers and embroidered skull-caps, but the other two were wearing the more traditional ankle-length robes and turbans.

As Nasruddin appeared the men's faces jerked guiltily towards him, as if they were a bunch of schoolboys caught playing cards behind the bicycle sheds. Recognition eased the faces somewhat, but the tension in the group was still palpable.

'Everything is going as expected,' Nasruddin told them, squatting down and looking across the circle at Talib Khamidov. His cousin gave him a tight smile in return, which did little to soften the lines of his hawkish face.

'They all came?' Akbar Makhamov asked anxiously, 'the Americans too?' Despite Nasruddin's assurances the others had feared that the two septuagenarians would sit out the side-trip to Shakhrisabz.

'Yes. I told you they would come.'

'God is with us,' Makhamov muttered. The bearded Tajik was the other third of the group's unofficial ruling triumvirate. He came from a rich Samarkand family, and like many such youths in the Muslim world, had not been disowned by his father for demonstrating a youthful excess of religious zeal. His family had not objected to his studying in Iran for several years, and on his return in 1992 Akbar had been given the prodigal son treatment. Over the last year, however, his father's patience had begun wearing a little thin, though nothing like as thin as it would have done had he known the family money was being spent on second-hand AK47s and walkie-talkies for a mass kidnapping.

'Everyone knows their duties?' Nasruddin asked, looking round the circle.

They all did.

'God be with us,' Nasruddin murmured, getting to his feet. He caught Talib's eyes once more, and took strength from the determination that he saw there.

He walked back to the tour bus, and found the driver behind his wheel, smoking a cigarette and reading one of the newly popular 'romantic' graphic novels. Nasruddin was angered by both activities, but managed to restrain himself from sounding it.

'I told you not to smoke in the bus,' he said mildly.

Muran gave him one contemptuous glance, and tossed the cigarette out through his window.

'We'll be picking up two more passengers on the way back,' he told the driver. 'A couple of cousins of mine. Just on the other side of Kitab. I'll tell you when we get there.'

Muran shrugged his agreement.

Nasruddin started back for the café, looking at his watch. It was almost six o'clock. As he approached the tables the Fiat drove out of the car park and turned up the road towards Samarkand, leaving a cloud of dust hanging above the cross-roads.

The group was ready to go, and he shepherded them back across the car park and into the bus, wondering as he did so which of them might make trouble when the time came. The ex-soldier and the builder looked tough enough, but neither seemed the sort to panic and do something stupid. Ogley was too fond of himself to take a risk, and the American was too old. Though neither he nor his wife, Nasruddin both thought and hoped, seemed the type to drop dead with shock.

Muran started up the bus, and Nasruddin sat down in the front folding seat. Once out on the road he sat staring ahead, half listening to the murmur of conversation behind him, trying to keep calm. He could feel a palpitation in his upper arm, and his heart seemed to be beating loud enough for everyone in the bus to hear.

He glanced sideways at the driver. There was a good chance the man would take the hundred American dollars and make himself scarce. But even if Muran went to the authorities, it wouldn't matter much.

Nasruddin took a deep breath. Only ten minutes more, he told himself. It was almost dark now, and the fields to left and right were black against the sky's vestigial light. Ahead of them the bus's headlamps laid a moving carpet of light on the asphalt road. In the wing mirror he had occasional glimpses of the lights of the following car.

They entered the small town of Kitab, and passed families sitting outside their houses enjoying the evening breeze. In the centre a bustling café spilled its light across the road, and the smell of pilaff floated through the bus.

Nasruddin concentrated on the road ahead as they drove out through the northern edge of the town. A hundred metres past the last house he saw the figures waiting by the side of the road.

'Just up here,' he told Muran.

Docherty's head had begun to drop the moment they started the return journey, but the jerk of the bus as it came to a halt woke him up. His eyes opened to see two men climbing aboard, each with a Kalashnikov AK47 cradled in his arms. A pistol had also appeared in Nasruddin's hand.

The three men seemed to get caught up in one another's movements in the confined space at the front of the bus, but this almost farcical confusion was only momentary, and all three guns were squarely pointed in the passengers' direction before anyone had time to react.

A variety of noises emanated from the passengers, ranging from cries of alarm through gasps of surprise to a voice murmuring 'shit', which Docherty recognized as his own.

2

A stunned silence had settled on the tour party.

'Mr and Mrs Ogley,' Nasruddin said politely, 'please move to the empty seats in the back.'

The academics stared at him for a moment, as if unable to take in the instruction. Nasruddin nodded at them, like a teacher trying to encourage a child, and they responded with alacrity, moving back down the aisle of the bus as if their lives depended on it. Elizabeth sat down next to Brenda Walker, while Charles took the single seat across the aisle from her.

Docherty was examining the two men holding the assault rifles. Both were in their late twenties or early thirties, and both, to judge by the slight body movements each kept making, were more than a little nervous. One wore a thin, dark-grey jacket over a white collarless shirt, an Uzbek four-sided cap and black trousers. His hair was of medium length and he was clean-shaven. Dark, sunken eyes peered out from either side of a hooked nose. His companion was dressed in a black shirt and black trousers, and wore nothing on his head. His hair was shorter, his Mongoloid face decorated with a neat beard and moustache.

'I don't suppose I need to tell you all that you have been taken hostage,' Nasruddin begun. Then, as if realizing that he was still talking to them like a tour guide, the voice hardened. 'You will probably remain in captivity for several days. Provided you obey our orders quickly and without question, no harm will come to any of you . . .'

There was something decidedly unreal about being taken hostage in Central Asia by a Pakistani with a Yorkshire accent, Docherty thought.

'We do not wish to harm anyone,' Nasruddin said, 'but we will not hesitate to take any action that is necessary for the success of this operation.' He looked at his captive audience, conscious of the giant step he had taken but somehow unable to take it in. It felt more like a movie than real life, and for a second he wondered if he was dreaming it all.

'Can I ask a question?' Mike Copley asked.

'Yes,' Nasruddin said, unable to think of a good reason for saying no.

'Who are you people, and what do you want?'

'We belong to an organization called The Trumpet of God, and we have certain demands to make of the Uzbekistan government.'

'Which are?'

Nasruddin smiled. 'No more questions,' he said.

'Can we talk to each other?' Mike Copley asked.

The bearded hijacker spoke sharply to Nasruddin – in Tajik, Docherty thought, though he wasn't sure. Their guide smiled and said something reassuring back. Docherty guessed that neither of the new arrivals spoke English.

'You can talk to the people next to you,' Nasruddin announced, deciding that conversation would do no harm, and that enforcing silence might be interpreted as a sign of weakness. 'But no meetings,' he added. He turned to Talib and Akbar, and explained his decision in Uzbek.

'So what shall we talk about?' Isabel asked Docherty in Spanish. She sounded calm enough, but he could hear the edge of tension beneath the matter-of-fact surface.

'Some ground rules,' he said in the same language. The two of them were used to conversing in her mother tongue, and at home often found themselves slipping between Spanish and English without thinking about it.

'OK,' she agreed. 'Number one – you don't try playing the hero. You're retired.'

'Agreed. Number two – don't you try arguing politics with them. These don't strike me as the kind of lads who like being out-pointed by women.'

'That doesn't make them very unusual,' she said, putting her eyes to the window. 'Where do you think they're taking us?'

'Somewhere remote.' Docherty was watching Nasruddin out of the corner of his eye, thinking that he would never have suspected the man of pulling a stunt like this. He suddenly remembered something his friend Liam had said the last time he'd seen him, that the more desperate the times, the harder it was to recognize desperation.

He turned his attention back to his wife's question. They seemed to be travelling mostly uphill, and the road was nowhere near as smooth as they were used to. He tried to remember the map of Central Asia he had examined before the trip, but the details had slipped from his mind. There were mountains to the east of the desert, and Chinese desert to the east of the mountains. Which wasn't very helpful.

He thought about leaning across the aisle and asking to borrow Mike Copley's guide book, but decided that would only draw attention to its existence and his own curiosity. Better to wait until they reached their destination, wherever that might be.

He turned round to look at Isabel, and found her angrily wiping away a tear. 'I was just thinking about the children,' she said defiantly.

He took her hand and grasped it tightly. 'It's going to work out OK,' he said. 'We're going to grow old together.'

She smiled in spite of herself. 'I hope so.'

Diq Sayriddin plucked a group of sour cherries from the branch above the *kravat*, and shared them out between the juice-stained hands of his friends. 'I have to go inside for a while,' he told them.

It was fifty-five minutes since he had received the call from Shakhrisabz at the public telephone in Registan Street. Nasruddin had expected him to make his own call from there, but somehow the place seemed too exposed. He had decided to use his initiative instead.

Sayriddin passed through the family house and out the back, climbed over the wall and walked swiftly down the alley which led to Tashkent Street. His father, as always, was sitting outside the shop in the shade, more interested in talking with the other shopkeepers than worrying about prospective customers. Sayriddin slipped round the side of the building and let himself in through the back door.

The whole building was empty – no one stayed indoors at this hour of the day – and the office was more or less sound-proof, but just to be on the safe side he wedged the door shut with a heavy roll of carpet. Exactly an hour had now gone by since the call from Talib – it was time to make his own.

He pulled the piece of paper with the number, name and message typed on it from his back pocket, smoothed it out and placed it on the desk beside the telephone. He felt more excited than nervous, but perhaps they were the same thing.

After listening for several seconds to make sure he was alone, he picked up the receiver and dialled the Tashkent number. It rang once, twice, three times . . .

'Hello,' an irritable voice said.

'I must speak with Colonel Muratov,' Sayriddin said. His voice didn't sound as nervous as he had expected it would.

'This is Muratov. Who are you?'

'I have a message for you . . .' Sayriddin began.

'Who are you?' Muratov repeated.

'I cannot say. I have a message, that is all. It is important,' he added, fearful that the National Security Service chief would hang up.

There was a moment's silence at the other end, followed by what sounded like a woman speaking angrily.

'What is this message?' Muratov asked, almost sarcastically.

'The Trumpet of God group . . .' Sayriddin began reading.

'The what?!'

'The Trumpet of God group has seized a party of Western tourists in Samarkand,' Sayriddin said, the words tumbling out in a single breath. 'They were with the "Blue Domes" tour, staying at the Hotel Samarkand. There are twelve English and two Americans among the hostages . . .'

Muratov listened, wondering whether this was a hoax, or simply one of his own men winding him up. Or maybe even one of the Russians who had been jettisoned when the KGB became the NSS. It didn't sound like a Russian though, or a hoax.

'Who the fuck are The Trumpet of God?' he asked belligerently.

'I cannot answer questions,' Sayriddin said. 'There is only the message.'

'OK, give me the message,' Muratov said. Who did the bastard think he was – Muhammad?

'There are eight men and six women,' Sayriddin continued. 'All will be released unharmed if our demands are met. These will be relayed to you, on this number, at eleven o'clock tomorrow morning. Finally, The Trumpet of God does not wish this matter publicized. Nor, it believes, will the government. News of a tourist hijacking will do damage to the country's tourist industry, and probably result in the cancellation of the Anglo-American development deal' – Sayriddin stumbled over this phrase and repeated it – 'the Anglo-American development deal . . . which is due to be signed by the various Foreign Ministers this coming Saturday . . .'

Whoever the bastards were, Muratov thought, they were certainly well informed. And the man at the other end of the line was probably exactly what he claimed to be, just a messenger.

'Is that all clear?' Sayriddin asked.

'Yes,' Muratov agreed. 'How did you get my private number?' he asked innocently. His answer was the click of disconnection.

In the office of the carpet shop Sayriddin was also wondering how Nasruddin had got hold of such a number. But his second cousin was a resourceful man.

He placed the roll of carpet back up against the wall, and let himself out through the back door.

In the apartment on what had, until recently, been Leningrad Street, Bakhtar Muratov sat for a moment on the side of the bed, replaying in his mind what he had just heard. He was a tall man for an Uzbek, broadly built with dark eyes under greying hair, and a mat of darker hair across his chest and abdomen. He was naked.

His latest girlfriend had also been undressed when the phone first rang, but now she emerged from the adjoining bathroom wearing tights and high-heeled shoes.

'I'm going,' she said, as if expecting him to demand that she stay.

'Good,' he said, not even bothering to look round. 'I have business to deal with.'

'When will I see you again?' she asked.

He turned his head to look at her. 'I'll call you,' he said. Why did he always lust after women whose tits were bigger than their brains? he asked himself. 'Now get dressed,' he told her, and reached for his discarded clothes.

Once she had left he walked downstairs, and out along the temporarily nameless street to the NSS building a hundred metres further down. The socialist slogan above the door was still in place, either because no one dared take it down or because it was so much a part of the façade that no one else noticed it any more.

Muratov walked quickly up the stairs to his office on the first floor and closed the door behind him. He looked up the number of the Samarkand bureau chief and dialled it, then sat back, his eyes on the picture of Yakov Peters which hung on the wall he was facing.

'Samarkand NSS,' a voice answered.

'This is Muratov in Tashkent. I want to speak to Colonel Zhakidov.'

'He has gone home, sir.'

'When?'

'About ten minutes ago,' the Samarkand man said tentatively.

The bastard took the afternoon off, Muratov guessed. 'I want him to call me at this number' – he read it out slowly – 'within the next half hour.'

He hung up the phone and locked eyes with the portrait on the wall once more. Yakov Peters had been Dzerzhinsky's number two in Leningrad during the revolution, just as idealistic, and just as ruthless. Lenin had sent him to Tashkent in 1921 to solidify the Bolsheviks' control of Central Asia, and he had done so, from this very office.

If Peters had been alive today, Muratov thought, he too would have found himself a big fish in a suddenly shrunken pond. And an even less friendly one than Muratov's own. Peters had been a Lett, and from all the reports it seemed as if the KGB in Latvia had actually been dissolved and had not simply acquired a new mask, as was the case in Uzbekistan.

Muratov opened one of the drawers of his desk and reached in for the bottle of *canyak* brandy which he kept for such moments. After pouring a generous portion into the glass and taking his first medicinal gulp the NSS chief gave some serious thought to the hijack message for the first time. If it was genuine – and for some reason he felt that it was – then it also represented a new phenomenon – hijackers who didn't want publicity. Their name obviously suggested some strain of Islamic fundamentalism, but could just as easily be a cover for men who wanted money and lots of it. Which it was would no doubt become clear when the demands arrived on the following morning.

Muratov walked across to the open window, glass in hand. The dim yellow lights on the unnamed street below were hardly cheerful.

The telephone rang, and he took three quick strides to pick it up. 'Hamza?' he asked. The two men had known each other a long time. Four years earlier they had been indicted together on corruption charges for their part in the Great Cotton Production Scam, which had seen Moscow paying Uzbekistan for a lot of non-existent cotton. The break-up of the Soviet Union had almost made them Uzbek national heroes.

'Yes, Bakhtar, what can I do for you?'

The Samarkand man sounded in a good mood, Muratov thought. Not to mention sleepy. He had probably gone home for an afternoon tumble with his new wife, whom rumour claimed was half her husband's age and gorgeous to boot.

'I've just had a call,' Muratov told him, and recited the alleged hijackers' message word for word.

'You want me to check it out?'

'Immediately.'

'Of course. Will you be in your office?'

'Either here or at the apartment.' He gave Zhakidov the latter's number. 'And make sure whoever you assign can keep their mouth shut. If this is genuine we don't want any news getting out, at least not until we know who we're dealing with and why.'

Nurhan Ismatulayeva studied herself in the mirror. She had tried her hair in three different ways now, but all of them seemed wrong in one way or another. She let the luxuriant black mane simply drop around her face, and stared at herself in exasperation.

The red dress seemed wrong too, now that she thought about it. It was short by Uzbek standards, far too short. If she had been going out with an Uzbek this would have been fine – he would have seen it as the statement of independence from male Islamic culture which it was intended to be. But she was going out with a Russian, and he was likely to see the dress as nothing more than a come-on. His fingers would be slithering up her thigh before the first course arrived.

She buried her nose in her hands, and stared into her own dark eyes. Why was she even going out with the creep? Because, she answered herself, she scared Islamic men to death. And since the pool of available Russians was shrinking with the exodus from Central Asia her choice was growing more and more limited.

There was always the vibrator her friend Tursanay had brought home from France.

She stared sternly at herself. Was that what her grandmother had fought for in the 1920s? Was that why she'd pursued the career she had?

She was getting things out of proportion, she told herself. This was a dinner date, not a life crisis. If he didn't like her hair down, tough luck. If he put his hand up her dress, then she'd break a bottle over his head. Always assuming she wasn't too drunk to care.

That decided, she picked up her bag and decided to ring for a taxi – most men seemed to find her official car intimidating.

The phone rang before she could reach it.

'Nurhan?' the familiar voice asked.

'Yes, comrade,' she said instinctively, and heard the suppressed amusement in his voice as he told her to report in at once. 'Hell,' she said after hanging up, but without much conviction. She hadn't really wanted to go out with the creep anyway, and after-hours summonses from Zhakidov weren't exactly commonplace.

She called her prospective date at his home, but the line was engaged. Too bad, she thought, and walked out to the balcony and down to the street. Her car was parked in the alley beside the house, and seemed to be covered in children. As she approached they leapt off and scurried into the darkness with melodramatic shrieks of alarm. Nurhan smiled and climbed into the driver's seat. Of the two Samarkands which sat side by side – the labyrinthine old Uzbek city and the neat colonial-style Russian one – she had always loved the former and loathed the latter. One was alive, the other dead. And the fact that she had more in common with the people who lived in the Russian city couldn't change that basic truth.

As she started up the car she suddenly realized that her dress was hardly the appropriate uniform for an NSS major in command of an Anti-Terrorist Unit. What the hell – Zhakidov had said 'now'. She pressed a black-stockinged leg down on the accelerator.

It took no more than ten minutes to reach the old KGB building in Uzbekistan Street. There was a light burning in Zhakidov's second-floor office, but the rest of the building seemed to be in darkness.

She parked outside the front door and climbed out of the car. As she crossed the pavement a taxi pulled up and disgorged Major Marat Rashidov, commander of the largely theoretical Foreign Business and Tourist Protection Unit. Rashidov had been a friend of Zhakidov's for a long time, and those in the know said he had been given this unit for old times' sake. The bottle was supposed to be his real vocation.

'My God, is it an office party?' he asked, looking at her dress.

She smiled. 'Not unless it's a surprise.' There was something about Marat she had always liked, though she was damned if she knew what it was. At least he was sober. In fact, his brown eyes seemed remarkably alert.

Maybe he had moved on to drugs, she thought sourly. There were enough around these days, now that the roads to Afghanistan and Pakistan were relatively open.

The two of them walked up to Hamza Zhakidov's office, and found the bureau chief sitting, feet on desk, blowing smoke rings at the ceiling, his bald head shining like a billiard-ball under the overhead light. He too gave Nurhan's dress a

32

second glance, but restricted any comment to a momentary lifting of his bushy eyebrows.

'We may have a hijack on our hands,' he said without preamble. 'Someone phoned the office in Tashkent claiming that a party of tourists has been abducted here in Samarkand . . .'

'Have they?' Marat asked.

'That's what you're going to find out. It's supposedly the "Blue Domes" tour . . .'

'Central Asian Tours – it's an English firm,' Marat interrupted, glad he had thought to do some homework on his way over in the taxi. 'They do a ten-day tour taking in Tashkent, Bukhara and Khiva as well as here. They use the Hotel Samarkand.'

Zhakidov looked suitably impressed.

'Has the hotel been contacted?' Nurhan asked.

'No. Tashkent's orders are for maximum discretion. The hijackers . . . well, you might as well read it for yourselves.' He passed over the transcription he had taken from Muratov over the phone.

Nurhan and Marat bent over it together, she momentarily distracted by the minty smell on his breath, he by the perfume she was wearing.

'Publicity-shy terrorists,' she muttered. 'That's unusual.'

'The tourists are probably all sitting in the Samarkand's candlelit bar, wondering when the electricity will come back on,' Zhakidov said. 'But just go over there and check it out.'

'And if by some remote chance they really are missing?' Marat asked, getting to his feet.

'Then we start looking for them,' Nurhan told him.

Zhakidov listened to their feet disappearing down the stairs and lit another cigarette. He supposed it was rather unkind

33

of him, but he couldn't help thinking a hijacked busload of tourists would make everyone's life a bit more interesting.

Her Majesty's Ambassador in Uzbekistan lay in the bath, his heels perched either side of the taps, a three-day-old copy of the *Independent* held just above the lukewarm water, an iced G&T within reach of his left hand. Reaching it without dipping a corner of the newspaper into the water was a knack gathered over the last few weeks, as the early-evening bath had gradually acquired the status of a ritual. The long days spent baking in the oven which served as his temporary office had required nothing less.

The British Embassy to Uzbekistan had only opened early the preceding year, and James Pearson-Jones had been given the ambassadorial appointment at the young age of thirty-two. His initial enthusiasm had not waned in the succeeding eighteen months, for post-Soviet Uzbekistan was such a Pandora's Box that it could hardly fail to be continually fascinating. It was 'the mullahs versus MTV' as an Italian colleague had put it at one of their unofficial EU lunches, adding that he wouldn't like to bet on the outcome.

'God save us from both,' had been a French diplomat's comment.

Pearson-Jones smiled at the memory. His money was on the West and MTV – from what he could see the average Uzbek was much more interested in money than God. And the trade and aid deals to be signed over the coming weekend would put more money within their reach.

His thoughts turned to the arrangements for putting up the junior minister and various business VIPs. He had been tempted to place them all in the Hotel Uzbekistan, where his own office was, just to give the minister an insight into what life was like in Central Asian temperatures while a hotel's air-conditioning was – allegedly, at least – in the process of being overhauled. But he had relented, and booked everyone into the Tashkent, which had the added advantage of being cheaper. After all, no one had said anything about increasing his budget to cover the upcoming binge.

There was a knock on the outside door.

He ignored it, and started rereading the cricket page. Cricket, he had to admit, was one very good reason for being in England during the summer. That and . . .

The knocker knocked again.

'Coming,' he shouted wearily. He climbed out of the bath, reached for his dressing-gown and downed the last of the G&T, then walked through to the main room of the suite and opened the door. It was his red-headed secretary, the delicious but apparently unavailable Janice. He had tried, but these days a man couldn't try too hard or someone would start yelling sexual harassment.

She wasn't here for his body this time either.

'There's been no call from Samarkand,' she said. 'I thought you ought to know.'

He looked at his watch, and found only an empty wrist. 'What time is it?'

'Eight-thirty. She should have called in at seven.'

'What were they doing today?'

'The Shah-i-Zinda this morning, and Shakhrisabz this afternoon.'

'That must be it then. It's a long drive – the bus probably broke down on the way back. Or something like that.'

'Probably. I just thought you should know.' She started for the door.

'Wait a minute,' Pearson-Jones said. There might be no brownie points for being too careful, but the Foreign Office sure as hell deducted them for not being careful enough. 'Maybe we should check it out. We have the number of the hotel?'

'It's in the office.'

'Can you get it? We'll ring from here.'

He got dressed while Janice descended a floor to the embassy office, thinking that he'd never heard her mention a boyfriend. Still, she handled the post, and for all he knew there were a dozen letters a day from England that arrived reeking of Brut.

Dressed, he poured himself another G&T, and took it out on the concrete balcony. In the forecourt below a couple of early drunks seemed to be teaching each other the tango.

Janice knocked again, and he went to let her in. 'You do the talking,' he said, 'your Uzbek is better than mine.'

Nurhan Ismatulayeva and Marat Rashidov arrived at the Hotel Samarkand some five minutes after leaving the NSS building. The coffee shop in the lobby was full of local youths, all of whom looked like bad imitations of Western rock stars. The hotel restaurant was almost empty, but one long table had been set and not used, presumably for a tour party.

Nurhan showed the receptionist her credentials, and got a scowl in return. One of these days, she thought, it would be nice to have a job which encouraged people to smile at her. Maybe she could join the state circus as a clown.

'The Central Asian Tours group,' she said. 'Are they in the hotel?'

The receptionist shook his head, his eyes apparently fixed on her black-clad lower thighs.

'Do you know where they are?'

He shook his head again.

'Look, friend,' Marat said cheerfully, 'let's have a little co-operation here.'

Reluctantly turning his attention to the male member of the duo, the receptionist gave him a pitying look. 'They're not back yet – that's all I know.'

'From where?' Nurhan asked patiently.

'I don't know. This is a hotel, not a travel agency.' Seeing the look on Marat's face, he added: 'You could try the notice-board in the lounge – they sometimes put the itineraries up there.'

Marat went to look.

'Which rooms are they in?' Nurhan asked.

He sighed and opened the register book. 'Three-o-four to 310.'

'Keys,' she said, holding out her hand.

'All of them?'

'All of them.'

He passed them over, just as Marat returned. 'Nothing,' the NSS man said.

They walked up the four flights of stairs to the third floor, and let themselves into the first room. Two open suitcases half-full of neatly folded clothes lay up against a wall. If the group had been hijacked it was without a change of underwear. A novel – *A Suitable Boy* – lay on the bedside table. Inside the front cover 'Elizabeth Ogley, May 1994' had been inscribed.

They had been through three of the seven rooms before Marat found what they were looking for. Inside another paperback – *Eastern Approaches* by Fitzroy Maclean – the folded piece of paper used as a bookmark yielded a hand-written copy of the tour itinerary. A trip to Shakhrisabz had been scheduled for that afternoon.

'That's it then,' Marat said. 'That road across the mountains is terrible. They've had a puncture, or driven into a ravine or something.'

Nurhan looked at the itinerary. 'Bit of a coincidence,' she said, 'that the only time they go off on a jaunt into the countryside we get a call to say they've been hijacked.'

'For someone in the know that would be the best time for a hoax,' he suggested, but with rather less confidence.

'I think it's for real,' she said, walking across to the window. A car was drawing up down below, not a tour bus. This would be her first real chance to prove herself, she thought.

'We'd better call Zhakidov,' Marat said.

They went back downstairs to the desk, and found the receptionist had disappeared. Nurhan used his phone to call in.

'You'd better drive over to Shakhrisabz,' Zhakidov said. 'If you meet them on the way, fine. If you don't, then find out if they ever got there.'

Nurhan was not pleased. 'Why can't we just phone our office there?' she wanted to know.

'Discretion, remember?

'It's a nice ride,' Marat added for good measure. And besides, he thought, it would remove him from temptation for a few hours.

Another phone suddenly started ringing in the office behind the counter.

'Maybe it's them,' Marat suggested. 'Maybe someone got taken ill and they had to find a doctor in Shakhrisabz.'

'Maybe,' Nurhan agreed. She moved towards the office's open door just as the receptionist re-emerged from wherever it was that he had been skulking.

'I'll answer that,' he said indignantly.

'If it's anything to do with the Central Asian Tours party I want to speak to them,' Nurhan said.

'OK, OK,' the receptionist said, picking up the receiver. 'Yes,' he said, in answer to some question, glancing across at Nurhan and Marat. 'Wait a moment,' he told the caller, 'the police want to speak to you.' He held out the phone for Nurhan. 'Who is that?' she asked.

'I am calling from the British Embassy in Tashkent,' a female voice said in reasonable Uzbek. 'I wish to talk to someone staying at the hotel. Brenda Walker.'

Nurhan cursed under her breath. 'The group has not returned from their trip yet,' she said.

'Do you know why they're late?' the woman asked.

'No. A problem with their bus, most likely. Do you wish to leave a message?'

'Why are the police involved?' the woman asked.

'We just want to talk to the tour operators,' Nurhan improvised. 'Is there no message?'

'No, I'll try again in an hour or so.'

Nurhan put the phone down. 'Why did you say "police", you idiot?' she asked the receptionist.

He shrugged. 'You didn't tell me not to.'

She looked at him. 'The woman will be calling back. You will tell her the same thing I told her – that you don't know why the tour group has not returned, but it's probably that their bus has broken down. Is that clear?'

'Of course.'

'Then don't fuck up,' Marat warned him. 'Or our next meeting will not be as convivial as this one has been. Now what sort of bus are they in?'

'A small one. Green and white.'

The two NSS officers headed out through the glass doors in the direction of their car, oblivious to the disdainful finger being raised to their retreating backs.

* * *

Four hundred kilometres to the north-east Janice Wood was trying to explain the tone of the policewoman's voice to James Pearson-Jones. 'I'm sure she was lying, or at least not telling the whole truth. Something's happened.'

Pearson-Jones sighed, thought for a moment, and muttered 'shit' with some vehemence. 'We'd better call London,' he said.

'And bring Simon in?' she asked. Simon Kennedy was ostensibly Pearson-Jones's number two at the embassy, with a portfolio of responsibilities which included that of military attaché. He was also MI6's representative in Central Asia.

'Yes, bring him in,' Pearson-Jones agreed. 'I'll go down to the office and make the call.'

3

In London it was nearly four in the afternoon, and the tall patrician figure of Alan Holcroft had just arrived back at the Foreign Office from the House of Commons. Prime Minister's Question Time had been its usual farcical waste of time, and Holcroft had sat on the front bench wondering why they didn't put a cock-fighting arena by the dispatch box, and give the two sides some real blood to cheer about. He was quite willing to agree that the occasion was a useful theoretical demonstration of democracy in action, but could see no reason why anyone with real work to do should have to sit through the damn thing twice a week.

And as Foreign Minister he had plenty of work to do. The rest of the world seemed even more of a mess than usual. The Americans had found something new to panic them – North Korea, this time – but at least for the moment they seemed to have dropped the idea of invading Haiti. Russia was still collapsing, the Brussels bureaucracy its usual irritating self, and the French as difficult as ever. Bosnia continued on its bloody way, despite losing top spot in the genocide league to Rwanda. And then there was the Middle East . . . If this was the New World Order, Holcroft thought, then he would hate to see chaos.

On his desk he found a memo waiting for him. The two British hostages held by the Khmer Rouge in Cambodia were getting a full-page write-up in tomorrow morning's *Independent*, and it was expected that the Labour MP championing their cause would be seeking a government response the following afternoon.

Holcroft sighed. What did they expect – a gunboat? That the government would send the hostage-takers to bed without any supper? The honest answer would be to say that Her Majesty's Government had no influence whatsoever on the Khmer Rouge, and to admit in addition that it had more important things to worry about than a couple of British citizens who had been stupid enough to travel in a country that was clearly unsafe. As far as Holcroft was concerned they were like transatlantic rowers or potholers – he had no objection to them taking risks, but every objection to their using taxpayers' time and money to pull themselves out of jams of their own making.

None of which he could say at the dispatch box. He settled down to read through the memo, confident that the author would have supplied him with either a more acceptable reason for doing nothing or a convincing explanation of how much he was already doing.

Holcroft was nearly halfway through the three-page memo when there was a sharp rap on his door. He looked at his watch – there was still at least forty minutes left of the one hour without interruption which he demanded each day. 'Come,' he snapped.

It was his Parliamentary Private Secretary, Michael Allsworth. 'Sorry to interrupt you,' the intruder said, 'but the embassy in Tashkent has been on the line.'

Holcroft felt the familiar mixture of anger and frustration seize him by the throat. 'What in God's name has she done now?' he demanded.

'No, it's nothing like that . . . it's . . . well . . .' Allsworth took a seat. 'It all seems a bit iffy, Minister. The gist of it is that the tour party your daughter is with seems to have disappeared. Or at least not returned to the hotel in Samarkand when it should have. As you know, the agent assigned to your daughter is supposed to report in each day at seven local time. Today she hasn't. But we have no actual reason to suspect foul play . . .'

'No *actual* reason?'

'Well, when the embassy tried to contact her at the hotel they were asked to speak to the police, which they found a bit odd.'

'Was there no reason given for the tour party not being there?'

'Just lateness. And that may be . . .'

'What's the time there now?' Holcroft wanted to know.

'About ten o'clock in Samarkand, eleven in Tashkent.'

'And they were due back when?'

'For dinner at eight o'clock.'

'So it's only two hours. That doesn't seem much.'

'No, it's just . . .'

'The police business. I understand.' Holcroft considered for a moment. The familiar thought of how much easier life would be, both for him and his wife, without their youngest daughter flitted across his mind, and for once induced a slight sense of shame. Rather more to his surprise, Holcroft also felt a tinge of panic. 'If they're not simply late, then what are the possibilities?' he asked Allsworth.

'An accident of some sort, a simple hold-up, a political hijack.'

Holcroft wondered which would be worst. 'So what do you suggest?' he asked.

'Get the intelligence boys working on it, just in case. After all, they've already got someone with the party, and MI6 have another man in Tashkent. MI5 or Special Branch can do any spadework that needs doing this end. The tour company operates out of Bradford,' he added, in response to Holcroft's raised eyebrow.

'Of course.' Sarah had told him as much when she'd announced this ridiculous jaunt. That was how he had managed to arrange the accompanying minder. 'Right,' he told Allsworth. 'Do that. And call me if any news comes in. I'll be at home.'

The secretary disappeared, leaving Holcroft with a sinking sensation in his stomach. 'They're just late,' he murmured to himself, but it didn't sound convincing. He wondered what, if anything, he was going to tell his wife Phyllis.

Marat Rashidov watched Nurhan's thighs shift as she changed gears and had a fleeting memory of being excited by his ex-wife in similar circumstances. 'What were you planning this evening?' he asked.

She didn't answer for a moment, being absorbed in circum-navigating a goat which had strayed into the middle of the road, and now seemed transfixed by the car's headlights. 'What did you say?' she asked, once they were past the belligerent-looking animal.

He repeated the question.

She smiled to herself. 'Just a dinner date,' she said.

'Who was the lucky man?' he asked.

She laughed. 'Mind your own business,' she retorted. 'What did you have planned?'

He grunted. 'Nothing much.' Another evening staring at the walls and wondering who he was staying sober for. He glanced across at Nurhan, whose black hair was now gathered at the nape of her neck and held by an elastic band she had found in one of the tourists' rooms. Marat had known of her for a long time, occasionally run into her when their professional duties overlapped, but he had no real idea of who she was. Rumour had it that she'd screwed her way to the position she currently held, but in the predominantly male world of the Samarkand NSS such an explanation of her success was almost inevitable. Marat doubted it was true. She didn't seem like the scheming sort. Or the sort who wanted to be beholden to anyone for anything.

'How did you get into this work?' he asked.

'It's in the family blood,' she said. 'My grandmother was in the Chekas during the Revolution.'

'Tell me about her,' Marat said.

She glanced across at him. 'It's ancient history,' she said. 'Why would you be interested?'

'It's going to be a long ride,' he said. 'Humour me.'

She shrugged. 'She was my mother's mother. Her name was Rahima Asankulova. She was the wife of one of the first Uzbek Bolsheviks, a very young wife. Of course he treated her like any Uzbek husband treated his wife in those days, and in 1921, when she was only about nineteen – she never knew exactly which year she was born in – she ran away to Moscow, to the headquarters of the Party women's organization, the Zhenotdel. There was a big fuss, but six months later she came back as a Zhenotdel worker, one of the first in Central Asia. You know what they went through?'

'I imagine they weren't too popular.'

'That's an understatement if ever I heard one. They campaigned against the veil, and for an end to the selling of brides, and in favour of education for women . . . the usual. Some were stoned to death, some were thrown down wells, one woman was actually chopped up. All these murders were committed by fellow family members, of course.'

Glancing to his left, Marat could see her staring angrily ahead.

'And your grandmother?'

'She survived until the thirties, then died giving birth in one of Stalin's prisons.'

'To your mother?'

'No, she was born in 1928. She worked for the Party too, though not for the KGB. She was a union representative for the Tashkent textile workers. She's retired now, but she still lives in Tashkent . . .'

She broke off as two headlights appeared round a bend in the mountain road.

'It's a lorry,' Marat said, rummaging in his pockets. A hand emerged holding a tube of mints. He offered her one.

She took it, wondering if she had been wrong earlier in assuming that the mint on his breath had been a cover for the smell of alcohol.

'I've just given up smoking,' he said, as if in answer to her unspoken question.

'Good idea,' she said.

He rearranged himself in the seat and asked her why she had joined the KGB.

She was silent for a few moments. 'I think the main reason was that I couldn't think of an alternative,' she said eventually.

'You're joking . . .'

'No. I got accepted at Moscow University, and could hardly believe my luck. I really wanted to get out of Tashkent. To get out of Central Asia, full stop.'

'Why? You're Uzbek . . .'

'An Uzbek woman. I don't expect any Uzbek man to understand . . . but for anyone brought up the way I was there's not many chances of fulfilment in this culture.'

'So why did you come back?'

'I missed the place.' She laughed. 'But that's only part of the story. I don't know how you feel about what's happened in the last few years . . .'

'Ambivalent, I suppose.'

'That sounds about right. I hated it in Moscow – it was so obvious there that the system only worked for a few people at the top. Back here it was different. Oh, I know it was far from perfect, and every time I turn on the TV now there seems to be some new horror story about what's been done to the environment, but . . . well, look at the place compared to what it was before the Revolution. We have education for everyone, and health care . . .'

'I saw what this place must have been like before the Revolution,' Marat said. 'In Afghanistan.'

'Exactly,' she said. 'I guess I wanted to preserve some of what had been achieved.'

'And the KGB seemed the best place?'

'One of the best. Advances in things like women's rights are enshrined in the state law. Which is what we're supposed to protect, among other things.'

'You're not too worried about the other things?'

'If you mean locking up fundamentalists, no I'm not. They're not interested in democracy.'

'What would you do if they came to power?'

'Leave, I expect. What would you do?' Islamic Republics were alcohol-free zones, after all.

'Probably the same. Though I've no idea where I'd go. America maybe, if there was a way to get in.'

'If they declared an Islamic Republic here I expect the West would bend over backwards to take in political refugees.'

He grunted with amusement. 'Maybe I should be voting for the bastards. If we ever get another vote, that is. As our beloved President is so fond of pointing out: "Do not destroy your old house until you have built another."'

'Makes sense to me,' Nurhan observed.

'Maybe. But only if people are allowed to start work on the new house. Bakalev is putting anyone who tries in prison.'

She looked at him. 'You've given up hope, have you?'

He smiled. 'Let's just say I'm not expecting too much from the next few years.' He put his hands in his pockets to conceal the fact that the left hand had begun to shake. Looking out of the Volga's window at the mountains and star-filled sky he had the sudden conviction that the ancient Greeks had got it wrong – Orion was holding a bottle opener, not a sword.

Simon Kennedy had left Tashkent about half an hour after Nurhan and Marat's departure from Samarkand. The main road between the two cities wasn't bad, and he reckoned he would be in Samarkand not much later than two in the morning. He didn't expect there would be a great deal he could do before daylight, but at least he would be on the spot.

Driving, in any case, was something he always enjoyed, especially at night. He had done quite a lot of it lately, usually with Janice, who seemed much more happy indulging her sexual appetite in some desert lay-by than in either of their rooms at the Hotel Uzbekistan. Kennedy wasn't complaining, though he did sometimes wonder what the local police would make of it if the two of them were ever caught in the act.

Janice had a brain, though, and he was inclined to trust her judgement in this business with Sarah Holcroft. There probably was something funny going on in Samarkand. Either way, he supposed he would know by morning.

* * *

The tour bus had been travelling for slightly more than three hours when it finally reached its destination. Its occupants had seen no other vehicles during the journey, and passed not a single light, either beside the road or off in the distance. They could have been driving across the moon.

'Please stay in your seats,' Nasruddin said.

'Until the plane has come to a complete stop,' Docherty added under his breath. He wondered if there had ever been such a courteous hijack as this one.

'The women will leave the bus first,' Nasruddin told them. 'They will have separate quarters from the men.' There was a muted wail of fright from Elizabeth Ogley at this news.

'There is no cause for alarm,' Nasruddin said, almost indignantly. 'On the contrary – such an arrangement is in accord with Islamic tradition.'

And will make it harder for any rescue operation, Docherty thought. He wondered what sort of 'quarters' were awaiting them outside in the darkness.

'The women will now leave the bus,' Nasruddin announced.

For a moment no one moved, as if in instinctive mutiny against the demand. Alice Jennings was the first to stand up. She leaned over to kiss Sam on the forehead, murmured something to him, and started down the aisle, head high. Docherty didn't see the look she gave Nasruddin, but their former guide looked as if he had been slapped.

One by one the others followed. Sarah Holcroft and Sharon Copley both looked frightened, Elizabeth Ogley close to panic. Brenda Walker showed no emotion, encouraging Docherty to believe that she was indeed what he had suspected. With any luck she would have the same training as he had in dealing with hostage situations.

Isabel was last, her face stern as she disappeared down the

steps at the front of the bus. Docherty prayed to any possible gods that might be up there that he would see her again.

Nasruddin disappeared, leaving just the clean-shaven man with them. The AK47 was held loosely, but its barrel was pointed right down the aisle between them. There was no sign of carelessness, and the previous hint of nervousness had given way to a watchful confidence. This man has seen military action, Docherty thought.

Several minutes went by. The men didn't speak, but their shared glances were eloquent enough. What a fucking mess, Copley's expression said. This can't have happened to me, was written all over Ogley's face. The Zahid men were trying to hide their anxiety behind stoical exteriors and failing. Their sons, like Sam Jennings, could not conceal the absurd sense of excitement which was bubbling up through the fear.

'Talib,' a voice said from outside, causing the clean-shaven man to prick up his ears. Words in a foreign language followed.

Talib gestured with his left hand for the men to follow him, and retreated down the steps. Docherty stood up quickly, intending to position himself at the head of the procession, but then thought better of the idea. A time might come for him to assume some sort of command responsibility, but it hadn't arrived yet.

They filed off the bus, stepping down on to a gravel surface. Ahead of them was a long, one-storey building with dim lights showing in two of the windows. Two men with automatic rifles stood on either side of the twenty-metre path which led to the front door, channelling their passage. Another two waited by the door. Since Nasruddin was not among them, this raised the number of the hijackers to at least seven.

While making this simple calculation, Docherty was also taking in the panoramic sweep of countryside to either side.

Though moonless, the clear sky offered enough illumination to make out the jumble of slopes which receded into the distance. The lodge had been built at the back of a wide shelf, at the upper end of a deep valley. Behind the building a bare rock-face rose almost sheer, while from its front the folds of the valley stretched away into the darkness. In the few seconds he had left before reaching the door Docherty searched for and found the North Star, low in the sky away to his left. The building faced west.

Not that it mattered. They seemed to be a long way from civilization. In more ways than one.

The interior of the building, though, exceeded all his expectations. It seemed to have been decorated and furnished to a higher standard than most of the Central Asian hotels they had stayed in, which perhaps wasn't saying much. Docherty had a glimpse of a large living-room with bear rug and open hearth, before passing down a long corridor full of closed doors. At the end they were ushered into a dormitory room. It was reasonably large, about four metres by six, with two-tier bunks on three of its four walls. Otherwise the room was empty, save for the cheap rug which covered most of the floor. Docherty was still wondering what the place was when he heard a bolt slam shut on the outside of the door. And then another.

He looked round at his fellow-captives. The two elder Zahids had begun talking animatedly in Urdu, with their sons looking on anxiously. They suddenly looked no older than adolescents, Docherty thought.

Ogley was sitting on one of the bunks with his head in his hands, Copley pacing up and down. 'Where do you think the women have been taken?' the builder asked nobody in particular.

'A room like this one,' Docherty said.

Copley looked at him with worried eyes. 'You don't think they'll . . .'

'No I don't,' Docherty said shortly. A year ago there would have been more inner certainty behind the denial, but the mission to Bosnia had shaken his sense of how much evil was loose in the world. 'If they're Islamic fundamentalists then we can expect some sort of moral code,' he added, with more conviction than he felt. But one of the worst things that could happen here would be for the men to sit around imagining what was being done to their wives. If they were to get out of this alive then they all had to remain rational and reasonably focused. Fear and anger led in the opposite direction.

'How do you know they are Islamic fundamentalists?' Ogley asked.

Docherty shrugged. 'The Trumpet of God doesn't sound like a bunch of communists. What else could they be?' He turned to the Pakistani contingent. 'Mr Zahid,' he said, addressing the elder brother, 'have you heard of these people?'

The mullah shook his head dismissively. 'They must be Shiites,' he said angrily. 'Lunatics from Iran. That is all I can think.'

'Hey, look,' Copley said from behind Docherty.

There was another door in the fourth wall. Copley tried the handle and it opened to reveal a bathroom and toilet. Admittedly the former comprised just a tap and the latter just a hole in the floor, but a full bucket of water was standing by one wall.

'I think we must be on a Magical Mystery Tour,' Copley said. He at least seemed to be recovering his composure.

'I wonder which of us is the Walrus,' Docherty murmured.

'Will you two stop gibbering,' Ogley snapped behind them. 'We've been kidnapped, for God's sake.'

'Tell us something we don't know, Professor,' Copley said drily. 'You know,' he went on, 'I wouldn't have believed it, but I actually feel hungry.'

'So do I,' Sam Jennings agreed. 'Do you guys mind if I take one of the bottom bunks?' The Zahid fathers had already laid claim to two of the four.

'Go ahead,' Docherty said, wondering what the place was normally used for. Maybe it was a youth hostel. Or a barracks for border guards.

He noticed Ogley sitting with his head between his hands, sighed, and went over to him. 'Are you OK, Professor?' he asked.

'I am not a professor,' Ogley said. 'And what do you care anyway?'

Docherty chose his words carefully. 'I care because experience has taught me that in a hole like this people need to pull together. I want to be alive a month from now, not a name in an obituary column.'

Ogley looked at him sideways, rather like a schoolboy who wasn't sure if he was being kidded. 'So do I,' he agreed slowly.

'Good. Now is that the bunk you want?'

The women's room was a mirror image of the men's, situated at the opposite end of the lodge. Once the bolts had clanged shut behind them, Isabel went round checking all the more obvious hiding-places for listening devices. She wasn't expecting to find any, but it was better to be safe than sorry.

Once she was reasonably certain there weren't any, she asked her five companions for a conference. Both Elizabeth

Ogley and Sharon Copley seemed close to hysteria, and Isabel thought developing a sense of solidarity could only help.

She also had something vital to ask. 'Sarah,' she began quietly, 'no one's mentioned it, but I think we all know who you are – or maybe I should say we all know who your father is . . .'

'I don't,' Alice Jennings said, surprise on her face.

'He's the British Foreign Minister,' Sarah Holcroft said.

'Oh boy,' Alice said softly.

'The point is, do they know?' Isabel asked, jerking her head in the direction of the door.

Sarah looked surprised. 'I . . . I don't know,' she said.

'Did Nasruddin ever say anything to indicate he knew?'

'No. At least, I can't remember . . . But he must have known, mustn't he?' A hint of a wry smile crossed her lips. 'He did live in England.'

Alice Jennings snorted. 'They're always doing polls in America that show eighty per cent of Americans don't know who the President is.'

'Nasruddin seems a serious young man,' Isabel said. 'The type who would read the *Guardian* rather than the *Mirror*. And your picture would have appeared in the tabloids, not the qualities.'

'What are you getting at?' Brenda Walker wanted to know. She had been eyeing Isabel with suspicion ever since their arrival.

'It's simple. Maybe they don't know who Sarah is. In which case we have to be damn careful not to let them find out.'

'They must know,' Elizabeth Ogley said, 'or why would they have hijacked us?'

'That would be a coincidence,' Alice Jennings agreed.

'They happen,' Isabel said. 'They may have hijacked us for no more reason than that we're British. Most of us, anyway.'

'But what difference will it make whether they know or not?' Elizabeth Ogley asked.

'Their demands will be higher if they think they have someone important,' Isabel said. 'And the lower they stay the better our chances of getting out of this.'

'You seem to know a lot about this type of thing,' Brenda Walker interjected.

Isabel was about to say that her husband had a lot of experience in these situations, but stopped herself in time. There didn't seem any point in letting Docherty's SAS background out of the bag. 'I do have some experience of this kind of thing,' she said. 'From the other side.'

'You don't mean you were a hijacker?' Alice Jennings asked with a laugh.

'I was involved in two kidnappings, nearly twenty years ago now, in Argentina. In England you had protest demonstrations, in Argentina things got a little more serious,' she added, trying to make light of it. The other women all looked dumbstruck, with the notable exception of Brenda Walker.

She already knew, Isabel realized. Hence the suspicion. Ms Walker must have some secrets of her own.

In fact, Brenda Walker had spent the last five minutes wondering whether to come clean about her own role, and deciding that she had no option. As a social worker her advice in this situation would be ignored; as an intelligence agent it would not.

'I also have a confession to make,' she began.

'My God,' Alice Jennings gasped. 'Is no one who they seem to be on this trip?'

'I am,' Sharon Copley said, with a noise that sounded half laugh, half sob.

They all laughed, and then there was a moment of silence as they realized what they had done.

'I work for the government,' Brenda Walker said quietly. 'My job was, well, it was to make sure Sarah didn't cause the government any embarrassment while she was abroad.' She looked across at Sarah. 'I've enjoyed your company,' she said simply.

'Christ!' was all Sarah could say.

'She was just doing her job,' Isabel said. It looked as if imbuing this group with a sense of solidarity was going to be an uphill task.

But Sarah sighed and gave Brenda a rueful smile. 'I've been enjoying your company too,' she said.

Sir Christopher Hanson, the head of MI6, poured himself a small glass of port and sipped at it, allowing the sweetness to smooth away his sense of irritation. Another twelve hours and he would have been on his way to Heathrow to begin a fortnight's holiday in St Lucia. At any moment now his wife would be receiving the news that he wouldn't be coming, and he was half expecting her cry of rage to be audible above the ten miles of rush-hour snarl-ups which separated them.

But one of his men – or woman on loan, to be precise – was apparently in a life-threatening situation, and he would not have felt happy deserting the helm at such a moment. Brenda Walker's file was supposedly on its way from MI5 Records, though it seemed a long time arriving. He was about to make further enquiries when an apologetic courier appeared in his open doorway.

Hanson took the discs and went to turn on his computer terminal, feeling, as usual, nostalgic for the bulging file of mostly illegible reports which had once served the same purpose. There was something real about paper and ink, something substantial.

Still, the new system was ten times as efficient, not to mention a damn sight easier to store. He accessed Brenda Walker's file and skimmed through it. The computerized portrait told him she had short dark hair and a face, which wasn't very much. Even in this brave new world there had to be a photograph somewhere, surely.

Hanson smiled, remembering one subordinate's tongue-in-cheek suggestion that they rename MI6 Rent-a-Bond.

Brenda Walker's personal details contained no surprises, unless you counted her working-class background and comprehensive education, but these days that was almost par for the course among MI5's foot-soldiers. She had done a lot of escort work with the royals, had a short stint with the embassy in Australia, and had then taken a specialist training course in immigration law. She had been working in that area for only a few weeks when given the job 'minding' the Holcroft girl, apparently because the previous candidate had abruptly fallen ill.

Was that suspicious? Hanson doubted it.

He printed out the file and then switched discs. The new one contained not only the 'paperwork' from her current assignment, but also the preliminary vetting reports on the tour group concerned and the other members of the party.

He went through the latter, his mouth opening with surprise when he read the information on Jamie Docherty and his wife Isabel. An SAS veteran and an ex-terrorist! Put them together with Brenda Walker, and that made three of the fourteen tourists who had first-hand experience of dealing, from one side or the other, with such volatile situations. If the party had indeed been hijacked, then that had to be some sort of record.

Assuming for the moment that they had been, one big question remained: whether or not the hijackers were aware of the fact that they had netted the Foreign Minister's daughter.

4

Isabel lay on the bunk, considering the irony of her situation. She wondered how many people in the world had personally experienced a hijack and kidnapping as both perpetrator and victim. She might well be the first.

Her thoughts went back to Córdoba in 1974, and the beginning of the war she and her comrades had been crazy enough to launch against the Argentinian military. The first man they had kidnapped had been a local glass manufacturer notorious both for his high living and for the low wages he paid his employees. They had kept him for three days in an apartment not two hundred metres from the city's central police station, blindfolded but otherwise not ill-treated. His family had paid the requested ransom – $60,000 worth of food and clothing for the city's poor. They had watched the man's wife hand out the packages on TV, and then let him go.

Two weeks later they had done it again. This time the victim was a member of the family which had ruled over the city for most of the century, their wealth amassed through land ownership, banking and several manufacturing businesses. The ransom demanded had been correspondingly higher – $1,000,000 in gift packages for poor schoolchildren, plus the reinstatement of 250 workers who had recently been locked out of the family's construction business.

The ransom had been paid, but the experience had not been so pleasurable the second time round. The victim had turned out to be almost likeable, and on several occasions the proximity of police teams scouring the city had made it seem likely that he would have to be killed. In the event this had not happened, but the probability had been enough to sow doubt and dissension through her guerrilla unit. It had made them look more closely at themselves and each other, and in some cases they hadn't liked what they had seen.

And now here she was among the victims. She wondered how Nasruddin and his comrades were getting on with each other. Maybe it was a crazy thing to think, but from the little she had witnessed The Trumpet of God didn't seem to be having much fun. So far, she hadn't seen a single smile on any of their faces. At the beginning of their war against the Junta, her group, the ERP, had treated it all like a mad adventure.

Though later, to be sure, there had been nothing to laugh about, only torture and death.

She had been lucky to survive, her body scarred but intact, her soul missing in action for many years thereafter. She wondered if Nasruddin and his friends believed in what they were doing as strongly as she and her friends had done, and whether they would still be alive in twenty years, and able to look back on what had happened the previous evening.

She wondered if she would be, or if her luck had finally run out. She thought about Docherty and hoped she hadn't held him for the last time.

In the men's room the light had abruptly gone out shortly after eleven o'clock.

'I guess that means it's bedtime,' Copley sighed.

'Aye,' Docherty said, remembering rooms like this in Highland youth hostels. In his early teens he and his friend Doug had spent many a weekend hitchhiking around from hostel to hostel, partly for the sheer joy of free movement, partly to get out of Glasgow and the parental orbit. After lights out they would talk in whispers and giggles until an older boy managed to shut them up.

He clambered up on to the bunk above Ogley, wondering if any of them would manage to sleep that night. He felt pretty strung out himself, and guessed that the others, none of whom had his previous experience of life-threatening situations, would spend most of the night listening to their hearts beating wildly inside their ribcages.

'The last time I was in a place like this,' Sam Jennings said, his soft drawl floating out of the dark, 'it was a police station in Mississippi. Back in the Civil Rights days, in the early sixties. We were helping to get black voters registered, which wasn't very popular with the local authorities. They arrested about twenty of us, though I can't remember what charges they dreamed up – it was something like walking on the grass with shoes on. Anyway, we were put in a cell a lot like this, except that the police dog pound was right outside, and every so often a dog's face would appear at the window, growling fit to bust and slavering something awful. We all started singing "We Shall Overcome", but I tell you, I don't think any of us felt too confident about it that night. I was scared.' There was a pause. 'I'm scared now,' he added.

'So am I,' one of the Zahid boys said, eliciting what sounded like a comforting sentence in Urdu from his father.

'What do you think, Jamie?' Copley asked Docherty. 'You must have seen some hairy situations in the army.'

'We're at the mercy of people we know nothing about,' Docherty said, 'and that's always scary. But I don't think they're madmen. I don't think they'll harm us for fun, or without what they would consider good reason. We mustn't give them any reason to act in anger – in fact, we should do everything we can to make ourselves human to them. In situations like this people are harder to k . . . harder to harm if you know them.'

A silence of several moments was broken by Copley. 'I wonder how the women are getting on.'

'Probably better than us,' Docherty said. He knew that women always found it easier to share their feelings, and in adversity that was a useful thing to do. Still, he was worried about Isabel. Though twenty years had passed since her nightmare incarceration in the Naval Mechanical School outside Buenos Aires, being imprisoned once more was bound to give the dreadful memories new life, no matter how different the circumstances might be.

For the first time since the men with the AK47s had climbed aboard the bus, Docherty felt anger welling inside him. Anger at the bastards who were holding them, anger at a world in which such happenings had become so commonplace, anger at himself for being so helpless to save her.

He lay on his back looking into the darkness above his head, willing himself back to the state of mind he would need for all their sakes.

The thought crept in unbidden that he would willingly sacrifice all the others if only she could walk away unscathed.

It was almost twenty past eleven when Nurhan Ismatulayeva and Marat Rashidov drove down Sholkoviput Street and into the mostly sleeping town of Shakhrisabz. The soaring remnant of Tamerlane's palace loomed out of the darkness on their right, and Nurhan brought the Volga to a halt opposite the entrance to the car park.

The chain-link gate was closed, and no lights were visible beyond them.

'Do you know this town?' she asked Marat.

'Not well.' He stared past her at the palace complex. 'There must be a caretaker somewhere around.'

'Yeah,' she agreed, and reached for the door handle.

They walked across to the gate, and found it attached by nothing more than a cheap padlock. Marat lifted himself up and over, breathing a bit heavily, and raised a hand to help her down. She ignored it, and then felt a bit churlish for doing so.

'I don't think much of their security,' she said, checking anxiously to see if her best nylons had been laddered. Tursanay had brought them back from Paris with the vibrator.

'They probably think thieves would have a hard job sneaking out of the country with this thing,' Marat said drily, looking up at the ruined entrance.

'There's always vandalism,' she said tartly. 'It's been getting worse and worse in Samarkand. There's graffiti everywhere.'

'True,' Marat agreed. 'Maybe we do need an Islamic Republic after all. Bring back some discipline, eh?'

She ignored him. The nylons seemed to have survived intact.

'We could cut off the artists' hands,' he went on, warming to his theme.

'Are you finished?' she asked.

'Sure,' he said, thinking how sexy she looked, standing there in a darkened car park with a short party dress on, hands on hips and eyes flashing. 'The museum building seems the best bet,' he added helpfully. 'It's that one over there.'

'What are we standing here for then?' she asked, turning on her heel and starting off across the pock-marked asphalt surface.

After knocking at two doors they found the caretaker, a man somewhere between middle and old age, asleep on a *kravat* in the trees behind the building. His eyes opened slowly from slumber, widened quickly at the sight of Nurhan standing over him, and then narrowed once more at the sight of her NSS identification.

'They were just small pieces,' he said. 'No bigger than this,' he added, bending his forefinger inside his thumb to indicate just how small.

'What are you talking about?' Nurhan asked him sternly.

He blinked up at her, opened his mouth and then closed it again.

'Pieces of pottery or tile,' Marat said wearily. 'Our friend here has been selling them to the tourists.' He shook his head.

'That's not why we're here,' he said, 'though I may come back to find out if you're still doing it. We're looking for the tour party who were here this afternoon.'

The man blinked again. 'There were three here this afternoon,' he said.

'This one came in a small green and white bus.'

'Ah, the last one. Is there a reward for this information?' he asked hopefully.

'There's a heavy penalty for selling state property,' Marat reminded him.

'Yes, yes. What do you want to know? I see them go into the museum, and I see them go out. The last time I see them they are sitting outside the café across the street.'

'When was that?' Nurhan asked.

The man shrugged. 'It was growing dark. Maybe six o'clock.'

64

'You didn't see the bus leave?'

'No.'

Nurhan looked at Marat. 'The café?'

He nodded, and turned to the caretaker. 'Cut out the side-line,' he told him, 'or you'll be out of a job.'

They walked back round the building and across the vast space towards the gate, with Nurhan wishing they had brought along the caretaker and his key. She doubted whether her nylons would survive another climb.

Still, there was a simple answer to that. She turned away from Marat, lifted the dress, unhooked the French suspenders and pulled down the nylons. 'They cost a fortune,' she muttered in explanation.

He said nothing, but this time failed to offer her a helping hand.

Human beings are ridiculous, she thought, climbing down to the road.

'That's the café,' Marat said, indicating a dark shape some fifty metres up the road. They left the car where it was and walked up. It was a one-storey building set back from the road, with a yard full of metal tables and chairs strewn beneath the large plum tree in its front yard.

The proprietor finally appeared in answer to their knocking, rubbing the sleep from his eyes. 'I was working out the back,' he said, 'but my wife will answer your questions.' He disappeared to fetch her.

'Working out the back,' Nurhan repeated to herself sarcastically. The man had probably been sitting around talking to his friends while his wife ran the place for him.

She appeared at the door, a diminutive woman with quick eyes and an aura of efficiency about her. She remembered serving the group in question, but had not actually seen them leave. For that they would need to talk to her son, who was responsible for selling the tickets at the gate. She disappeared in search of him.

'I think I'll go back and break a pot over that caretaker's head,' Marat muttered, as they waited once more on the café veranda.

This time, though, it was worth it. The son had seen the bus drive out of the park, and seen it turn right on to the Samarkand road. 'And the car left right behind it,' he added.

'Which car?' Nurhan asked.

The boy described the black Volga, and the rusty black Fiat which had spent most of the afternoon alongside it. He had assumed they must be waiting for something. The Fiat had left just before the bus. He thought that each car had contained two or three men, but he couldn't be more precise than that. During the afternoon the men had sat down together under the trees behind the two cars, but it was over a hundred metres from the gate, so he had not been able to see them very clearly. Most were wearing Western dress, but at least one man was wearing a traditional robe.

'You didn't catch the number of either car?'

No, he had not.

They thanked him and started back towards their own vehicle.

'We've got a hijack on our hands,' Marat said. It felt strange saying it – hijackings were things that happened somewhere else. Still, this one should keep him busy for the next few days.

'We should talk to Zhakidov,' Nurhan said, opening the door and reaching for the radio receiver. Despite the intervening mountains the signal was loud and clear. She waited while the duty operator went to fetch Zhakidov, then told him what they had discovered. 'There's no indication of where they went,' she said. In fact, as she suddenly realized, the hijackers could have left Shakhrisabz at six and got back to Samarkand before she and Marat had left. She suggested as much to Zhakidov.

'It's possible, I suppose,' he said doubtfully. 'You two had better stay in Shakhrisabz tonight, and start trying to pick up the trail at first light.'

'At the hotel?' Nurhan asked hopefully.

'At tourist prices? You must be joking,' Zhakidov said. 'It's only about five hours till dawn. Just pretend you're on a stake-out.'

'Thanks a lot,' Nurhan said under her breath.

'And keep me up to date,' Zhakidov was saying.

'Will do,' she started to say, but he had already cut the connection.

'I take it we're not sleeping between clean white sheets tonight,' Marat said.

'You got that right,' she told him, reaching over into the back seat for the rug. 'You're in your bed right now. At dawn we're supposed to find the hijackers.'

'And rescue the tourists?'

'If we're in the mood.' She let her seat back with rather more suddenness than she intended, and almost knocked the breath out of herself.

He looked down at her with a grin. 'I don't suppose I get to share the rug,' he said.

She smiled sweetly up at him. 'You got that right too.'

Nasruddin Salih was sitting in the large living-room, his foot resting on the bear's head, a bottle of lemonade in his hand. Talib Khamidov was slumped in another chair, his AK47 within easy reach, while the bearded Akbar Makhamov was almost perched on the edge of the large leather sofa, as if fearful of being contaminated by such decadence. Of the other four members of the group, Farkhot and Sabir were on guard outside the hostage's rooms, Shukrat and Chunar out front of the lodge, some fifty metres down the approach track.

The hunting lodge itself had been built and half finished under the last government of the Uzbek State Socialist Republic, and had been intended for the use of both the local Party bigwigs and any visiting cronies from Moscow. Though the same people were still in power in Tashkent and Samarkand, they had become rather more discreet about enjoying the perks of office, and the lodge had not been used for over two years. Nasruddin had been able to date the abandonment of privilege with some accuracy – among the pile of pornographic magazines found in one of the furnished bedrooms the most recent issue had been that of August 1992. Akbar had burnt the magazines out on the hillside, along with the mass-produced portrait of Red Army Marshal Frunze which had held pride of place above the hearth.

'Two of us should sleep,' Nasruddin said, though without much conviction. A day of anxious waiting had given way to that sense of liberation which came with an irrevocable leap into the unknown. He had started a new life that day, and the adrenalin was still pumping through his veins in celebration.

'Have we no decisions to take?' Akbar asked. Neither Nasruddin's manic calm nor Talib's stoicism seemed to have rubbed off on the Tajik.

'I don't think so,' Nasruddin said. 'Everything has gone exactly as we hoped.'

'God willing,' Talib murmured.

'What about the hostages?' Akbar asked. 'Do we have anything to fear from them? The soldier, for example.'

'I don't think so,' Nasruddin said. He had liked the Dochertys – they were the only members of the party who had not treated him differently because of his race. The Americans, being liberals of the old school, had overcompensated.

'I think it might be better to keep him separate from the others,' suggested Akbar.

'Then we would have to guard him separately as well. The fact that his wife is here will keep him from doing anything foolish.'

'Should we not discuss what we intend to do if our demands are not met?' Akbar asked.

Nasruddin considered. A tendency to talk too much was one of the perils of shared leadership, but it was a relatively harmless one. And in one way Akbar was right: the more eventualities they had mentally prepared themselves for, the easier it would be to take difficult on-the-spot decisions.

But at that moment he did not want to consider the possibility of such a setback. Today marked the end of his fifteen-year struggle to find a way of fighting back, and he wanted to let his heart revel in the moment. In the morning he could apply his mind to the practicalities once more.

'I think tomorrow will be soon enough for that,' he said, looking at Talib.

His cousin took the hint. 'And let us hope that God spares us from such a choice,' he said softly.

In Talib's sunken eyes Nasruddin caught an unwelcome premonition of pain both given and endured.

President Yegor Bakalev had had a premonition of disaster the moment he heard Bakhtar Muratov's voice on the other end of the line. Just when things were going so well, and the West was ready to put some serious money into the Uzbek economy, this had to happen.

It wasn't just the money, but what it represented. If the West invested in the future of a secular Uzbekistan, then he would have a powerful ally against the fundamentalists. On the one hand an improving economy would give the people less desire for change, while on the other there would be no serious criticism of the way he dealt with the Islamic dissidents. The Americans and the British knew what democracy had served up in Iran, and they weren't about to make the same mistake again. The bleeding-heart organizations like Amnesty International might complain, but they complained about everybody. The people who mattered would turn a blind eye in the interests of stability. On his last visit to London, Bakalev and the British Prime Minister had been united in the belief that a prosperous Uzbekistan would keep the fundamentalists at bay throughout Central Asia.

And now this, just four days before the deals were due to be signed. Maybe a miracle would happen, and they could keep the matter quiet for those four days. Maybe it could be resolved in such a way that confidence in his country and government would even be increased.

Maybe camels would fly. The chances of keeping this business off the world's TV screens seemed remote. He wondered who these people were and what they wanted. He hoped they were foreigners, and preferably Iranians. He hoped they would ask for something utterly ludicrous, and thereby brand themselves as lunatics. After all, every country had its share of them, and no one would expect Uzbekistan to be any different.

* * *

In England it was still only seven o'clock, and Detective Sergeant Dave Medwin was one of the many whose plans for the evening had been interrupted by the disappearance of a bus in far-off Samarkand. His had included taking Ben to see the comedy movie *Mrs Doubtfire*, but the call from Special Branch Central in London had put an end to that. Maureen had not been pleased. He wondered how long it would be before she gave him another opportunity to spend a whole evening with their twelve-year-old son.

His own people in London had hardly spoken to him before handing over the phone to an MI5 smoothie. The man had given him his instructions in triplicate, and then faxed the relevant papers to the Leeds office.

Now he was on his way to Bradford, and the registered office of Central Asian Tours Ltd in Westfield Street. At least the rush hour was over. And once he was finished with this errand he could see if Lynn fancied a drink in the Dog & Biscuit.

He found the office in question occupying the top half of a two-storey building, above a newsagent's, in a street mostly populated by Asian fabric shops. There were no lights showing upstairs, and the newsagent's was in the process of closing.

Medwin showed the man his warrant card, and said he would like to ask a couple of questions about the business upstairs.

'They are closed,' the man said.

'For how long?'

The Asian looked at his watch. 'Three hours?' He shrugged. 'I didn't see the girl leave today.'

'But she was there today?'

'Oh yes. Of a certainty.' He grinned. 'She is not so light on her feet, you know.'

Medwin went back to his car. If Pinar Ishaq Khan had been there that day, it seemed unlikely she was involved in any major villainy that was under way in Samarkand. Wherever the hell that was. And it also meant she had a key to the office. The MI5 man had told him to make as few waves as possible, and breaking into the office across the road might well generate some, at least in daylight. He looked up the secretary's address in the vetting report which had been faxed to him, found out where it was in the *A–Z*, and started up the car.

She lived with her mother in a rather nice old house on the outskirts of Bradford. It was the older woman, looking rather worried, who showed him in. She, as Medwin had already learnt from the vetting report, taught in an elementary school in the centre of the city. Her son Imtiaz lived with his wife in Leeds.

Medwin waited while Pinar was summoned from the depths of the house, idly noting that the *Guardian* on the table was open at the women's page. This was not a traditional family.

Pinar, despite the newsagent's unflattering comment, was only slightly plumper than average, and had a face which made Medwin think of princesses in the *Arabian Nights*. He told her there was probably nothing to worry about, but that there was a chance the current 'Blue Domes' tour party had run into trouble. They were still waiting for details from Samarkand.

She looked stunned.

'I have to ask you a few questions,' he went on.

She looked at him blankly, and then nodded.

'Was there anything unusual about this particular tour?'

'No. Well, this was the only one which Mr Salih escorted personally. The Jordan/Syria and Pakistan tours are escorted by local employees. But . . .'

'I meant this particular group of people,' Medwin said. 'You do handle the bookings?'

'Most of them.' She thought. 'I can't remember,' she said at last. 'I'm taking bookings almost all the time – the next five trips are already fully booked.'

Medwin handed her his copy of the list. 'Does this help?' he asked.

She studied it. 'There's one thing I remember,' she said. 'The Jenningses. Mr Salih was pleased we had some Americans at last. They were the first we'd ever had book with us.'

Medwin wondered whether it was worth giving the office the once-over, and decided not. If it was still functioning as normal, he found it hard to imagine finding anything relevant, and Pinar looked intelligent enough to ask if he had a warrant, which he did not.

He thanked her for her help, went back to the car, and consulted his street guide again. Nasruddin Salih's home was not far from the office, back towards the centre of the city.

He reached it in twenty minutes, a small terraced house in a dead-end street. After parking the car a hundred metres or so away he checked round the back, and found a path running along between a playing field and the back entrances. There was still too much daylight for a surreptitious forced entry, so he went looking for a pub.

An hour and two pints later he was walking back towards Salih's house. Reaching it, he counted the houses to the end and then walked down the back path, counting them off in reverse. A couple of lights showed and a dog barked, but the neighbourhood seemed almost deserted.

The back door presented no problem to his customized piece of plastic. He took a few seconds to let his eyes grow used to the darkness, then walked through the kitchen to the living-room and pulled the curtains before taking out the torch he had brought from his glove compartment. The room looked incredibly tidy, as if Salih had been expecting guests. Maybe he had been expecting a visit from someone like me, Medwin thought.

He went slowly through the house, touching as little as possible. There was no sign of a woman's presence, and no sex magazines either. There was no alcohol.

There were a lot of bookshelves, both downstairs and up, most of them full of books about religion and politics. An incongruous group of books about railways caught Medwin's attention. He took one down and fingered through it. It was full of pictures of British Rail diesel locomotives, photographed in and around Leeds. Inside the front cover the name Martin Salih had been written.

Did Nasruddin have a son? he wondered. There had been no mention of it in the vetting report. And anyway the diesels were mostly painted the old blue colour – the book had to be fifteen years old.

He tried some of the political books, all of which had the name Nasruddin Salih inscribed inside their front covers. It was a mystery, Medwin thought, but probably not a relevant one.

It was ten minutes later that he found the photograph album, and recognized Nasruddin as one of the children in the family group pictures. There he stood, his face fifteen years younger but otherwise strikingly similar, next to a brother and sister, and behind his seated mother and father. Martin, Sheila, David, Ma and Pa, the caption read.

Medwin stared at the photograph for several seconds before inspiration struck. He picked up the telephone, called West Yorkshire Police Headquarters, and asked for the Records

Department. Once connected, he asked for Rose or Mary. Rose was there. 'I need a name checked out,' he told her.

'How thrilling,' she said.

'Martin Salih,' he said patiently. 'S-a-l-i-h.'

'Your wish is my command.'

He could hear her fingers on the keyboard. 'One arrest,' she said eventually. 'Vandalism,' she added. 'He went on a window-breaking spree in the middle of Bradford. He was only thirteen. Got put on probation.' There was a silence lasting several moments, followed by a muted 'wow'.

'What is it?' Medwin asked.

'The poor little bugger had his reasons. His mother had just been killed in an arson attack. Somebody tossed a fire-bomb through their front door, and the house burned down with her in it. She was probably too afraid to come out.'

Medwin sighed. 'Thanks, Rose,' he said. 'I'll see you around.'

'Make sure you remember your wallet next time.'

Medwin smiled and sat back on Nasruddin's sofa. His parents must have done what many immigrant parents did, and given their children English names in an attempt to smooth their passage in an adopted country. At some point after his mother's death, unable to bear the shame of an English name, Martin had rechristened himself Nasruddin. And the violence in his past had slipped between the cracks of the vetting procedure.

If there had indeed been a hijacking in Samarkand, it seemed more than possible that Nasruddin Salih had been one of its perpetrators.

5

Nurhan Ismatulayeva woke to find the new day's light filtering through the window above her head. The Volga's dashboard clock said it was six-fifteen. In the adjoining seat Marat was snoring gently. His face looked a lot younger in sleep, she decided, much more at peace. He probably wasn't much older than she was.

She reached forward for the door handle, eased open the door, and levered herself out into the dawn air. It was quite cold, and she reached back in for the rug to wrap around herself. Across the road the sun suddenly alighted on the very top of the ruined entrance gate, like a match catching fire. The birds were singing up a storm in the trees.

She stood there for a moment, savouring the scene, remembering mornings like this at the family dacha in the Tien Shan foothills north of Tashkent, and then started walking slowly across the park, her thoughts turning to who the hijackers might be, and what they might want. They might be nothing more than bandits, but she thought it much more likely that they would prove to be Islamic terrorists of one sort or another. She hoped so. If anything could set back the rise of Islam as a political force in Uzbekistan it was a bunch of psychopathic loonies masquerading as the children of Allah.

She should be back in Samarkand, she thought, where the decisions would be taken about who was to handle the potential hostage situation. By rights it should be her, but her male superiors would probably need reminding of that. She strode back to the car, pulled her seat back up and poked her colleague in the stomach.

He opened one eye, and didn't like what he saw. 'I thought you had gone for coffee,' he said.

She turned the key in the ignition. 'We can grab a cup at the bus station in Kitab,' she said, sliding the gear lever into first and bumping the car back on to the road, as he struggled to get his seat into the upright position.

'Hey, what's the hurry?' he asked.

'Why don't you call Samarkand and find out if there's any news,' she suggested.

'They'd have called us.'

'We might not have heard them over your snoring,' she said brutally.

He grimaced. 'I can't have been snoring that much – I was only asleep for about five minutes. You don't have anything for a headache, do you?'

'There's some pills in my bag.'

He reached into the back seat for it, and looked inside for the pills.

'A small brown bottle,' she said.

'Got it.' He had just noticed the pack of condoms she carried. A woman of the nineties, he thought, and wondered how happy she was behind the beautiful mask. He used thumb and forefinger to place two pills at the back of his throat, and swallowed.

'Are there any roads off this one before Kitab?' she asked him.

'Not that I know of.'

'Where would you go if you had just hijacked a tourist bus in Shakhrisabz?'

He thought for a minute. 'That would depend on what I wanted,' he said at last. 'If I wanted the maximum publicity splash I suppose I'd drive back to Samarkand and take over one of the tourist sights – one of the Registan *madrasahs*, maybe.'

'If they're Muslims wouldn't that be like defiling holy ground or something?' She should know something like that, she told herself. She should know more about Islam if she was serious about fighting it.

Marat didn't know either. 'Maybe Tamerlane's mausoleum then,' he suggested. 'The whole world's heard of him.'

'And it would be difficult to use force without damaging the building,' she thought out loud.

He reached for his first mint of the day. 'There's one problem with all this,' he said. 'If they wanted to make their stand in Samarkand then why go to all the bother of taking them hostage in Shakhrisabz. Whatever they did, they could have done it just as well before they left the city. Or at least a few miles outside.'

'And if they're not in Samarkand?'

'Simple choice,' he said. 'They either turned left for the desert or right for the mountains. In the desert they'd be easy to find, but it would be hard to sneak up on them. In the mountains vice versa.'

'It would be easier to stay alive in the mountains,' she suggested.

The first houses of Kitab slipped by, and a minute later Nurhan brought the Volga to a halt beside the crossroads at the centre of the small town. Even at this hour there were quite a few people on the streets, and the cafés were already doing a roaring business in morning glasses of tea. Marat and Nurhan walked across to the nearest establishment and ordered coffee. Sitting down, she became conscious of the angry looks she was getting from the men occupying the *kravats*. Short red dresses obviously weren't too popular in Kitab.

Marat had noticed too. 'I could tell them I've arrested you for prostitution,' he said, and wished he hadn't. The look she flashed him was mostly of rage, but if he was any judge of women there was also an element of hurt.

Of course, his ex-wife had always told him he wasn't. 'Sorry,' he said instinctively.

She gave him another look, more pitying this time, which he didn't find much of an improvement. 'But I shouldn't stray off on your own,' he added, looking round.

'I won't.'

He drained the last of his coffee. 'Let's start asking questions then.'

They began with the staff, moved on to the clientele, and then went through the same process at the establishment across the street. Half an hour and many sullen silences later they had found four witnesses to the passage of the bus the previous evening. All of them had seen it go straight across the crossroads, on to the road which led back to Samarkand.

They went back to the Volga, and Nurhan steered the car slowly out of town, past the bus station and a mosque under construction. She kept an eye on the alleys to the left as Marat scoured those to the right. There was no sign of a bus.

They emerged from the town alongside the river which had created it, now no more than a trickle of water between sun-baked stones.

'How many turn-offs do you reckon there are between here and home?' Marat asked.

'I don't remember any proper roads,' she replied. 'But it's a long time since I did this journey in daylight.'

The fields soon petered out, as the road climbed steadily into the dry hills. After two or three kilometres it was joined by a dusty track from the east. One or more vehicles turning right had left tyre tracks on the bend.

'Let's try it,' Marat suggested.

She gave him a withering look. 'There's thousands of square kilometres of wilderness out there, and I'd rather explore it with a map and some proper supplies. We could drive around all day without seeing anyone. Or of course, if we were really lucky, we could meet up with half a dozen heavily armed terrorists.'

He smiled. 'Point taken. But let's drive up it for a mile or so – just to get a sense of the lay of the land.'

Looking at him, she realized he was serious. 'All right,' she agreed reluctantly, and started the car up the surprisingly smooth track.

Half a mile later they came to an unmarked forking of the ways. Ahead of them the yellow hills rose into grey mountains, and the mountains into distant snow-covered peaks beneath a deep-blue sky. It was as beautiful as it was daunting.

'This is a job for a helicopter,' she said.

'I guess you're right,' he conceded.

Docherty's first thought on waking was to wonder why he was sleeping alone. Then realization dawned. He lay motionless for a moment, grateful that he had at least managed to get some sleep. Light was filtering in through the cracks in the boarded-up window. He looked at his watch and found that it was twenty past six.

Someone was in the bathroom, and since everyone else was visible from where he lay, it could only be Ogley. Docherty poked his head over the edge of the top bunk and confirmed as much.

He wondered if the children knew what had happened. He couldn't imagine his sister would tell them, but kids had a way of knowing something was wrong without being told. Docherty rubbed his eyes and decided he'd rather be doing something than lying there thinking.

He went to take a daylight look at the room's only window. Somewhat to his surprise, it slid open. Beyond the glass there was a mosquito screen, and beyond that planks had been nailed across the aperture. It wouldn't take much effort to break out, but it would be hard to do it quietly. The real problems would begin once they were outside. Even without any idea of where they were, one or two of them might be able to escape across the mountain wilderness, but not fourteen.

Still, he thought, it would serve as an escape hatch in an emergency. He turned away from the window and almost walked into the elder of the two Zahid brothers.

'Can you see the sun?' the man asked. 'Or any shadows?'

'I don't think . . .' Docherty began, and then noticed the rolled-up prayer mat Ali Zahid was holding in his hand. 'But the window faces east,' he said. 'I noticed the North Star when we got off the bus last night,' he added in explanation, just as the sound of cursing came from the bathroom. Ogley's voice sounded almost hysterical.

Docherty and Ali Zahid exchanged glances, and the Scot strode across to the door. He tried to open it, but Ogley had wedged his sweater between door and floor, and he had to push hard to open up a six-inch gap. Through it, he saw Ogley scrambling on a flooded floor without his trousers on, apparently trying to wipe himself with what remained of the fast-disappearing water. The bucket lay on its side. 'Get out!' Ogley shouted at him. It was almost a sob.

Docherty closed the door. Behind him Ali Zahid had laid out his mat, and was now prostrating himself in the general direction of Mecca. It had to be ironic for a Muslim priest like Zahid, the Scot thought, being hijacked by people of his own faith who claimed to be holier than he was. In his own case it would be akin to being held hostage by a bunch of Celtic's skinhead supporters.

'What have you got to smile about?' Copley asked him. 'There's no breakfast, no newspaper, and there probably won't even be a morning post.'

'You haven't heard the worst of it – the professor's just spilt our entire water supply.'

'Shit, he hasn't.'

'But I think we're going to have to be kind to him. This room isn't big enough to accommodate someone having a nervous breakdown.'

'Well, I don't suppose he can help it. And I guess we're all going to be prone to the odd fart of alarm. I was just lying there thinking about Sharon and the kids. I think she only comes on these jaunts to keep me company. Maybe next year we'll go to Majorca.'

'And you'll probably get mugged by a gang of Spanish teenagers.'

'Yeah, right.' He looked at Docherty almost as if he was seeking reassurance. 'You've never been in a spot like this before, have you?'

'Nope. But I suppose I've been in physical danger enough times to know that getting excited only gets in the way. And I guess it becomes second nature after a while.'

'Well, I'm glad you're here even if you're not.'

'Thanks,' Docherty said wryly, just as Ogley reappeared.

The lecturer walked between them without saying anything, and threw himself on to his bunk.

'Is all the water gone?' Docherty asked, trying to keep any note of accusation out of his voice.

'You shouldn't have walked in like that,' Ogley said in a shaky voice. 'If we don't respect each other's privacy then we become animals like them.'

'Sorry. I thought you needed help. Now, is the water all gone?'

'Yes. It was an accident. I couldn't . . .'

'OK. We'll get some more.' Docherty went through to the bathroom, where Ogley's incontinence was much in evidence, both in the air and on the ground. He collected the bucket and took it back through to the door which led to the corridor. He rapped once, and was about to do so again when the wooden hatch was pulled back to reveal two eyes.

Docherty held up the water bucket.

The hatch slammed shut, and the seconds turned into a minute. Docherty was just coming to the conclusion that they had had their answer when the hatch opened again. 'Leave bucket by door and stand back,' a voice said in English. Docherty did as he was told, and the door slowly opened inwards to reveal a man holding an AK47 aimed straight into the room. The man's eyes darted from right to left and back again, and then he nodded, whereupon a second man appeared with a new bucket of water, and exchanged it for the empty one. He pulled the door shut behind him, and the familiar clang of bolts followed.

Docherty took the bucket to the bathroom door and then turned round. 'I think you've got some cleaning up to do,' he told Ogley.

The lecturer opened his mouth to reply, but the look on Docherty's face obviously made him think better of whatever it was he intended to say. Yet he made no move to do as he was asked.

'Like you said, we have to have respect for each other,' Docherty pointed out, as gently as he could. Ogley was going to clean up his own shit if the Scot had to force him, but it would be a hundred times better if the man realized that here and now – maybe for the first time in his life – he had the responsibilities which went with membership of a group of equals.

For several seconds the two men looked at each other, and then it was Ogley who looked away, climbed out of his bunk, and carried the water through into the bathroom.

Thirty metres away, at the northern end of the lodge, the women's day began with a crisis. Sharon Copley had woken sometime before dawn, and rather than wake anyone else, had allowed her anxiety to build, right up to the point where an asthma attack seemed imminent. She told Isabel and Alice Jennings as much between wheezing breaths. Her inhaler was in the bag which she had left on the bus.

Alice went immediately to the door and started beating out a tattoo on it. When no one appeared she simply upped the violence of her assault, her face a study in wrathful indignation. Isabel was torn between admiration and a fear that the old woman would pay for such temerity.

Eventually one of the hijackers' faces appeared at the hatch. It took several minutes of mime to explain the situation, whereupon the face disappeared. Another minute later, with Sharon's inability to suck in breath worsening by the second, the man called Talib appeared, and raised one finger to indicate that one of the women should accompany him.

Isabel looked round, saw no one else was keen to volunteer, and put herself forward.

'Go to bus?' she asked.

The man nodded, and gestured her to walk in front of him. She retraced their steps of the night before, down the corridor which ran the length of the building from north to south. On the right were guest rooms and the large lounge with the bearskin rug; on the left what seemed to be store rooms. One wall was lined with skis.

The sun had not yet risen above the mountain behind the lodge, and the valley stretching out in front of her was still cast in shadow. It was a beautiful morning, and she felt buoyed up by it in spite of everything.

On the bus she quickly found Sharon's bag, and checked that the inhaler was inside it. Through the window she could see Talib waiting for her, his eyes seemingly fixed on the valley below. He had a sad face, she thought. And an intelligent one. These were not a bunch of mindless maniacs. But was that good or bad?

She stepped back down to the ground, and he stepped politely aside to let her pass. A minute later she was back in their room, handing over the inhaler to Sharon. For the next few minutes it was all smiles, as Sharon recovered her breath and they all shared in their small victory over adversity. But soon the basic truth of their situation reasserted itself, and Isabel found herself wondering what she could do to counter the creeping fear that seemed to be infecting them all, herself included.

They all expressed it in different ways, of course. Elizabeth Ogley talked too much and too bitterly, and often only to herself. Alice Jennings was finding it easier to be angry than admit to herself how worried she was about her husband.

Sarah Holcroft seemed to be slowly sinking into a sea of self-pity, and Brenda Walker had lost all her brisk certainty of the evening before.

As for herself, Isabel seemed unable to counter the feeling – the ridiculous feeling – that she was paying for the transgressions in her past. Maybe her unconscious was still mired in the Catholicism of her childhood; maybe it even remembered every word of the homilies she had sat through in the small wooden church which overlooked the Beagle Channel.

She lay on her bunk drifting through the conscious memories – the joy of leaving the heavy air of the church and emerging into a landscape of sea and sky which seemed to go on for ever.

It felt wonderful and wrong at the same time. She levered herself up into a sitting position and started applying her mind to the problem of how to lift the collective spirits of six terrified women.

Simon Kennedy had arrived in Samarkand at half-past two in the morning. He had not seen a single soul on the streets as he drove across town towards the missing tourists' hotel – even the drunks had bedded down for the night. The hotel was no livelier. After parking his car, rather against his better judgement, on the street outside, Kennedy had almost needed to knock the doors down in order to raise the night receptionist. Once a room had been grudgingly found for him, the MI6 man set about determining the whereabouts of the Central Asian Tours party.

The receptionist's token resistance had collapsed at the sight of a ten-dollar bill. The tour party, he said, had not yet returned from Shakhrisabz. A vehicle breakdown was doubtless the cause, and there was no need for concern – his brother worked at the tourist hotel in Shakhrisabz, and it was excellent. When asked by Kennedy about the involvement of the police, the man had denied all knowledge of any such thing.

Kennedy had phoned the lack of news to Tashkent and gone to bed, wondering if he had just driven four hundred kilometres for nothing.

He was woken four hours later by the clamour of a pneumatic drill, and almost fell out of bed in his haste to reach the window. His car was still in one piece, but major roadworks seemed to have started all around it. Kennedy dressed hurriedly, waited three minutes for a lift that never came, and ran down the six flights of stairs to the ground floor. Ignoring the ironic jeers of the Uzbek workmen, he extricated his car from under the shadow of a bulldozer, and drove it through into the hotel's now-open car park. In the lobby he checked that the keys to the Central Asian Tours party's rooms were still hanging on their nails behind the reception desk. They were. And according to the sign on the dining-room door breakfast was about to be served.

Twenty minutes later it arrived in all its neo-Soviet glory. Various cold meats with bread, jam from distant Russia, ersatz coffee courtesy of Nescafé. The only genuine Central Asian touch was a delicious glass of *lassi*, which almost made up for the rest. Kennedy was sitting with his second cup of appalling coffee, daydreaming about fresh Danish pastries and cappuccino, when a blonde woman walked past and took a seat at the table furthest away from him. He smiled hopefully in her direction, and she smiled back, but neither of them said anything.

He had the vague feeling he had seen her before, but he couldn't for the life of him remember where, and he found it hard to admit he would have forgotten anyone quite so striking. Her hair was cut fairly short – it was called an urchin cut, he thought – and she had a pixie-ish face, with a perfect small nose and mouth beneath blue eyes. There was nothing pixie-ish about her body though: she was at least five foot nine, with long legs and pronounced hips and breasts. Classic English upper class, Kennedy thought. She'd probably played hockey at Roedean.

For all he knew she was a German or a Swede. Probably waiting for her husband to finish his morning crap and join her. Slow crappers, the Germans, but thorough.

He had things to do, like find out if a busload of Brits had really been hijacked. He got up, gave her one last glance and found she was smiling across at him.

Maybe she didn't have a husband, he thought. If she was still here that evening he would have to find out.

Annabel Silcott had a better memory for faces than Simon Kennedy. She had seen him the previous week at a party in Tashkent, and though they had not been introduced, their semi-drunken Russian host had included Kennedy in the witty thumbnail sketches of other guests which he had treated her to. 'He's a paradox,' the host had said. 'Intelligence without it.'

So what, she idly wondered, was an Intelligence man doing in Samarkand? Probably nothing, but if by any chance he was gainfully employed, then the nature of that employment was bound to be more interesting than her current project, which was writing an article on 'Women under Islam around the World' for one of the Sunday tabloid colour supplements back home.

It was not an assignment she was enjoying. All her editor really wanted were horror stories of women oppressed by the dreadful Muslims, preferably with elements of romance and bondage thrown in. A sort of modern-day sheikhs-and-harems piece, but written in a balanced, multicultural style. She had to be careful to point out how fulfilling some of these women found sexual slavery.

Annabel didn't much like the way Muslim men, by and large, treated their women, but then she didn't much like the way tabloid editors treated them either. The main problem, though, was that there was nothing new to say. She could find some juicy stories – or make them up if all else failed – but no one was going to take any notice, or at least not for any more time than it took this week's paper to become next week's cat litter. This was not the way for her to become the next Kate Adie.

Something to do with Intelligence work might be. Serious news, not news as soap opera. She remembered that the British and Americans were signing some sort of trade deal in Tashkent over the coming weekend. Maybe there had been an assassination threat, or something like that.

In which case, why would Kennedy be here in Samarkand? It couldn't be that. In fact, he was probably on holiday, and she was just indulging in wishful thinking.

But she would make a few enquiries, just the same.

Nurhan and Marat arrived back in Samarkand around eight-thirty. They had counted thirty-seven turn-offs between Kitab and the intersection with the Pendzhikent road just outside the city. Twenty had led east, seventeen west. None had been metalled. They had encountered only four people on the trip across the mountains, and though two of them had seen the bus heading south the previous afternoon none had seen it return.

'How about a bath before we report in?' Marat suggested.

'Why not?' she agreed. The chance to change into something more suitable would be worth any slight delay in re-establishing their claim to lead this investigation.

89

She dropped him outside his apartment building – a grey Russian block on what used to be Engels Street – and drove back across to her flat in the Old Town. The water supply was acting up again, but she managed to bathe herself in two inches' worth, and then selected a pair of loose-fitting black trousers and a kaftan-style blouse to wear. The latter was loose enough for her to carry the SIG-Sauer P226 automatic concealed in the small of her back.

Marat was waiting by the kerb when she returned to pick him up, wearing what she hoped was another white shirt – it looked crumpled enough to be the old one – and dark-blue trousers.

'How long have you lived here?' she asked.

'About two years. Since I separated from my wife,' he added, as if that provided a more accurate dating.

'Where's she?'

He looked at her with a wry smile. 'You do enjoy asking questions, don't you?'

She shrugged. 'I'm just curious. You don't have to answer.'

'She and the children are in an apartment on Mirshazapova. An expensive apartment.'

'I didn't know you had children.' They were approaching the NSS building.

'I'm not sure I do any more,' he said, reaching for the door handle.

They found Hamza Zhakidov in the position they had left him, sitting behind his desk. The tiredness in his face and the still made-up camp-bed against one wall suggested he had spent all night at the office. Or maybe he had been home to the delectable Susha, Marat thought cynically.

They told him what they had discovered – or rather not discovered – since calling in from Shakhrisabz.

90

'So what's your guess?' Zhakidov asked them.

'The mountains,' they said almost as one voice.

'We need to take a helicopter up there and have a look,' Nurhan argued.

Zhakidov looked at her doubtfully. 'Have you any idea where to start looking?'

'We'll do some research first,' Marat said. 'Have a look at the map and see what the possibilities are. Then work out a search plan to cover the most likely places.'

Zhakidov nodded. 'OK, do it. But make sure you keep in contact.' He looked at his watch. 'In about seventy-five minutes we should be hearing from the terrorists.'

6

According to Docherty's watch it was almost nine o'clock. The atmosphere in the men's room was better than it had been two hours earlier, largely, he suspected, for the simple reason that they had been fed. It had not exactly been a feast, but it was better than Docherty had expected – the bread was only slightly stale, the tea highly refreshing, and he had always liked his yoghurt on the sour side anyway. Whoever the terrorists were, there was nothing sadistic in the way they were treating their hostages.

And everyone had managed to use the bathroom, showing exemplary restraint in the amount of water they used.

That was the good news. The bad news was that Sam Jennings seemed to be having trouble with his heart. Docherty knew that the sheer stress of such situations tended to create particular medical problems, and that the cardiovascular system was one of the main areas at risk. The respiratory system, as he unwisely told Mike Copley, was another. Sharon was apparently prone to asthma attacks.

Sam Jennings himself said there was nothing to worry about. 'Who's the doctor here?' he asked indignantly. 'I'm going to outlive these bastards if it's the last thing I do.'

Docherty hoped it wouldn't be, and not just for Sam Jennings's sake. For one thing, a doctor was always useful to have around. For another, there was no telling how the hijackers would react to the death of one of their hostages. They would, after all, be blamed for it.

In the meantime, Copley had been pacing up and down the room for several minutes. He had started off making jokes about Colditz and *Porridge*, and was always ready with a grin, but left to its own devices his face settled into the grim mask it was wearing now. Some people used humour to keep them going, Docherty thought, while others used emotionalism. He preferred the former – it was kinder on the others involved.

The initial shock was wearing off, he realized. Now everyone was getting a bit restless. Maybe this was the time for him to give his version of the Counter Revolutionary Warfare Wing lecture on hostage situations and how to survive them. Always assuming he could remember any of it.

Flexibility, adaptability . . .

At that moment the sliding panel on the door jerked back. 'Stand back,' the familiar voice said, and almost immediately the door opened inwards. 'Exercise time,' the man with the AK47 said, gesturing with the gun for them to leave the room.

Everyone looked at Docherty, who said: 'Let's go.' If the hijackers wanted to shoot them, they could do so a lot more easily where they were.

The man with the gun pointed him back down the corridor they had used the previous evening, and the eight males walked in single file towards the centre of the lodge, where they took the right turn, which led to the front entrance. Docherty tried repressing his hope that the women might already be outside, but the sense of disappointment could hardly have been more acute when he discovered they were not.

Instead there was only the natural beauty of the mountains that rose up behind the lodge and reached out on either side to enclose it. By daylight it was clear that the lodge stood at the head of a west-facing valley, almost a bay, that was gouged from the side of the range. Ahead of him wooded mountainsides sloped away into brown foothills, which in turn tumbled down to a distant yellow-brown plain.

It was a beautiful place for a prison, he thought.

No one had told them where they could walk, but the four armed men positioned on the corners of the rectangular space in front of the lodge seemed to offer a pretty good clue. Docherty recognized the man who had answered to the name Talib on the bus, and walked slowly towards him, making sure that both his hands were visible to the hijacker. He stopped when still five metres away.

'Can I ask a question?' he said.

The man looked at him impatiently. 'No speak English,' he said shortly.

'Do any of the others speak English?' Docherty asked, pointing at each of the other three men in turn.

'No speak English,' Talib said again. He seemed almost amused, Docherty thought. Maybe he did speak English.

It was more than frustrating, almost like a slap in the face. It made him feel impotent, and reminded him of the way he had always felt as a young man, when girlfriends retreated into silence in the middle of a fight.

He turned away from Talib, so as not to show the angry frustration he was feeling. The man who had let them out of the room, and who at least knew the words 'stand back' and 'exercise', was nowhere to be seen. Nor was Nasruddin, whose English was as good as his own. Probably better, if you liked the BBC version.

This was policy, Docherty realized. Someone had done their homework on hostage situations, and decided on a policy of minimal communication between hostage-takers and hostages. That was depressing enough in itself, since often the communication between the two was instrumental in saving the latter's lives. But it was also depressing in what it said about the prospects for a successful negotiation to end this business. These men did not seem likely to fold, and presumably the Uzbek government would have little more reason to make concessions. Not unless the British government was putting pressure on them, and everyone knew their policy on giving in to terrorism.

Except, he suddenly realized, that this time one of their own was caught up in the net. A cynic would expect that to make a difference. He supposed he should hope it wouldn't, but to hell with that – they needed all the help they could get.

A cynic might also think that the Zahids were prostrating themselves on the ground as a way of demonstrating their Islamic credentials. Or maybe they were praying for a rescue mission.

It suddenly occurred to Docherty that with Sarah Holcroft among the hostages his old regiment might be brought into this. Now there was a thought . . . He started scouring the horizon for suitable places to put an observation point. The SAS could hardly be here yet, but by this time tomorrow . . .

He noticed for the first time that the others were just standing idly around, and walked across to join them. 'We should be keeping moving,' he urged them. 'There's no way of knowing how long it'll be before they let us out again.'

'You should write a book,' Ogley said sarcastically, but he accompanied the other three as they began circumnavigating the available space.

Docherty asked the American how he was.

'I've been better,' Sam said, 'but I'll be OK.'

'What did you ask the guard?' Copley asked.

'I asked if I could ask a question. The answer was no. He said he didn't speak English, but I think they've decided to keep contact to a minimum.'

'Why?' Copley wanted to know.

'Ever heard of the Stockholm Syndrome?' Docherty asked. 'Well, it was named after something that happened in Sweden, oh, about twenty years ago now. A man tried to hold up a bank, but the police arrived too quickly for him to get away, so he gathered together about half a dozen hostages and holed up in the bank's vault. They were there for six days. And during that time a bond developed between the man and his hostages. A practical bond which seemed completely crazy to those who weren't directly involved. They stood guard for him when he slept, and protected him with their bodies when he surrendered, just in case the police were feeling trigger-happy. One of the women hostages fell in love with him, and married him later in prison.

'I guess it's easier to see why he co-operated with them than the other way round. In some ways they were in the same sort of situation as a pet would be towards its owner – utterly dependent – and some psychologists reckon people do regress when they feel that powerless . . .'

'Jesus, are we going to start getting up on our hind legs and begging for dog biscuits?'

'Probably. I guess the other side of the equation is the important one for us to worry about. The hostage-taker in Stockholm ended up being unable to harm his hostages for the simple reason that they had become real human beings to him.'

'And you think that's what these people are trying to avoid?'

Docherty shrugged. 'Maybe. On the other hand they could just be rotten linguists. But any chance we get to talk, we should. Even the odd smile will help.'

Nurhan and Marat stood shoulder to shoulder over the 1:250,000 scale map of Kashkadar'inskaya Oblast, studying the mosaic of unmade tracks in the areas to either side of the Samarkand – Shakhrisabz road.

'There's nothing up there,' Marat muttered.

'What did you expect – a new housing estate? There's a hell of a lot of caves.'

'OK, so where do we start? This map doesn't seem to have a symbol for caves large enough to hide a bus in.'

She sighed. 'Christ knows.'

'Well, I vote for following that first track outside Kitab. It was the only one on that side of the mountain with definite tyre marks.'

'The other tracks weren't so dusty. But OK, it's as good a place as any.'

Marat looked for it on the map. 'It's not marked,' he decided. 'Unless this is it,' he added, pointing out a track which wound its way up a steep valley and abruptly ended. 'But there's no sign of the fork we came to.'

'These maps are hopeless,' she said. 'In the old days all they cared about were the border areas. They got them right.'

'It's all we've got,' he said, rolling it up. 'Let's go.'

It took them fifteen minutes to reach the airport, where the Ka-26 helicopter was waiting for them, the contra-rotating rotors hanging limp above the squat fuselage. Its blond Russian pilot was morosely smoking a cigarette on the cab running board of a fuel tanker nearby. Marat showed him their destination.

'What are we looking for?' the pilot asked.

'A bus,' Nurhan said shortly.

'There are plenty of those in the city.'

'Ha ha. Let's get moving.'

The pilot grinned and ushered them aboard. Almost instantly, it seemed, they were rising swiftly into the sky, Samarkand laid out in its bowl beneath them, the blue domes sparsely scattered across the brown city, like cornflowers in a desert.

After their walk in the mountain air the room seemed almost unbearably stuffy. 'I'm sticking to my shirt already,' Copley complained, 'and it's not even ten o'clock. I think hijackers should be obliged to provide fresh underwear on a daily basis.'

'They could put it in the Geneva Convention,' Sam Jennings agreed. The American seemed better, Docherty thought. The colour in his cheeks was back to normal.

'It's a serious point though,' the Scot said. 'In these conditions we're not going to be able to stay as clean as we'd like, but it is important we keep ourselves as clean as we can.' He stopped, thinking that he sounded like a preacher. Everyone was looking at him, including the Zahids. Docherty found them harder to read than the others, particularly the two older men. The young men seemed to have bounced back from the initial shock with typical adolescent bravado.

'I've done courses in how to deal with situations like this,' Docherty went on, 'though mostly from the point of view of those outside the situation. Still, I picked up a few tips on the way which might come in useful. So . . .'

'Enlighten us, Doc,' Copley said with a grin.

Docherty grinned back. 'Most of it's common sense. The basic thing is to keep active and keep flexible, both mentally and physically. We have to keep ourselves as together as we can. That means eating whatever food they give us, whether it tastes like what we're used to or not. It means wiping our arses whichever way we can, and not freaking out at the absence of toilet paper. It means accepting that we're not going to get a nice hot bath each day, and not using that fact as an excuse to get slovenly. We're in a situation where we're denied all respect from the rest of the world, so we have to get it from ourselves and each other.

'The same thing goes for our minds. We have to keep them active, one way or another. For a start, how many books do we have?'

'One guide book,' Copley said.

'A biography of Tamerlane,' Sam Jennings volunteered.

'Nothing,' Ogley admitted.

'A Koran,' Ali Zahid said with a smile. 'But in Urdu, I'm afraid.'

'Last year's *Wisden*,' Javid said.

'OK. So by the end of this we should all be experts in something. How about paper and pens? I have one ballpoint.'

There were three others, one of which had already succumbed to the heat.

'We can play word games,' Docherty said. 'We can make a draught-board and pieces. We can argue about which footballers or cricketers are the best who ever played. We can write tortured poetry. Anything is better than sitting around wondering what's happening in the world outside. Our chances of influencing the authorities are non-existent, and our chances of influencing this lot outside are not much better. But even given that, like I said before, we shouldn't miss any chance we get of making human contact with these men. Though it's wise to keep in mind the old saw about not discussing religion or politics.'

He paused for a moment. 'I don't want to scare anyone, but just remember that even a split second's hesitation – that split second most people seem to need before they can open fire on someone they know – might save your life in the event of a rescue attempt . . .'

'What are the chances of one?' Sam Jennings asked.

Docherty shrugged. 'Most situations like this end in either the terrorists' surrender or an attack by the authorities. If it comes to the second, then remember, get down on the floor and stay there. In these situations more hostages have been killed by the authorities than by their captors, and nearly always because they've stood up when they shouldn't.'

'We should try and tell the women,' Copley said.

'They should already know,' Docherty said. 'I think Brenda Walker works for Intelligence, so . . .'

'Looking after Sarah Holcroft,' Ogley said. 'That makes sense.'

'Well, it never occurred to me,' Copley admitted. 'She seemed kind of nice.'

In the women's room things had slowly improved over the last few hours. Isabel, with help from Brenda Walker, had bullied the others into talking with each other. They were not the most homogeneous of groups, in age, class or interests, but once started, the conversation, like a ball on a downhill slope, had just kept rolling.

Sarah Holcroft, rather nervously for someone with her tabloid reputation, had suggested that the four married women tell the story of how they met their husbands, and before anyone could object Alice Jennings had launched into the tale of how she had met Sam nearly sixty years earlier, in New York's Central Park. She had slipped when getting off her horse on the famous old carousel, and he had grandly come forward, parting the crowd with the words 'Make way – I'm a doctor.' In matter of fact he had only just entered medical school, but her ankle had only been slightly sprained, and they had even managed to go out dancing the same night.

Sharon's account of meeting Mike was not quite so romantic. They had met when Sharon was asked to sing with a Coventry-based punk band called The Hump. Mike was the drummer. 'He had a Mohican then,' Sharon said, 'and I thought what a dipstick! I still do sometimes. Anyway, we sort of started talking to each other a lot about my boyfriends and his girl-friends, and then one day we just started kissing each other. Just like that. It was weird. But nice.'

Isabel had half expected Elizabeth Ogley to decline to take part in this sharing of personal histories, but the lecturer seemed more than willing. 'It was a very sixties meeting,' she said drily. 'A party in Ladbroke Grove in the summer of '68. I was lying stoned out of my mind on one of the beds upstairs listening to a Cream record coming through the floor. This guy was sitting on the floor with his back to the bed telling me about the demonstration he had been on that day, and how "Ho, Ho, Ho Chi Minh" was a modern mantra. I must have fallen asleep because the next thing I knew he was on the bed beside me with his hand inside my bra. And the next thing after that he was pulling himself out, apologizing for coming too soon, and promising that he would do better next time.' Elizabeth grimaced. 'So it started with a lie,' she said matter-of-factly. Then her face softened momentarily. 'But it hasn't been all bad,' she said.

'Your turn, Isabel' Sarah said.

Isabel hadn't been sure whether this group was ready for her story, which she sometimes had trouble believing herself. She knew the disclosure of her career as a political kidnapper had shocked the others, and she wasn't at all sure whether she wanted to re-underline the extraordinariness of her younger life. But then again, it was a good story, and as far as the other women in the room were concerned, she'd at least been on the side of the angels that time round.

So she had told the story of her meeting with Docherty, of how she, an Argentinian exile in London, had agreed to work for MI6 in Argentina during the Falklands War, and how Docherty, himself leading a British unit behind enemy lines on the Argentinian mainland, had come to the hotel in Rio Gallegos to warn her that her cover might have been blown. Together they had escaped the country, hiking their way across the southern Andes into neutral Chile.

'You have had an exciting life,' Alice Jennings said, and the looks on the faces of the other women expressed much the same thought.

'The last twelve years it's just been bringing up the kids,' Isabel said.

'I thought they were all great stories,' Sarah Holcroft said, with a brusqueness which seemed to hide more than a trace of wistfulness. 'Have you ever been married?' she asked Brenda Walker.

'No,' was the answer, and there was sadness here too, Isabel thought. Both of these young women had been unlucky with men, she decided. Either with fathers or lovers or both.

Bakhtar Muratov noticed that the President was staring at the Georgia O'Keeffe print, an enormous red flower which seemed to be reaching out to suck him in. He had bought it in New York several years earlier, and the print had occupied pride of place on his living-room wall ever since. He had fallen in love with the original at first sight, without really knowing why until a fellow gallery visitor had explained the implicit sexuality. This visitor had then taken him back to her Lower East Side apartment for a coffee and twenty-four hours of the explicit version, entangling the print with memories of such pleasure that Muratov felt good whenever he looked at it.

The President was not impressed. 'I could have painted this,' he muttered.

Muratov scowled at Bakalev's back and looked at his watch again. It was one minute to eleven. He had the feeling that – Uzbekistan Telephone willing – the call would come on time.

It did.

Muratov switched on the tape and picked up the receiver, holding up a finger to indicate the need for Bakalev to remain silent. The President's presence in the room was the last thing he wanted the hijackers to know. 'Muratov,' he said.

'Good morning, Colonel,' a voice said. It was not the same man Muratov had spoken to the day before – both the tone and the accent were different. 'My name is Nasruddin Salih. I am the spokesman for The Trumpet of God.'

'Then speak,' Muratov said.

Nasruddin ignored the sarcasm. 'Have you verified what you were told yesterday?' he asked.

'The tour party is missing.'

'It is here with us.'

'And where are you?'

'In the Fan Mountains. I am sure you will work out the exact location soon enough.'

There was amusement in the bastard's voice, Muratov thought. It was the first time he could remember one of these Islamic zealots having a sense of humour.

'These are our demands,' Nasruddin told him abruptly. 'Our organization's programme is to be printed in full in tomorrow morning's *Voice of the People*. And the following men are to be released from your prisons – Muhammad Khotali, Timur Lukmanov, Akhmadzhon Pulatov and Erkin Saliq.'

Muratov waited several seconds, expecting more.

At the other end of the line, Nasruddin had been diverted by the sound of an approaching helicopter and the sudden appearance of Talib to tell him about it.

'Visitors,' the Uzbek said. 'In an army helicopter. But they're only looking, I think. It's only a Ka-26. There can't be many people up there.'

But they would have seen the bus, Nasruddin knew. It didn't matter a great deal – he had never expected that their location would remain undetected for very long.

'Colonel Muratov,' Nasruddin said. 'It seems you have discovered where we are . . .'

'What?'

'There is an army helicopter in the sky above us. Since we have the means of shooting it down, I suggest you recall it to base immediately. I will call you again in ten minutes.'

Muratov rubbed his eyes, and dialled a new number. In the Ka-26 Nurhan and Marat were staring down at the lodge nestled at the top of the valley. The bus was sitting outside like a trophy, and three armed men were staring up at them as they hovered some two hundred metres above.

'It's not marked on the map,' Marat was saying. But then the approach road had not been marked either.

The pilot was more interested in the visible guns. 'Can we go now?' he asked anxiously.

'No,' Nurhan ordered. She had taken about a dozen photographs so far of the building and the surrounding area, but wanted more close-ups. Through the zoom lens she could see a man emerge from the lodge's front door with what looked distinctly like a shoulder-held missile launcher.

'What's that?' she asked Marat calmly, passing him the camera.

'It's a fucking Stinger,' he said. 'Get the hell out of here,' he told the pilot.

Nurhan carried on taking pictures until the lodge was out of sight. A few seconds later Zhakidov's voice came through on the radio, advising their immediate withdrawal.

'Happy?' Muratov asked Nasruddin.

'I have no desire to needlessly take human life,' Nasruddin retorted.

'I hope not,' Muratov said. 'Shall we get back to your demands?'

'You have heard them. You will find a copy of our programme in the Hotel Samarkand safe, where I deposited it under my own name yesterday. Once it has been printed in the newspaper – and we shall know if it has or has not – the four released prisoners are to be brought here by helicopter – an Mi-8. They, ourselves and the hostages will then fly across the border to Tajikistan. You will announce that the prisoners have been granted exile, and we shall release the hostages. By then the deal with the Western governments will have been signed, and no one will be very interested in such a benign act of terrorism. I am sure you will come up with a half-convincing explanation for it all – an anti-terrorist exercise which went wrong, perhaps.'

Muratov raised an eyebrow. 'That will be easier if the hostages are all alive and in good health,' he said.

'They are.'

'You understand that I cannot say yes or no to you myself?'

'Yes, but I am sure you will have no difficulty in reaching the President.'

Muratov smiled to himself, looking across at Bakalev's angry face. 'How can I reach you with a reply?'

'I will ring you at three p.m. In the meantime the hostages' well-being depends on your behaviour. We do not wish to see anyone within a mile of here, either on the ground or in the air. Is that clear?'

'Perfectly. I . . .' Muratov began, but the call had been disconnected. He stared at the phone for several seconds, before replacing the receiver. It was the first time he had ever talked to a hijacker, but even so he had the distinct impression that Nasruddin was not typical of the species.

'Well?' Bakalev asked him.

Muratov told him the hijackers' demands, and how they were supposed to be met, adding that he was surprised they hadn't asked for more.

The President looked at him. 'These are not insignificant demands,' he said sarcastically. 'Khotali has been a thorn in our side for years, and I like him where he is. And how do we explain our sudden decision to print these lunatics' programme?'

Muratov thought for a moment. 'The second wouldn't be too much of a problem. We could print it as the first of a series – every mad group's manifesto that we can find. Though of course we won't say that it's part of a series until the second one is printed, by which time the hostages will have been released.' He smiled. 'And you'll get extra credit from the West for your determination to support democracy.'

Bakalev grunted. 'Are they that stupid? Maybe they are.' He exhaled noisily. 'But . . . you now what Khomeini did from exile . . .'

'Khotali's not in the same class.' And if that many people in Uzbekistan supported the clerical zealot, Muratov thought, then he and Bakalev were both wasting their time anyway.

'So you think we should just give them what they're asking for?' Bakalev said. He had begun to pace up and down.

'It looks better than the alternative. We need the Western deal and we need tourism. If The Trumpet of God' – Muratov curled the words derisively on his tongue – 'starts killing these tourists then we can say goodbye to about a quarter of our foreign-currency earnings for the next few years.'

'The deal would probably still go though,' Bakalev replied. 'After all, the English and Americans are not in it for charity – they want it as much as we do.'

'They want it, we need it.'

'Yes, yes . . . wait a minute,' Bakalev said, stopping in his tracks. 'Once the hostages are released, what's to stop them telling the newspapers? Our tourism income will be affected anyway.'

'It will be damaged much more if people are seen to die. If everyone is rescued then we can use it as proof of how efficient our police are, how safe this country is.' Muratov paused, wondering whether he really believed what he had just said. 'The only alternative,' he added sardonically, 'would be to kill the tourists ourselves after their release by the terrorists.'

Bakalev stopped once more. 'Or we could kill them all now,' he said softly. 'We know where they are, don't we?'

'They're in the new hunting lodge.'

The President looked surprised, and then almost indignant. 'The bastards,' he said, and then shrugged resignedly. 'Well, there was no way we were ever going to be able to use it again. And it's certainly a long way from anywhere. What's to stop us launching an air strike? Who will know? We can say their bus went over a cliff and exploded.'

7

After putting the phone down Nasruddin sat there for several seconds, feeling his heart thumping like a steam hammer. He had never imagined that it would feel like that – the exhilaration of talking on equal terms to someone who was probably the second most powerful figure in the country. He had told the man to get his helicopter away and he had done so, just like that.

And yet, having experienced the feeling, he knew where it came from. Any sociologist could write reams on the sense of powerlessness endemic in oppressed minority cultures, and his personal history had accentuated that sense.

My mother is dead, went the forgotten voice inside his mind, and I can't bring her back.

'Well?' Akbar asked explosively.

'You heard what I told him. He will put our demands to the President.'

'The son of Satan was probably sitting there beside him,' Talib said. 'I wonder how they found us so quickly.'

Nasruddin shrugged. 'Guesswork, perhaps. Once they worked out we were in the mountains then the choices were limited.' He still seemed to be shaking inside from the experience.

'How did he sound?' Akbar asked.

'The way you would expect – clever, condescending, sarcastic.'

'You got no sense of what they will do?'

'None. They will not know themselves yet. They must weigh the costs of acceptance against those of rejection. And we must wait four hours.'

It sounded like eternity. Nasruddin was conscious of the dizzy sense of power slipping away, and in its place a growing awareness of the hard choices that might yet be forced upon them.

'Do you think it was one of ours?' Copley asked.

'If it didn't land I think we can assume it was,' Docherty said. Whoever 'ours' might be in this context. He hadn't said anything to the others, but the old Soviet Union had not been slow to take on terrorists in situations like this, often with scant regard for the hostages concerned. Sometimes it had worked: one group of Lebanese Shiites who had kidnapped four Soviet diplomats had been sent a finger from one of their relatives, and had hastily released their captives. Sometimes it had not, and a hostage's chances of survival had come down to how adept or lucky they were when it came to dodging the bullets of both terrorists and authorities.

Of course, there was always the hope that the new Uzbekistan had not inherited such KGB propensities, but somehow Docherty didn't feel optimistic. He still felt their best chance rested on Sarah Holcroft's involvement drawing in help from home.

'It didn't seem to be moving,' Sam Jennings was saying.

'No,' Docherty agreed. The helicopter had been hovering. And presumably watching.

'Well, it's gone now,' Copley said.

'At least they know we're here,' added Ogley, as if a weight had been lifted from his mind.

'They always knew we were somewhere,' the American said unhelpfully.

This is just the beginning, Docherty thought. Despite his own pep talk he felt almost consumed by powerlessness. They didn't know what the hijackers wanted, or whether it could be granted, or what the authorities were planning. They were the ones at risk, and they were the ones who knew the least.

When the sound of the helicopter had faded into the distance, the women had drawn much the same conclusions as the men.

'They know where we are,' Elizabeth Ogley said, unaware that her husband was saying much the thing thirty metres away.

'But what does that mean?' Sharon wanted to know. 'Isabel?'

Isabel pulled herself out of her reverie. During the flying visit her mind had gone back twenty years, to the room in Córdoba where they had held the industrialist whose name she had long since forgotten. There had been no helicopter whirring above them, but she remembered the sound of sirens on the streets outside, and the strange blend of thrill and fear which they had evoked in her and her comrades. She wondered if Nasruddin and the others had watched the helicopter with the same intense emotions, and found herself feeling almost sorry for them.

'Isabel?' Sharon repeated.

'I don't know,' Isabel replied. 'But it can't be bad news.' Docherty would know, she thought, and felt the fear of loss wash through her mind once more.

Simon Kennedy wiped his brow and stared across the car park at the Ak Saray Museum. Maybe there would be someone over there he could question about the missing tourists.

It had taken only one and a half hours to reach Shakhrisabz on the mountain road, but it had still been cool when he started out, and the wind blowing behind the moving car all the way had not prepared him for the heat of the day. And he had forgotten his hat. As he approached the museum, the patch of shade under the overhanging acacia looked positively paradisal.

The *kravat* which occupied this space was home to an ageing Uzbek. Throwing English reticence to the winds, Kennedy took a seat without being asked and wiped his brow again. 'Do you speak Russian?' he asked, without much hope.

'*Da*,' the man said.

Kennedy explained about the missing tourist party. The Uzbek said he had information, and unselfconsciously extended his palm. The MI6 man gave him a five-thousand-rouble note, thinking that he would claim it back on expenses under the heading 'greedy peasant'. The old man told him about his visit from the police the night before, and then pulled several pieces of mosaic tile from somewhere within the robe he was wearing. 'Only a dollar each,' he said in Russian. 'Genuine fifteenth-century.'

Kennedy walked back across the car park, wondering how long it would be before someone noticed that the tiles on the gateway were growing fewer day by day. It was probably his imagination, but the boy on the gate seemed to smile knowingly at him.

The café across the street was just opening, and he went in search of coffee and an interpreter. The former was available, if almost undrinkable, and he had to wait over half an hour before a customer arrived who spoke both Russian and Uzbek. The man initially looked at Kennedy as if he was mad, but was persuaded to humour him by the sight of a five-thousand-rouble note. They walked across the street to interview the boy on the gate, who told Kennedy, through the bewildered interpreter, the same story he had told the NSS man and woman the night before, and generously added that he had seen the two of them head off in the same direction as the bus soon after first light that morning.

All of which seemed pretty decisive, Kennedy thought, once more ensconced behind the wheel of his car. He suddenly remembered the black Volga he had seen parked on the side of the road on the other side of the mountains. A rather striking-looking woman in a short red dress had been talking to two men, one of whom had been dressed in Western clothes, the other not. They must have been the police in question, he realized, though there had been no reason to think so at the time. The KGB had never been noted for its fashion sense.

Like the two of them, he could see no reason for lingering in Shakhrisabz once he had reported in. 'The Mystery of the Disappearing Bus,' he murmured to himself. What would Poirot make of it? he wondered, and wished he hadn't. His staff college instructor's remark – that he would make the perfect Hastings – had not yet ceased to rankle.

Still, even Hastings could probably put two and two together. Kennedy had no direct evidence that the bus had been hijacked, but the circumstantial facts – the disappearance, the security police interest, the cars which left with the bus – seemed conclusive enough. He told Janice as much when he finally managed to get through to Tashkent from the Shakhrisabz post office. Five minutes later she was walking through to see Pearson-Jones in the adjoining room. He listened, sighed, and asked her to connect him with London once more.

* * *

There were only three men gathered around the table in the Cabinet Office – the Prime Minister, Alan Holcroft and Sir Christopher Hanson. All three looked decidedly bleary-eyed. The last-named had just finished briefing his political masters on what had happened over the previous eighteen hours, beginning with Brenda Walker's failure to check in and ending with Kennedy's report from Shakhrisabz. He stressed that most of what they knew was educated guesswork, but added that in his opinion they were dealing with a real hijack.

'All right,' the Prime Minister said quietly, 'the first question has to be: why have the Uzbek authorities not contacted us?'

'Two possibilities,' Hanson said precisely. 'One, they don't yet know about the hijack. Two, they have reasons of their own for keeping silent. The first seems possible but unlikely. I don't know of any reason they might have for keeping silent.'

'I do,' Holcroft said. 'The trade deal is due to be signed this weekend. They may think this counts as bad publicity.'

'Really?' the Prime Minister said, as if he found it hard to believe. 'All right, assuming that is the case, what are we to do with our knowledge?'

'There is another question,' Hanson interjected. 'Why have the hijackers not publicized the abduction?'

'Perhaps the Uzbek government is keeping a tight lid on all the channels of information,' Holcroft suggested. It felt strange talking so logically about the problem when his own daughter was involved. For most of a sleepless night his brain had assaulted him with pictures of Sarah at every conceivable stage of her childhood and youth.

'Perhaps,' Hanson agreed, 'but usually hijackers work this sort of thing out in advance. The last thing they want is to pull off a stunt like this and have no one know about it.'

'So what is the answer?' the PM asked petulantly.

Hanson shrugged. 'I don't know. The third question, of course, is whether they know that one of their captives is the Foreign Minister's daughter.'

'You think it's possible that they don't?' Holcroft exclaimed in surprise. It had to be better if they didn't know, he thought. And then again . . . she would have more value as his daughter, and therefore be less likely to be harmed. If one hostage was selected for killing, he thought, remembering the *Achille Lauro*, then they would be less likely to choose her if they knew who she was.

'It does seem unlikely,' Hanson was saying, 'and something of a coincidence, but until we know for certain . . .'

'So what are we to do?' the PM asked Hanson.

'Well, the first thing we need to know is what the hijackers want and whom they want it from. If, for example, they do know that they have the Foreign Minister's daughter, then their demands will almost certainly be levelled at us rather than the government of Uzbekistan. If they don't know, then it's a different matter.'

'But what if the demands are levelled at us, but the Uzbeks are not passing them on?' Holcroft asked, thoroughly alarmed.

'A good question,' Hanson agreed.

'We have to inform the Uzbek government that we are aware of the situation,' Holcroft said, trying to keep a pleading tone out of his voice.

'Knowing that we know may reduce their anxiety,' Hanson agreed. And prevent them from charging in with guns blazing, he thought to himself.

'All right,' the PM agreed. 'I had better talk to President What's-his-name.' He picked up the nearest internal phone and asked his private secretary to get hold of an interpreter and the relevant number.

114

The ensuing silence was broken by Holcroft. 'Prime Minister,' he said formally, 'we could offer the Uzbeks help in dealing with a hostage situation. We do have the best people in the world in that department.'

'We'll see, Alan,' the PM said coolly. 'Let's wait until we know more about the situation.'

A long ten minutes went by before the interpreter arrived from elsewhere in the Whitehall labyrinth. The private secretary then started the laborious task of linking them, through Moscow, with Tashkent.

The call from London reached President Bakalev's office just as he returned from his meeting with Bakhtar Muratov. The moment he was told the British Prime Minister wished to talk with him the President realized the cat was out of the bag. While the interpreters wished each other good morning he congratulated himself on allowing Muratov to talk him out of ordering the air strike.

Then he picked up the waiting receiver. 'Mr Prime Minister,' he said, realizing he had forgotten the man's name.

'Mr President,' came the eventual reply. Probably the Englishman had forgotten his too. 'We have reason to believe,' Balalev's translator passed on, 'that a group of our British citizens has been the subject of a terrorist kidnapping in your country. In Samarkand, to be precise.'

'That is correct,' Bakalev agreed. 'We have only just been informed of this ourselves,' he lied. How the hell had the English already found out? he wondered. And what would they want now they knew?

'Do you have a list of those taken hostage?' the Prime Minister asked.

'No, only the numbers of men and women . . .' He was

about to add 'and their nationality', but thought better of it. Maybe no one else knew that Americans were involved.

In London, the PM, Holcroft and Hanson shared glances. It seemed that the Uzbeks were unaware of Sarah Holcroft's presence among the hostages. 'We can supply you with a list,' the PM told Bakalev.

'Thank you.'

'Do you know who these terrorists are?'

'They call themselves The Trumpet of God. They are religious fanatics.'

'Have they told you what they want in exchange for the hostages' release?'

'We received their demands half an hour ago. They wish to have their programme printed in our state newspaper, and they are demanding the release of four other zealots from prison.'

There was a slight pause as the Prime Minister sought out the most sensitive phrasing. 'This is clearly an internal matter for the government of Uzbekistan,' he said eventually, 'but I am sure you will understand, Mr President, that the safety of British citizens is a matter of great importance to us, wherever they may be in the world.'

'Of course,' Bakalev agreed. 'But I am fully aware of British policy as regards such situations – "no surrender to terrorism". Were those not the words of your illustrious predecessor?'

'Yes, yes, they were,' the PM agreed. 'And as a general rule we hold to that policy very firmly. But there can be exceptions, special circumstances to consider . . . It is not for the British to dictate the government of Uzbekistan's response. I can only say that the British government would consider it a most friendly act, and I would consider it a personal favour, if the government of Uzbekistan could do its best to secure the peaceful release of these hostages.'

The translation of this last sentence ushered in a lengthy silence. In London, Holcroft gave the PM a grateful glance. In Tashkent, President Bakalev wondered if he had really heard what he thought he had heard.

'I would naturally like to help,' he began cautiously, 'but conceding these demands could be very costly for my country. As you must be aware, a semblance of political stability has been hard to achieve for many of the newly independent states in this region, and to be seen to give ground to the Islamic fundamentalists would be profoundly destabilizing. And an increase in political problems will of course exacerbate our existing economic difficulties. As I said, I personally would be happy to offer assistance, but I must think first of my country and the people who elected me.'

Hanson rolled his eyes at the ceiling. Holcroft found he was clenching his fist. The PM bit the bullet. 'I realize that no price can be put on such things,' he began, 'but I think it would be possible for the British government to offer compensation for any problems which arose as a result of this situation.'

Bakalev smiled to himself. 'I think $200 million would be a reasonable sum.'

'I will need to discuss such an arrangement with my colleagues,' the PM said.

'Of course.'

'If we can keep this line open then I will talk to you again in fifteen minutes.'

'Very well.'

The PM signalled his secretary to cut off the extensions, and looked round at Holcroft and Hanson.

'It's a lot less per person than we paid out for the Falkland Islanders,' Hanson said drily.

'It's a drop in the bucket,' the PM said. 'And in any case, as long as it's tied to development deals this country won't be any the poorer. The only problem will be hiding the transaction in the public accounts.'

'There's always a way,' Hanson said cynically. 'And in any case, who could object to expenditure aimed at saving lives?'

'The people who say we should never give in to terrorism?' Holcroft asked wearily.

'Nobody cares who runs Uzbekistan,' Hanson insisted. 'It could just as well be the Muslim loonies in government, the communists doing the hijackings. We worry too much about these small countries. They're basically irrelevant to how we do in the world.'

'Maybe,' the PM said. 'But in any case, no one has made any demands of the British government, so there's no way we can be giving in to terrorism.' He looked thoughtful for a moment. 'But just in case – I think your earlier suggestion was a good one, Alan.' He nodded, as if agreeing with himself.

In Tashkent, President Bakalev had been smoking a cigarette, unable to believe his luck. Perhaps next time, he thought ironically, his own people could do the kidnapping and cut out the middlemen.

He wondered why the British government was so concerned about the fate of these fourteen hostages. Maybe there was an election coming up – after what had happened to Jimmy Carter in the USA no one wanted to face one with a hostage crisis under way.

Bakalev sighed with satisfaction, blowing smoke at the fan spinning round above his head. 'They're on again,' an aide called to him from the open door.

The Prime Minister wasted no time. 'The sum you suggested is acceptable,' he began. 'It will of course be in the form of development grants, with half the sum tied to the purchase of British products.'

Bakalev grimaced, but concurred. 'And the deal already agreed will be signed here this weekend, as arranged?'

'Yes. But there are two further conditions. First, we expect to be consulted at all levels throughout the duration of the hostage crisis. After we two have finished speaking I would like your operational commander to get in touch with our embassy, so that a British liaison officer can be attached to his team.'

'Is this really necessary?' Bakalev asked. 'The situation should be resolved by this time tomorrow, and the hostages on their way home.'

'I hope you are right,' the PM agreed. 'But there is no way we can be sure. The second condition is that you accept help from us in dealing with the hostage situation. I intend no disrespect to your country, Mr President, when I say that the British Army has more experience of dealing with such situations than anyone . . .'

'How many men?' Bakalev asked bluntly.

'Two,' the PM said, picking a figure out of the air. 'They will serve only in a consultative capacity, of course.'

'Of course,' Bakalev said, wrinkling his nose. After all, what difference could it make? By the end of the week these two soldiers and all the hostages would be back in England, leaving behind a richer Uzbekistan and a more popular President.

'Are these two conditions acceptable?' the Englishman was asking.

'They are,' Bakalev said.

8

On his way to see the President, Muratov realized how relieved he was that the English had suddenly intervened. The idea of taking out the hostages and hijackers in one explosive swoop had certainly had an appealing simplicity to it, but over the years experience had taught him that such schemes had a habit of rebounding on their architects. And, he had to admit, while fourteen innocent deaths might represent no more than an average week's murder toll in a large American city, it still seemed an excessively large burden to put on one's conscience.

Muratov wondered whether he was succumbing to the new religious mania. This is where seventy years of enforced secularism leads a culture, he thought. Right down the throats of the hungry mullahs.

He found the President smoking a cigarette and gazing happily out of the large picture window at the opera house across the square. Bakalev lost no time in filling him in on all the delightful details.

'Two hundred million dollars, plus the trade deal,' he gushed, 'and all for letting a few madmen out of prison and printing some idiotic religious drivel. If the whole business gets out we can say we conceded to the demands on humanitarian grounds, and because the British asked us to.'

'What interests me is why they asked us to,' Muratov said, mostly to himself.

'Who knows? Maybe they have an election coming up and don't want any bad publicity. It's not as if they're giving up anything, is it?'

'Except $200 million.'

Bakalev shrugged. 'It's hardly anything to them. I probably should have asked for more.'

You probably should, Muratov thought. 'So I just tell the hijackers we accept their demands?' he said.

'Yes. Arrange the prison releases and the printing of their programme. Ah, I almost forgot – the British did insist on sending two experts in hostage situations to help us. They will arrive early tomorrow. Until then they want one of their embassy staff to liaise with your people.'

'What's the point? If we're giving the hijackers what they want . . .'

'That's what I said. They claim they want people here in case something goes wrong, or the hijackers change their minds. Whatever.'

'Our people are going to love this.'

Bakalev smiled. 'And I had an idea,' he said. 'That Ismatu-layeva woman is in charge of the Anti-Terrorist Unit, right? Her mother was always a pain in the arse. Anyway, put her in charge of this operation, responsible directly to you. If anything does go wrong, then having a woman in charge will be good publicity for us in the West.'

Muratov frowned but said nothing.

'And I've been wondering,' Bakalev continued, 'should we contact the Americans? Do you think they would pay another $200 million for their two hostages?'

'No,' Muratov said. He still wasn't at all sure why the British had suddenly become so terrorist-friendly. Until he did understand their reasons – or lack of them – it felt better not to further complicate matters. He told Bakalev so.

The President was in too good a mood to argue with him.

Nurhan and Marat drove back into town from the airport in silence. Her mind was fully engaged with the problems posed for her unit by the terrorists' location, while his was still recovering from the sudden recognition of the Stinger on the man's shoulder. The last time he had seen one had been eight years earlier, on a two-helicopter patrol in Afghanistan. A split second after visual identification the missile had been fired, turning one of the helicopters into an instant ball of flame. This explosion had sent Marat's helicopter into a spin which the pilot was still struggling to right when the ground intervened. Marat had spent one month in a field hospital and several more in a convalescent unit in Tashkent. He had never enjoyed a helicopter flight since.

They arrived back at the NSS HQ for the second time that day shortly before noon. The temperature was in the low thirties and still rising, but all the shady parking spaces had been taken. They left the Volga to bake and walked into the cool of the building.

Zhakidov's office was the only one with an air-conditioner, an ancient machine which, according to the manufacturer's plate, had been made in Springfield, Massachusetts, and had somehow contrived to spend its working life in the service of the KGB, deep in the heart of Asia. To judge from the noises which emanated from it, that life was almost over. The machine seemed to gulp rather than simply ingest electricity, because every now and then the noise would suddenly rise to a tumult and every light-bulb in the building would momentarily flicker and dim.

The air in the office, though, was almost cold, and Zhakidov was actually wearing his jacket. He gestured them into chairs with a wave of his hand and carried on writing something into some sort of ledger. He looked vaguely pissed off, Marat thought, and wondered if the new young wife was proving more trouble than she was worth.

'Do you know what that place is?' Zhakidov asked abruptly.

'No idea,' Nurhan answered, assuming he meant the lodge where the terrorists were holed up.

'It's Bakalev's personal hunting lodge. Or at least it was intended to be. It was built a few years ago, for the Party bosses. Gorbachev was going to be the first invited guest to spend a weekend there.'

'Surprise surprise,' Marat murmured. Lately he had begun to wonder whether the Party leadership had done anything other than feather its own nest during the final thirty years of Soviet rule.

'But he was too busy dismantling the country,' Zhakidov went on. 'Anyway, it was only used once or twice, and it hasn't been used at all since the break-up.'

'Too embarrassing,' Marat murmured. He wondered if Zhakidov had ever made use of the facilities, and decided to risk asking. They would need a first-hand description of the place from somebody.

But Zhakidov had never been invited.

'What's been decided?' Nurhan interjected. Zhakidov had let them know what the terrorists were demanding during the return helicopter flight, and she had assumed that Bakalev's answer would be a cross between outright refusal and delaying tactics. Then it would be up to her to dream up a workable rescue attempt while the terrorists were stalled in negotiations.

Zhakidov punctured the balloon.

'What!?' she exclaimed angrily. 'We're just going to let them get away with it? Why?'

Zhakidov simply shrugged, which infuriated her even more.

'What's the point of setting up an anti-terrorist unit and then not using it the first time it's needed?' she demanded to know.

'You won't be idle,' Zhakidov told her calmly. 'The agreement may break down, the terrorists may change their minds, who knows? Make contingency plans. Get your people in position and ready to go if the need arises. And be prepared for visitors.' He told her about the embassy official and the experts flying out from Britain.

She exploded a second time. 'You mean I'm going to have two Englishmen leaning over my shoulder?'

'Maximum co-operation,' Zhakidov said.

Marat remembered reading about the Iranian Embassy siege in London. 'Are they from the SAS?' he asked.

'I wasn't told,' Zhakidov said.

'What difference does it make?' Nurhan said automatically, though a small voice at the back of her mind admitted to an interest in meeting them if they were. Several of the hostage-release operations she had studied had involved the SAS.

'There's one other thing,' Zhakidov told her. 'You have been given command of the situation on the ground. From now on you will report directly to Colonel Muratov in Tashkent. Is that understood?'

'Yes, sir,' Nurhan said. She felt elation at the implicit promotion, but it was tinged with annoyance at the emptiness of the context – she was being placed in command of a surrender to terrorism, after all – and sorry for the implied slight to her immediate boss. She didn't exactly like Zhakidov, but she had always respected his professionalism.

'Congratulations,' Marat said drily. 'Who am I supposed to take orders from?'

'You're still mine,' Zhakidov said. 'And I want you to track down any contacts Nasruddin Salih has in the city. His tours have been coming here for several months, and he must have been here before that to set things up. He may even have relations here. Find out. I'm assuming,' he added to Nurhan, with an air of slightly mocking deference, 'that the more we know about these people the better.'

'Yes, sir,' she agreed.

It was almost two o'clock when the three men gathered again in the lodge's living-room. Talib had taken his first few hours of sleep since their arrival, and was still rubbing the tiredness out of his eyes.

'Any sign of the enemy?' he asked the others.

'None,' Akbar said, almost smugly.

'If they're not out there now they soon will be,' Talib said. 'If Bakalev rejects our demands we shall have to start making it more difficult for any watchers. I told you what happened at Djibouti.'

They remembered. All four terrorists had been taken out simultaneously by accurate long-range fire. It was a sobering thought.

'And they may have thermal imaging,' Talib went on remorselessly. 'We must keep at least some of our men close enough to the hostages to confuse the picture.'

Nasruddin glanced across at Akbar and realized why Talib was bringing this up now. The Tajik was getting overconfident, and needed reminding that some of the futures beckoning them were decidedly less rosy than others.

'If we have calculated correctly,' Akbar said, 'then our demands will be accepted . . .'

'God willing,' Talib murmured.

'But we have to consider rejection,' Nasruddin insisted reluctantly. What with Akbar's optimism and his cousin's fatalism he sometimes felt compelled to shoulder the burden of all their doubts.

'We will have a simple choice,' Talib said. 'To abandon the game or to up the stakes.'

'How do you mean?' Nasruddin asked softly. In their discussions and arguments prior to setting this operation in motion they had always skirted around this point. All three men had voiced their theoretical willingness to face a martyr's death, but on the subject of killing there had been a unanimous silence.

Talib broke it. 'We will have to kill one of the hostages.' He looked at each man in turn. 'I have questioned myself on this matter, and prayed for clear guidance. None has been given to me. But if, on balance, it seems that we can only achieve our goals by doing so, then I do not see how we can shrink from it. In the end, God will decide if we were clear-sighted or blind.'

'How would we choose which hostage to kill?' Akbar wanted to know.

'We can worry about that if and when it becomes necessary,' Nasruddin told him bluntly. He had struggled with his own conscience, and, like his cousin, had found it hard to reach a clear decision. Being with the tour party for almost a week, getting to know them as people, had, as expected, strengthened his doubts. But seventeen hours had passed since he had last set eyes on them, and already their reality as human beings was fading. 'I think we have no choice but to countenance such a step,' Nasruddin said slowly, 'but until . . .'

'We all hope it will not be necessary,' Talib interrupted. 'There is no joy in killing.'

'"You shall not kill any man whom God has forbidden you to kill, except for a just cause,"' Akbar quoted from the Koran. 'And ours is a just cause.'

'That is for God to decide,' Talib reminded him.

Lieutenant-Colonel Barney Davies, Commanding Officer 22 SAS, had rarely been more surprised. He had met the Foreign Minister before – several times in fact – but had never expected to have the man stride into his own office at the Regiment's Stirling Lines barracks on the outskirts of Hereford. Nor, in all their previous meetings, had he ever thought of Alan Holcroft as anything other than utterly certain of himself. An arrogant bastard, through and through.

But not today. The Foreign Minister looked almost shellshocked. Maybe the man had found God. Or caught AIDS off a rent boy, like that politician in *Prime Suspect*, which Davies had watched on video a few evenings before.

Or maybe not. Holcroft sat down, looked round the office, abruptly stood up again, and asked if the CO would take a walk outside with him.

'Across the parade ground?' Davies asked.

'Anywhere where we won't be heard,' Holcroft said.

Davies raised an eyebrow but said nothing. He led the way out of the building, noting in passing Holcroft's chauffeur leaning against the ministerial limousine. His opinion of politicians, never high, had not really recovered from his first run-in with Holcroft five years earlier, during and after the Colombian mission. The man had not only personally intervened to make sure that no public recognition was given to the two SAS troopers whose lives had been lost, but neither had he offered any private recognition of their sacrifice. Like countless soldiers before them, those two men had deserved better of their political masters.

Davies smiled to himself, remembering Trooper Eddie Wilshaw's utterly insubordinate face.

'This is a delicate matter, Lieutenant-Colonel,' Holcroft began. He stopped, as if collecting his thoughts. 'I will be as concise as I can. A British tourist party has been hijacked, kidnapped – whatever the right word is – in Uzbekistan. That's one of the successor states of the Soviet Union . . .'

'I know where it is,' Davies said coldly, keeping to himself that this knowledge was a fairly recent thing, stemming as it did from the secret mission to Kazakhstan undertaken by the SAS the previous year. They had lost three men on that one. He hoped to God this was not going to be a rerun.

'Good,' Holcroft was saying. 'Well . . .' He quickly went through what was known of the events of the past twenty-four hours, concluding with a mostly uncensored blow-by-blow account of the Prime Minister's conversation with President Bakalev.

'I see,' Davies said when he was finished, though he still didn't understand why they were discussing it all in the middle of a parade ground on a decidedly cool summer day. So the government was leaning on the Uzbeks to give the local opposition some breathing space, and getting some hostages released in the process. He had no argument with that.

Holcroft took a deep breath. 'There's one other thing,' he said. 'My daughter is one of the hostages.'

'Oh.' Suddenly the whole business made more sense. 'I'm sorry about that,' Davies murmured.

128

'But the kidnappers don't know who she is,' Holcroft went on. 'And of course it's important that they don't find out. Which is why I'm here in person. At this moment only the Prime Minister, myself and Christopher Hanson are aware of the full situation. And now yourself, of course. I'm relying utterly on your discretion – and those of the two men who are chosen to go.'

'You can take that for granted,' Davies said coolly.

For a moment Holcroft looked decidedly human. 'I know,' he said. 'But . . . this is hard for me. And my wife, of course.' He managed a smile. 'Look, I won't take up any more of your valuable time. Hanson has all the information about the hijack you will need . . . he already has a man out there. And Special Branch is covering the Bradford end.'

They had retraced their steps almost to the limousine. 'Ah, by the way,' Holcroft said suddenly. 'I forgot – one of your old boys is one of the hostages. James Docherty? Does that name ring a bell?'

'He led the team we sent into Bosnia last year,' Davies said dully. He couldn't believe it.

'Ah yes, a good man,' Holcroft said. They had reached the limousine. 'Keep me informed,' he added as he climbed inside.

'Of course.' Davies watched the car glide out of sight. Docherty! The man seemed destined for adventures, even when he no longer wanted them. Only eighteen months earlier Davies had coaxed him out of retirement to undertake the mission in Bosnia, and the Scot had come back with the bitterness woven a little more tightly through his smile. Davies knew all too well that you could send a soldier to war once too often, particularly a soldier who refused to close his conscience down for the duration.

In any case, Docherty had retired for good after that one, and Davies had heard nothing of what he was doing until now. The card he had received the previous Christmas from Glasgow, though very welcome, had been lamentably devoid of information.

Davies wondered whether Docherty's wife and children were also among the hostages. He walked back towards his office, stopping to ask his aide to find and summon Major Jimmy Bourne, the long-time commander of the Regiment's Counter Revolutionary Warfare Wing. Once behind his desk he called a number in Whitehall, and asked to be called back on a secure line. Then he ordered tea and a rock cake from the mess.

The call came first. Hanson gave him a brief verbal update, faxed the relevant information, and said he would call again in half an hour to see if there were any questions. The tea arrived when Davies was still on the first page. In his relief at finding that Docherty's children weren't on the list of hostages he bit with inadvisable vigour on the rock cake, causing a chain reaction of vibrating fillings.

A rap on the door was followed by Bourne, who was carrying his own mug of tea. 'Good morning, boss,' he said, eyeing the rock cake with distrust.

'Trouble,' Davies began, and went through what Holcroft had told him from start to finish, before handing over the reports from Hanson.

'Two men,' Bourne murmured to himself when he had finished reading. 'May I?' he asked, reaching for Davies's computer keyboard.

'Be my guest,' Davies said. He hated the damn thing. 'I think they should be relatively senior men,' he decided. 'We need to pull out all the stops on this one. No,' he said, seeing Bourne's expression, 'I don't like thinking that way either, but the bastards have us by the throat these days. And I don't mean the hijackers,' he added, somewhat superfluously.

'Well, I don't think there'll be a wide choice anyway,' Bourne said. 'They'll have to be Russian-speakers . . .'

'We're not out of Uzbek-speakers, are we?'

'Surprisingly, yes.' Bourne had the personnel of G Squadron on screen – this was the squadron currently on twenty-four-hour standby in case of terrorist incidents. He shook his head. 'I think we should send a couple of my lads,' he said.

'No objection from me,' Davies said, watching Bourne's two index fingers flashing to and fro on the keyboard.

'OK, then. Rob Brierley for one. He teaches the "Hostage Situation" course, and he's one of the three Russian-speakers. The other two are Terry Stoneham and Nick Houghton.' He paused a moment. 'I'd go with Stoneham, mostly because he gets on well with Brierley.'

'Fine. Brief 'em and kit 'em up. I'll get started on the transport arrangements.'

Terry Stoneham couldn't believe it. 'You're kidding me, right?' he asked his brother.

'Wish I was,' Mike Stoneham said. He was phoning from the cinema he managed in the West End.

'Tell me again,' Terry demanded.

'We've been fined half a million quid, banned from the FA Cup, and had twelve points deducted before we start next season in the League.'

'We start with minus twelve points!?'

'Right.'

'We'd be better off relegated. At least there'd be something to play for.'

'There still is – survival.'

'But the management's different now, the owner's different. How can they be blamed for what the fuckers before them

131

did? And why should the fans suffer? Why should I suffer, for fuck's sake – I didn't do anything wrong.'

'Yeah. Anyway, I just thought you'd like to hear the bad news from your brother, and not a total stranger.'

'Ha-bloody-ha.' He still couldn't believe it. They'd only escaped relegation by four points last season, and now they'd be starting off with a twelve-point handicap.

'How are you otherwise?' Mike asked.

'Fuck knows. OK, I suppose . . .' He knew it was only football, but somehow he hadn't needed this.

'Have you seen the baby yet?'

'Yeah, once.'

There was a few moments' silence at both ends of the line.

'Why don't you come up to town for the weekend?' Mike suggested.

'Maybe. Don't worry about me, OK? I'm all right. Really.'

'OK, we're here if you feel like a laugh.'

'I know. Thanks.' He put down the phone, and slumped back on to the sofa. The clock on the mantelpiece said he had another hour before teaching his 'Hearts and Minds' class to the latest bunch of insolent newly badged bastards.

'Only football' – he could remember Jane aping the words sarcastically. He thought about the baby, their son. The boy didn't even have a name yet, or at least not as far as he knew. Maybe she and her boyfriend had come up with one.

Terry thought about the boyfriend. Don his name was, but he would always be 'the boyfriend'. Was the guy really willing to take on someone else's kid and be a proper father to it? Jane obviously thought so, but it seemed a lot to ask. Terry wasn't at all sure he could do it if the situation was reversed.

Maybe Don could. He didn't seem such a bad bloke, much as Terry had wanted him to be. And if he was prepared to be the boy's father then maybe Terry should just back out of the situation, pretend he hadn't got a son. That was what Jane had asked him to think about. That was obviously what she wanted. It would be easier, no doubt about it. But was it right? He was buggered if he knew. In fact, when it came down to it, he didn't really know what he felt about it all. When he'd seen the baby, the little face and all the little limbs, he hadn't really felt any connection with himself. But maybe men didn't, at least not straight off.

He sighed and looked round the one-room flat. It still felt cramped, even after five months. He thought about all the work he'd put into their house, and felt the familiar anger well up inside him. I didn't deserve this, he thought, and felt instantly ashamed of feeling so sorry for himself.

It was time to get moving. He got to his feet, walked through into the tiny bathroom, and picked up the reusable razor which Jane had foisted on him as ecologically correct. He studied his face in the mirror, the blue eyes beneath the short, straw-coloured hair. 'And Tottenham didn't deserve it either,' he told his reflection.

The door broke open with a crash, and the room suddenly filled with smoke. The leading members of the rescue team burst into view, looking like *Star Wars* rejects in their flame-retardant hoods and respirators.

The red dots from the aiming-point projectors on their MP5s searched and found the two terrorists standing by the wall to the left. They opened fire, killing them before their guns were even half raised into the firing position.

The terrorist by the hostages had his arm round one of their necks, and was in the act of pulling the man towards him when the tell-tale red dot appeared just above his waist.

Good, Brierley thought, very good.

But there was still the terrorist behind the door. His SMG had reached the firing position, and was spewing bullets around the smoke-filled room. One hostage went down, and another, before one of the rescuers pumped upwards of fifty bullets through his torso.

'OK,' Brierley shouted, and everything came to a halt. 'That was better. Far from perfect, but better.'

But it was a good thing the room on the screen was really two. Ever since an NCO playing hostage had been tragically killed by rescuers in a similar exercise, the Stirling Lines 'Killing House' had been a very different place. Now those playing the hostages and terrorists occupied one room while the rescuers attacked another, with cameras and wraparound wall screens giving each group the illusion that they were all in the same room. Both sides were able to riddle the bullet-absorbent walls, while their instructors kept score on film.

The system worked so well that American Special Forces had copied the idea lock, stock and wraparound screen. And it offered the sort of training that a few years before had only been possible at enormous risk to life and limb.

Brierley waited for the participants to file in through the door for debriefing. On this particular morning he was feeling more than usually pleased with life. He enjoyed his teaching work, despite originally expecting not to. He had a whole weekend of flying coming up, and Margie had finally accepted that he wasn't going to give her the sort of commitment she wanted. He supposed it was kind of sad that they couldn't go on the way they had started – like friends who enjoyed sex together – but the way things had been going lately her decision to stop seeing him was also something of a relief. When all was said and done they just didn't want the same thing, and all the resulting hassles had taken a lot of the fun out of being together.

It was better to be single. Even most of the happy couples he knew told him so.

Watching the group of young men now taking their seats in front of him, he wondered how many of them had been stupid enough to replace their mothers with a wife.

'Two hostages were killed,' he began. 'The first question is why.'

'Because they stood up,' one man said.

'They weren't *trying* to get shot,' Brierley began, before his attention was captured by the adjutant who had appeared in the doorway.

'Major Bourne wants to see you immediately,' the man said.

Brierley acknowledged the message with a wave and handed the class over to a fellow-instructor. Two minutes later he was walking into Bourne's office. Terry Stoneham was already sitting in one of the two chairs facing the CRW boss's desk.

'Right,' Bourne began the moment Brierley sat down, 'you two are leaving today for the middle of nowhere.' He turned the opened atlas around, placed it in front of them, and jabbed a finger at the map. 'Samarkand. Ever heard of it?'

'It was on the old Silk Road,' Brierley said.

Bourne tried not to look impressed. 'It was also in the Soviet Union until a couple of years ago. Now it's in Uzbekistan. Lots of tourists go there apparently, though I have no idea why. Lots of monuments, I suppose.'

'The Registan is supposed to be one of the finest pieces of Muslim architecture in the world,' Brierley told him. 'There was a documentary about it on the TV a few weeks ago,' he added. 'They've run out of money for the restoration work since the Russians pulled out.'

'Are we taking them the Regimental savings, boss?' Stoneham asked with a straight face.

'There aren't any. Fourteen of these tourists – all but two of them Brits – have been hijacked, and you two are being sent out as advisers to the Uzbek authorities.'

'Who are the hijackers?' Brierley asked.

Bourne shrugged. 'They call themselves The Trumpet of God . . .'

'Fundies,' Stoneham murmured.

'Probably.'

'What do they want?'

'Publicity and some friends out of jail. The government has agreed, and it should all be over by eleven a.m. their time tomorrow. Samarkand is five hours ahead of us, by the way.'

'I don't understand, boss,' Stoneham said. 'We're flying all that way just to watch a handover? They don't need advice on how to cave in, do they?'

'You're flying all that way at the taxpayers' expense just in case,' Bourne said. 'And the reason you're going, just between us, is that one of the hostages happens to be the Foreign Minister's daughter.'

'Not Sarah Le Bonk?'

Bourne smiled wryly. 'The very same.'

Stoneham's eyes narrowed. 'Excuse me for saying so, boss, but . . . are you saying that we're only going out there because her dad's got clout? If so, it stinks.'

'It does,' Bourne agreed. 'But we do what we're told. And in this instance we do it knowing that Alan Holcroft will have an important voice in whether we get the funding we need over the next few years.'

Stoneham said nothing, but the expression on his face was lucid enough.

'There are also a couple of good reasons for going,' Bourne said mildly. 'First off, the other thirteen will get the same luxury treatment from Her Majesty's Government as Miss Holcroft. And by the way, from what we can gather the hijackers haven't twigged who she is.'

'That's a bit of luck.'

'Looks like it. Second, one of those thirteen also happens to be one of our old boys. Jamie Docherty. I trust you agree he deserves our best shot.'

'Of course, boss. Why didn't you tell us that first?'

'Do either of you know him, personally I mean?' Bourne asked.

Neither did, but both knew of his reputation. 'I wonder if he's enjoying captivity with Sarah Le Bonk,' Stoneham wondered out loud.

'I doubt it,' Bourne said drily. 'His wife is with him.'

'Oh Jesus.'

'Exactly.'

'When do we leave?' Brierley asked.

Bourne was about to say he didn't know when his phone rang. He jotted down the times on his notepad and put back the receiver.

'We're in luck,' he told them. 'Uzbekistan Airways flies direct to Tashkent three nights a week, and this is one of the nights. Twenty hundred hours from Heathrow, arriving 0730 their time in Tashkent. The locals will fly you down to Samarkand from there.' He looked at his watch. 'That gives us more than nine hours to get you kitted up and on to the plane.'

'More than enough,' Brierley said. 'What sort of set-up is it? I mean, where are the hostages being held?'

'In a hunting lodge up in the mountains, that's all we know at the moment.'

137

Brierley grimaced. 'It would be nice to have an idea of the terrain. Still . . . I take it our equipment will be cleared through customs at Heathrow?'

'If it isn't we can always hijack the plane,' Stoneham observed. 'We have the expertise.'

9

In Leeds a slight rain had just begun to fall, and Detective Sergeant Dave Medwin was able to savour the cooling drops on his face as he walked across the police station car park. This sense of relaxation was short-lived – he had barely poked his head through the front doors of the building when the duty officer barked out that London had been calling him every five minutes for the last half an hour.

'Bloody Londoners think they're the only people with a rush hour,' Medwin snarled back, and walked slowly upstairs. He had only downed three and a half pints on the previous evening, so it could hardly be the alcohol to blame for another semi-sleepless night. Maybe he was allergic to something. Celibacy, perhaps.

The phone was ringing as he entered his office. It was London, telling him to mount a full-scale investigation of Nasruddin Salih. They wanted personal history, psychological profile, estimates of intelligence. They wanted any evidence of who his contacts might be in Central Asia. They wanted anything he could find. The local CID had been instructed to issue him with any search warrants he required, but had not been told anything. Nor would they be. Complete discretion was still required, right up to the point where it might hamper the investigation. If that point was reached, then Medwin should call London for fresh instructions.

He sat there for a few moments trying to focus his mind, before reminding himself that such a difficult process required coffee. He walked down the hall, inserted his coins, and kept his thumb jammed on the extra sugar button as the machine coughed up its usual 'fresh-brewed' monstrosity. Back in the office he started with the obvious, calling British Telecom to check on Nasruddin's long-distance phone calls over the last few years, both from home and the office. There were none from the former, and all the latter were apparently to hotels. He took the numbers down anyway.

He then called Records and asked them to send up copies of both Nasruddin's personal file and the incident report on the arson attack. While he waited for these to arrive he called the local probation service, and found out that Nasruddin's officer had recently retired to Ilkley. He took down the address and decided against the hassle of demanding a copy of their file. He could do that song and dance later, if and when it proved necessary.

The copies arrived from the basement. He read through the arson incident report, and found nothing much more than Rose had told him the previous evening. The father and two elder children had been watching a Leeds game at Elland Road, and young Martin had gone to answer a knock on the front door. A youth in a crash helmet had thrown the Molotov cocktail over his head, and it had smashed on the living-room door jamb, setting both the hall carpet and wall hangings ablaze. His mother had apparently been trapped in the downstairs back room, on the other side of the flames from Martin. By the time the fire engines arrived most of the house had been consumed or blackened, but the spray-painted words 'Paki scum' were still visible on the front gate.

Medwin sighed and picked up Nasruddin's personal file. There was nothing much new here either – the boy had just gone berserk one evening, smashing windows in what seemed to be a paroxysm of grief. God only knew why they had put him on probation. If someone had done that to his family, Medwin thought, he would have gone and killed somebody.

He locked the two copies in his desk and walked down to the car park. The rain was still falling gently, almost like a lawn sprinkler. Once in the car, he turned on the local radio station, and spent most of the next half hour wondering why pop music sounded so much the same these days. Was he just too old to hear whatever subtleties it might contain? No, he didn't think he was. Lynn's fourteen-year-old son spent half his time listening to Hendrix and Dylan. The music really had been better twenty-five years ago.

He drove to Bradford and parked outside the newsagent's in Westfield Street, found the travel agency was open for business, and walked upstairs to find Pinar Ishaq Khan sitting and looking industrious behind her desk.

'Do you have more news?' she asked immediately.

'No, I'm afraid not.' With her lustrous hair and beautiful skin colour Pinar looked even better than she had the evening before. Even the faint shadow-line on the upper lip, which Medwin usually found a little off-putting, seemed part of her attractiveness.

'I tried to ring Samarkand a little while ago,' she said, 'but there's a problem with the line.'

I bet there is, Medwin thought. 'I have to take a look through the office,' he said, hoping she wouldn't want to see his authorization.

'Shouldn't you have a search warrant?' she asked politely.

He reluctantly retrieved the paper from his inside pocket and passed it over. She examined it with interest. 'This is serious, isn't it?' she said.

He shrugged and began methodically working his way through Nasruddin's desk.

'Can't you tell me any more?' she asked.

'No,' he said. There was nothing in the desk, and, as it turned out, nothing in the office. At the end of twenty minutes Medwin knew a bit more about travel agenting but nothing new about Nasruddin. 'Have you got a phone number for his sister, brother or father?' he asked Pinar.

'No,' she said.

'Do you know where they live?'

'Sheila lives in Bradford, I think. He didn't . . . he doesn't talk about his family much.'

'OK, thanks for your co-operation.'

'Should I just carry on?' she asked, as he made for the stairs. Medwin stopped and thought about it. He could hardly say no without giving her more of an explanation. 'You might as well,' he said. 'When I hear anything definite I'll let you know.'

She smiled without much conviction.

His next stop was Nasruddin Salih's local police station, where he picked up a constable to stand guard during his second search of the hijack leader's house. It was an easier job in daylight, but as on the previous evening he was close to conceding defeat when he finally found what he was looking for. Having failed to discover either an address book or a hoard of letters, he lifted a large, unmarked volume from a shelf, only to have several empty envelopes fall out to the floor. The volume was a stamp album, and two of the envelopes bore return addresses in Samarkand.

* * *

After the meeting with Zhakidov, Nurhan used the phone in her own office to call the city's army barracks, where the twelve men in her unit had been on alert since earlier that morning. The Anti-Terrorist Unit was in fact considerably less grand than it sounded. Nurhan was its only permanent member; those under her command were regular army soldiers who had been given special training in anti-terrorist situations, and placed on permanent standby should one such arise.

She filled in the ranking NCO Sergeant Abalov on what they were up against, and went through the list of what would be needed in the field, both for daily survival and completion of the task in hand. Most of what they required would be stored at the barracks, and if it wasn't then there was little likelihood of their finding it anywhere in Uzbekistan. Night-sights and goggles unfortunately fell in the latter category, as did stun grenades. Nurhan told the sergeant to gather together what he could and get the men to the airport, where she would meet them in an hour.

She then unrolled the map they had taken to the mountains, weighed it down at the corners on her desk, and studied it once more. During their flight that morning Marat had drawn in both the unmarked road and the lodge where it ended, high up the steep-sided valley. The terrorist leader had forbidden anyone to approach within two kilometres, so she drew a rough circle centred on the lodge with the appropriate radius. There were only a couple of points outside this circle from which the lodge and its approach road could be kept under long-range observation – in most directions visual contact was lost in considerably less than the specified distance.

There was only the one approach road, so if anyone wished to reach or leave the lodge in a vehicle that was the way they had to go. On foot the options were more numerous, in fact almost infinite for anyone fit enough to cope with the broken terrain. The border with Tajikistan was about sixty kilometres away to the east, perhaps two days' journey for a group of determined young men. With the hostages it would be more problematic. And probably impossible for the two American septuagenarians.

She sighed and stared straight ahead for a moment. It was all academic anyway, since the terrorists' demands had been granted. Still, it would be good practice for the next time, and maybe by then she would have political masters with backbones.

Nurhan decided she would put three men in each of the observation points, and spread the other six, in pairs, in a rough semicircular cordon to the east of the lodge. When darkness fell two men from each observation post could begin scouting out the land immediately in front of the lodge, to see if a surprise approach was possible from that direction. They could also pinpoint any guards the hijackers had posted on the road, and ascertain how easy their silent removal would be, before a direct approach at speed up the road itself.

The lodge itself was another matter. She needed more information, either through talking to people who had been there or through tracking down the architectural plans. Both options probably involved treading on sensitive toes. She seemed to remember that the Chairman of State Construction had been one of the big names in the last of the Soviet-era corruption trials.

She looked at her watch, and decided that the lodge could wait; it was more important to get the unit out into the mountains before nightfall. Downstairs she made a dozen photocopies of the relevant portion of the map, and then headed out for the car. As expected, it felt like climbing into

144

an oven. In America, someone had told her, you could even get cars with air-conditioners.

At the airport the twelve men were still sitting in the lorry that had brought them from the barracks. A few of them managed a welcoming smile but most maintained the distance she had come to expect from them. She thought they had been disabused of any notion that she was incapable of running the unit, but the fact remained that they weren't used to taking orders from women in general, and generally uncomfortable with a woman who was so aggressively modern by Uzbek standards. And then there was the additional psychological complication of her sexual attractiveness. Wanting to fuck one's infidel boss was probably a hard thing to live with. Sometimes Nurhan almost felt sorry for them.

She took the austere Sergeant Abalov aside and swiftly briefed him on the entire situation. As usual he absorbed the information in silence, with the minimum of questioning. Fifteen minutes later she watched two Ka-26 helicopters carry the twelve men and their equipment off into the eastern sky.

After their meeting with Zhakidov had broken up, Marat had also felt more than a twinge of disappointment. The last eighteen hours had been among the most diverting of his NSS career – there had even been fifteen-minute stretches when he had forgotten he wanted a drink. And he had been finding Nurhan's company more than a little enjoyable.

He remembered the look on her face when Zhakidov had said she was in charge, and smiled to himself. She was so transparent in some ways. But, he had to admit, they would have to go a long way to find someone better able to run such a unit. And next time around maybe she really would get the chance to show all the men how good she was.

Marat reminded himself that, for the moment, they were pretending that the terrorists would still be in Uzbekistan this time tomorrow. He picked up the phone, called Immigration Control in Tashkent, and asked the woman who answered to check the arrivals and departures of Nasruddin Salih. Once armed with a list of dates, he phoned round all the major hotels in Samarkand and got them to check their registers against it. Over the previous two years the terrorist leader had stayed three nights in every month at the Hotel Samarkand, presumably as part of his own tour group. Before that none of the major hotels had any record of a stay, although the list from Immigration showed that he had been making regular visits to Uzbekistan for at least two years more.

Marat drew the obvious conclusion – Nasruddin had stayed either at one of the small hotels or in a private home.

He laboriously worked his way through the former to no avail. He then tried checking through the phone book for the name Salih, also in vain. Finally, he went through the old Soviet electoral register for the city, and drew a blank for the third time.

Marat checked his drawers for cigarettes and was pleased to find there weren't any. He leaned back in his chair and yawned, just as a tall blond man in obviously foreign clothes appeared in his doorway. 'Major Marat Rashidov?' the man asked.

'That's me.'

'Simon Kennedy,' the man said, walking forward with hand outstretched. 'From the British Embassy,' he added in Russian. 'I am told you can take me to Major Ismatulayeva.'

Marat shook the proffered hand. 'I don't know where she is at the moment,' he said in the same language, realizing with some surprise how long it had been since he had spoken Russian.

146

A sign of the times. 'But you can either wait here, or I can tell her you called in. She can reach you at your hotel?'

Kennedy frowned. He had been warned that the NSS might give him the runaround, and told to be brutal if they did. 'She must be in touch with this building,' he said.

Marat scratched the back of his neck. 'I'll see,' he said, and picked up the phone to ask the operations room where she was. From the expression on the Englishman's face Marat guessed he didn't understand Uzbek. As he waited for the operations room to find her he suddenly had a brilliant idea.

The voice on the other end told him Nurhan had just left the airport and was on her way back to the office. He replaced the receiver and smiled at Kennedy. 'She'll be back in about twenty minutes,' he said.

'Then I'll wait here, if that's all right . . .'

'Of course. Mr Kennedy, I understand we are to share . . . I think "pool" is the English word, yes? To pool all the information we have?'

'So they tell me,' Kennedy said breezily.

'Good.' He told the Englishman that he was trying to find out where Nasruddin Salih had stayed on his earlier visits to Samarkand. 'I presume your police have searched his house in England. Can you find out whether they have discovered anything which might help me – an address book, perhaps, or letters?'

Kennedy considered, and could see no harm in it. In fact it might win him the Uzbeks' trust. 'I'll do what I can,' he said, and gestured towards the phone with a questioning look.

Marat pushed it towards him.

Kennedy dialled the Tashkent number, and Janice answered. He passed on Marat's request and the number he was on. 'They'll phone here direct from England if they have anything,' he said.

Marat smiled at him.

147

'Now if you can give me a rundown of what's been happening,' Kennedy said.

Marat wondered whether Nurhan would consider that her job, and decided that she would probably have more important demands on her time. He went through the official version of the story so far, which carefully omitted any governmental knowledge of the hijack prior to that morning. Kennedy, who knew better after his fact-finding trip to Shakhrisabz, chose to let sleeping dogs and NSS agents lie. As far as he could tell, the only thing they knew which he had not was the exact location of the hostages.

Marat was just describing the lie of the land around the mountain lodge when the call arrived from London. He handed the phone to Kennedy and watched him write down two names and addresses on the piece of paper he pushed his way.

'These . . .' Kennedy started to say once his call was over, but the phone rang again. It was the operations room telling Marat that Nurhan had returned. He pocketed the piece of paper, and walked Kennedy down a floor just in time to intercept her on the way back out again.

She shook Kennedy's hand distractedly, and just about noticed a large-boned Englishman with an arrogant red face and straw-like blond hair cut short at the back and sides. At the same time he was confirming the impression gained at a glance from his car that morning. The revealing red dress was unfortunately gone, but even in the baggy black blouse she looked much sexier than a Soviet policewoman was supposed to.

'Marat, can you. . .?' she pleaded, but to no avail.

'Mr Kennedy wants to see the lodge,' Marat said. 'And I have a lead,' he added, moving towards the stairs. 'I'll see you later.'

* * *

Annabel Silcott's eyes roamed round the courtyard, noting the grey-brown walls, the dresses drying on the line, the broom with its fan of twig bristles leaning against a balustrade, and the pomegranate tree under whose shade they were sitting. A moment ago a small boy had stuck his head round the edge of the open doorway in front of her, dark eyes full of curiosity. He had probably never seen a blonde goddess before, she thought.

Reluctantly she refocused her attention on the woman she was interviewing. Jenah, the senior wife of Samarkand's head imam, was putting the case for Islam as the best thing that had happened to women since sliced bread. 'Adam and Eve equally guilty,' Annabel had written in her notebook – apparently Islam didn't share the Christian penchant for loading all the blame on poor old Eve and her seductive wiles. Nor were Muslim women's prayers – their link to God – mediated through men, as they were in the Catholic Church. And women had control over their own possessions – they could conduct business without their husband's consent.

So why are you stuck in this courtyard, Annabel wanted to ask, and only able to go out dressed up like the Invisible Man in drag?

But she didn't ask it. Jenah seemed so content with her lot, sitting there in her beautiful courtyard, wearing her gorgeously coloured, flowing silk *atlas*. And why shouldn't she be? The imam no doubt had a bob or two stashed away, so his wife would hardly be wanting for any of the necessities of life. In fact her worries were probably as few and far between as they seemed to be.

Thinking about her friends in London, most of whom had dysfunctional relationships with their partners, their own bodies, their jobs and – if they could afford it – their therapists, Annabel had no difficulty understanding the attraction of a life like Jenah's. In fact this woman was a much better advert for Islam than the hotshot liberal she had interviewed earlier had been for secularism. That particular woman had spent the first half of the interview talking about how wonderful it was that Uzbek women were coming out of the dark ages, and the second half complaining about how hard it was to get decent cosmetics in Samarkand.

I'm too young to be this jaded, Annabel thought.

The interview over, she decided to brave the heat and walk back up Tashkent Street to the hotel. Eyes followed her every step, and what were probably ribald comments floated past her ears. She ignored it all, stopping occasionally to look at the rugs hanging outside the carpet emporiums, and feeling her appetite respond to the smell of skewered meat being barbecued on the braziers.

The sun was halfway down in the western sky, but it was still hot, and the shade offered by the Bibi Khanum mosque was too much to pass by. She paid a few kopeks at the small office and walked in under the huge ruined arch. The interior courtyard seemed almost the size of a football pitch; at its far end a group of Western tourists were having something explained to them. Annabel sat down in a shady corner and stared up at the half-restored dome filling half the sky above.

She didn't want to write this story. It had seemed like a good idea at the time: a vital contemporary theme – she had said so in her original submission – and lots of free travel to exotic places, all on expenses. She had already been to Egypt and Saudi, with India and Indonesia still to come. Most people would give their eye-teeth for a job like this, she thought. She felt bored by it, bored by its predictability, its sleazy opportunism, its utter inconsequentiality. Filling newspapers and magazines these days was like painting the Forth Bridge. No one had anything new to say, so it was just a matter of endless recycling. There would be an article on 'Women under Islam' in some magazine or other every three months, all saying much the same thing with different pictures. What was the point?

Earning a living – that was the point.

She walked out of the mosque and continued up Tashkent Street to the Registan, where she turned right towards her hotel. The man from British Intelligence intruded on her consciousness. What was he doing in Samarkand? Come to that, what did any of them do anywhere these days, now that the Cold War was over and the old enemy laid low? Who were the new enemies? Drug smugglers and terrorists, prob-ably. It could be either around here.

At the hotel she took her key from the receptionist, turned away and then, on a whim, turned back. 'The Englishman who is staying here on his own,' she said.

'Mr Kennedy?'

She described him.

'It is Mr Kennedy.'

'Can you tell me about him?' she asked. 'I will pay for information.'

The receptionist looked around, satisfied himself that they were alone, and leaned forward confidentially. 'How much?'

'That depends on the information. Can you tell me why he is in Samarkand?'

'Yes.'

'Ten dollars.'

'Twenty.'

She smiled. 'All right.'

He waited for her to produce it from the purse tied around her waist. 'He is looking for the tourists.'

'Which tourists?' she asked, more sharply than she intended.
'The ones who do not come back from Shakhrisabz.'

Bakhtar Muratov lay full length on the sofa in his apartment,
reading a copy of The Trumpet of God's manifesto. The original,
which had been faxed from Samarkand an hour before, was
now *en route* to *Voice of the People*. God knew what they would
think of the order to publish it. Muratov supposed they were
lucky the editor still did what he was told, as was no longer the
case in some of the neighbouring ex-Soviet republics.

He had to admit that whoever had written the manifesto
knew what he was doing. It was not couched in terms only
likely to stir the already faithful, and it didn't claim that
Islam would solve all the people's earthly woes. It simply put
forward, with some coherence, the argument that an Islamic
Republic would provide a better moral, political and economic
framework for the people of Uzbekistan. Though a distinct
whiff of puritanism seemed to seep out between the words,
there was little in the words themselves that most Uzbeks
would object to.

It was a more dangerous document than he had expected,
Muratov decided. But it was too late to worry about that now.

And maybe releasing Khotali and his acolytes would actually help to undo the damage. Khotali had never shown this
much subtlety.

The timer on his VCR said two fifty-nine. Muratov levered
himself into a sitting position and reached for a cigarette.

In the hunting lodge nearly six hundred and fifty kilometres
to the south Nasruddin Salih was watching the second hand
on his watch cover the last minute before three o'clock, his
hand poised over the telephone. He supposed they should

be grateful that the Party leaders had wasted so much of the people's money stringing a fifty-kilometre line across the mountains for their personal convenience, though they could always have communicated by radio. Still, Nasruddin preferred using technology he was familiar with.

He dialled the number.

Muratov let the phone ring twice, and then picked up.

'Good afternoon,' Nasruddin said.

'Good afternoon.'

'What is your answer?' the Englishman asked, his voice sounding more nervous than he would have liked.

Muratov allowed a few seconds of silence, just for the hell of it. 'We have accepted your demands,' he announced coldly.

'The prisoners are being released, and our programme printed in full in *Voice of the People*?'

'Yes'

'I am glad,' Nasruddin said. And he was. Another day and it would be over. As long as Muratov was not lying to him.

'The prisoners will arrive at the specified time in the helicopter you requested,' Muratov added.

The NSS chief sounded almost indifferent, Nasruddin thought, as if none of it mattered. It felt suspicious, somehow. 'We have heard your helicopters this afternoon . . .'

'None has approached within the two kilometres you specified.'

'Perhaps. I will just tell you again that if anyone, whether on foot or in the air, attempts to get any closer then one of the hostages will pay the price. Am I making myself clear?'

'Very.'

'It would serve no purpose for anyone to be hurt when we have already reached an agreement.'

'I understand.'

Nasruddin put the phone down, a huge smile spreading across his face. 'They agreed,' he told the others. 'No questions, no time-wasting, no demands to speak to one of the hostages. They just agreed. Our manifesto will be in the paper tomorrow morning, and the Imam Khotali will be here at eleven o'clock in the morning.'

'And the others?'

'All of them. They agreed,' he repeated, as if unwilling to believe it.

'Maybe they are saving the time-wasting for later,' Talib suggested pessimistically.

'Maybe we asked for too little,' Akbar retorted. When they had been planning the operation he had consistently argued for increasing their demands.

'Maybe it worked out exactly as we planned it would,' Nasruddin argued. 'If they have no idea what a great man the Imam Khotali is, then they are bound to think exile will be just another prison for him.' He smiled. 'They cannot see the threat. Whereas losing out on development deals and tourist revenue – they know what a collapsing economy will do to their popularity.'

Talib let a rare smile cross his lips. 'It just seems too easy, somehow,' he said.

'You overestimate them,' Akbar said. 'What are they? Just a few communists clinging to power, that's all.'

That angered Talib. 'I fought them in Afghanistan, remember? And the power they are clinging to is real enough. We must stay alert, particularly tonight but tomorrow as well. The helicopter could be booby-trapped . . .'

'With their pilot flying it?' Nasruddin asked.

Talib gave him a look which told him not to be so naïve. 'And expect there to be "unavoidable delays". They are bound

154

to test us at some point. I'm only surprised that they haven't already.'

His cousin might be right, and Nasruddin was more than prepared to act as if he was, but neither he nor Akbar had heard Muratov's voice. There had been more than a trace of repressed anger in the tone, as if the NSS boss was bitterly resenting every word he was forced to utter.

Nasruddin was convinced they had got it right. He and the others might be outlaws everywhere but Iran for the next few years, but during their exile there seemed every chance that Central Asia would fall to a resurgent Islam for only the second time in thirteen hundred years.

10

Brierley and Stoneham spent the last hour of the morning deciding what to take and the early afternoon gathering it all together. Their role was to be purely advisory, so equipping themselves fully for a combat role was obviously out of the question, but both men knew enough SAS history to realize that 'advisory' could be pretty loosely defined. Sometimes a teacher just had to show his pupils how something should be done.

For personal armament they agreed on a well-tested combination – a Browning High Power 9mm handgun and the silenced MP5SD variant of the Heckler & Koch sub-machine-gun. The latter had been specially fitted with laser guidance to pick out targets in darkened rooms. They also decided to take one Remington 870 pump-action shotgun. Men in purely advisory roles weren't usually given the task of blasting open doors, but who knew what might happen in a crisis?

By the same token they packed two sets of GPV 25 body armour, pouches for the spare ammo, stun and CS gas grenades, two AC100 helmets, and a pair of respirators fitted with CT100 Davies communications gear. Working on the assumption that the Uzbek authorities would lack such equipment, and that their hosts might be grateful to receive some, Stoneham added three more helmet-respirator combinations to the pile. 'It's like kids in the park,' he explained. 'If you turn up with a better ball then they tend to let you join the game.'

To Brierley's insistence on their including two abseiling harnesses Stoneham retorted: 'Why not? We can hang outside the windows offering advice.'

Clothing was more of a problem. Uniforms were not to be worn, in case some local bright spark started wondering out loud what the SAS were doing in Central Asia. 'Dress like tourists,' Bourne had told them. But how did tourists dress?

'Camera, dark glasses and a straw hat,' was Brierley's suggestion.

'You'll cause a sensation. I'm wearing clothes. I take it it's hot in Samarkand at this time of the year.'

'Very. Which reminds me – mosquito repellent. And I assume we're not going to need any jabs for this one.'

Stoneham shrugged. 'Doesn't look like it. The whole business seems a bit iffy, if you ask me.'

'I'm glad I didn't.'

'*The Crow*,' Javid Zahid said, grinning at his cousin.

'Never heard of it,' Copley said.

'I have,' Ogley said surprisingly.

It was almost three-thirty, and seven of the eight male hostages were almost an hour into a game dreamed up by Copley. The first person had to think up a film beginning with A, the second one beginning with B, and so on. When Z was reached the next person started again with A, and anyone failing to come up with a title had a point deducted. X, they soon realized, had to be omitted.

Docherty and Nawaz Zahid were tied for last place. Ali Zahid had had the sense not to play.

The panel on the door abruptly swung back, a piece of paper was pushed through and the panel swung shut. The paper floated slowly to the ground.

They all looked at it. 'And I said we wouldn't get any post,' Copley said wonderingly.

Docherty walked over and picked it up. 'The government of Uzbekistan has agreed to our demands,' he read. 'Providing everything goes according to plan you will all be released around noon tomorrow. The Trumpet of God.'

There was a short silence, which Sam Jennings broke. 'Sounds good to me,' he drawled.

'It sounds bloody fantastic,' Copley agreed, then noticed the look on Docherty's face. 'What's the matter, Doc?'

'Nothing.' It just seemed too good to be true. You're frightened of hope, he told himself.

'You don't look happy,' Copley insisted. 'Don't you think this is kosher?'

They were all looking at him, Docherty realized. Whether he liked it or not he'd been elected guru of this particular bunch of hostages. 'They've no reason to lie to us,' he said, choosing his words carefully. 'But the authorities may have reason to lie to them. I think this may be good news, but I don't think we should let ourselves get too carried away.'

'You think the authorities are going to attack?' Javid asked.

'I don't know. We don't know what these people asked for. Maybe it was a price the government didn't mind paying.'

'We will know tomorrow,' Ali Zahid said, making one of his rare pronouncements.

'Aye, that we will.'

It was a pleasant, well-shaded dead-end street on the northern outskirts of the city. On one side of the road an irrigation channel carried water to the cotton fields stretching out across the plain. On the other, behind a line of cherry trees, sat a row of relatively new houses.

Marat walked up to the door of number eight, and rapped loudly. The uniformed militiaman beside him sucked his teeth and shifted from foot to foot as if he needed a toilet.

An adolescent Indian boy opened the door and looked up at him enquiringly.

'Please get your father,' Marat said, stepping forward into the archway that led through to the courtyard.

The boy disappeared through a doorway into the house. Soon several voices could be heard in conversation, and a minute or so later a man appeared through the doorway. He was about thirty-five, with hair thinning on top and gold-rimmed spectacles. He was used to deference, Marat decided.

'How can I help you?' he asked confidently.

'Are you Mahmoud Ali Shahdov?'

'Yes.'

Marat showed him identification, and asked the man if he knew Nasruddin Salih.

'He is my cousin. Why do you want to know?' he asked, suddenly looking worried. 'Has there been an accident?'

'No,' Marat said, thinking furiously. In his haste to interview Shahdov he had forgotten that no public mention could be made of the hijacking. Yet no serious questioning would be possible without revealing at least some notion of what Nasruddin was involved in. He realized that he had no alternative.

'Mr Shahdov, I must ask you to come with us to police headquarters. There are a number of questions we need to ask about your cousin's business . . .'

159

A little of the man's self-assurance ebbed visibly away. 'The tour company. There is nothing wrong there, surely . . .'

'If you would come with us . . .'

'But can't . . .'

The uniformed man moved his hand to the butt of his holstered gun, as if he was following the script of a bad movie. It worked.

'Of course. I will happily help you to clear up any misunderstanding. May I tell my wife? . . .' He waited for permission.

'Yes.'

A couple of minutes later the Volga was on its way back into the city, the Indian sitting nervously in the back seat. At the NSS building Marat led him down to the basement, where the cells and interrogation rooms were. Nowadays they were more often empty than not, but on each of his rare visits to this nether region Marat had thought he could smell the legacy of fear. Terrible things had been done in this basement, particularly during Stalin's reign of terror.

The Indian seemed to sense it too. He had not said a word since entering the Volga, and all his previous confidence seemed to have vanished. Maybe there was something wrong with his business, Marat thought.

'What business are you in, Mr Shahdov?' he asked.

'Import and export,' the Indian said. 'Mostly from Pakistan,' he added as an afterthought.

Marat ushered him into one of the interview rooms. It had no windows, one desk and two chairs. The lighting was provided by one glaring fluorescent tube.

Shahdov took the seat in front of the desk without waiting to be told. Marat sat down opposite him. 'Your cousin, along with several other men, has hijacked a busload of Western tourists. I would like you to tell me everything there is to know about Nasruddin Salih, starting with the first time you laid eyes on him.'

The rain had cleared away in Bradford, leaving the sun struggling to break through. Dave Medwin's next port of call was the local comprehensive, which all three Salih children had attended. He searched in vain for a legitimate parking space and settled for leaving the car smack in front of the main entrance.

The headmaster's secretary wondered out loud whether he had time for an interview, but then discovered a 'window of opportunity' five minutes hence. Medwin tried hard not to show too much gratitude. He didn't expect much out of this visit – from what he had gathered at his son's school, these days headmasters rarely even knew their pupils by name. Still, the school should at least have academic records.

Despite Medwin's fears, the headmaster turned out to be one of those ageing teachers of the old school who had somehow refrained from quitting the system in disgust over government mismanagement. He had taught Martin Salih history, both in the boy's second and fifth years at the school, and remembered him well.

'Partly of course because of the tragedy,' he admitted. 'It had a marked effect on his schoolwork, as you can imagine. Before it happened, he was one of the best pupils in his year. After it, well, he struggled. Not through any lack of intelligence, mind you. He was bright. He even worked. And he passed a couple of A levels, I think. But the will to excel was gone, the sense that it was worth it. I often used to wonder whether he would shake it all off one day, you know, rise like a phoenix from the ashes. I take it he hasn't, or at least not in one of those ways that society finds acceptable.'

'No, I don't think so,' Medwin admitted. He found himself liking this man. 'I'm afraid I can't tell you anything . . .'

'I'll probably read it in the papers, will I?'

'Maybe. Can I ask you . . .' He paused for a moment. 'This may sound crude, but when I'm trying to put a personality to a name I've often found it useful to differentiate between three types of intelligence. The first one is intellectual – you know, an ability to juggle ideas. Abstract thinking, I suppose you could call it. The second one is practical – knowing how to get something done efficiently. And the third is something like wisdom, which I guess you could define as knowing what's worth doing. Now when you say Martin Salih was intelligent, which of these did you mean?'

The headmaster smiled at him. 'He was intellectually bright, or at least as much as an adolescent boy can be. Let's face it, none of us know very much about anything at that age. But he certainly wasn't a dreamer – he was very organized as I remember. As for wisdom, well, I think I'm too young for that.'

Medwin thanked him and walked back down to find his car being scrutinized by a caretaker. 'You can't park there,' the man said.

'I know,' Medwin said, and climbed back in behind the wheel.

It wasn't even noon by the dashboard clock, but he was already feeling hungry. After the probation officer, he told himself – there were several nice pubs in Ilkley.

The trip across the moors, along a narrow, madly winding road which seemed to bring out the worst in his fellow-drivers, took a hair-raising half an hour. Finding the probation officer's house took another fifteen minutes, thanks to some idiot constable giving him the wrong directions. He walked up the path to the door, rang the chimes, and stood admiring the roses in the front garden.

Norma Cummings opened the door. She had to be over sixty, but didn't look it. He explained why he was there, and she seemed to think about it before inviting him through thè house and out into an equally attractive back garden. 'Take that one,' she said, indicating the blue deck-chair, 'the other one's not too sturdy.'

He sat down and waited for her to speak, but she seemed more interested in staring into space. 'Martin Salih,' he reminded her.

'I know,' she said. 'Well, I remember him, of course. I remember most of the younger ones. What exactly do you want to know?'

'Anything you remember.'

She seemed to find that amusing for a moment. 'He was a sensible boy,' she said at last. 'He knew that breaking windows was no answer to anything. He was simply angry, and with good reason. The police never caught the ones who killed his mother.' She looked at Medwin, almost as if seeing him for the first time. 'He did everything that was required of him while he was seeing me. But who knows where an anger like that can take someone?' she asked.

'Do you think he could kill someone?'

She made an exasperated noise. 'I met him when he was thirteen or fourteen. What is he now, about thirty?'

'Twenty-eight.'

She shrugged. 'And in any case, I don't think there are many people on this planet who are incapable of killing someone, provided they think they have a good enough reason. My late husband killed four Germans in the war – four that he knew about, that is. And he had no crisis of conscience about it.' She looked at him again. 'I know – I'm not helping. You want to know what Martin Salih is capable of, and I

163

don't know. I don't expect he does either. All that distinguished him from other boys his age was his anger. Maybe he got over it. But then I suppose the fact that you're here asking me about him means that he didn't.'

'Will you have dinner with me?' Kennedy asked, as they waited at the side door of the airport building for the security people to let them in.

He was standing too close to her again. All afternoon he had either been brushing up against her breasts or staring at them.

'I'm busy this evening,' Nurhan said curtly, thinking that his mother had a lot to answer for.

'Tomorrow maybe.'

'Maybe.' Tomorrow she'd have two more oversexed Englishmen to deal with.

It had been a frustrating last couple of hours. Extracting the architectural plans of the hunting lodge from State Construction had been like trying to drag blood out of stone. She had finally been given a copy, but only after being given the runaround through several departments, with Kennedy following her around like a sex-mad puppy. She had half expected him to straddle a desk leg and start pumping.

Then Muratov had run her to earth with fresh instructions. There were to be no attempts to penetrate the terrorists' self-proclaimed security perimeter that night – her unit was simply to stand by, where it was, in case the situation changed.

She had taken another helicopter ride out to the mountains – with Kennedy almost pinning her to the door – and climbed up the steep path to where Sergeant Abalov and two other men were keeping the lodge under observation. The NCO had shared her disappointment at the ban on taking a closer look that night. All fourteen hostages, he told her, had been brought out for exercise shortly before she arrived, the women first, and then the men.

Both she and Kennedy had examined the lodge through the binoculars, but there had been nothing new to see. She had guessed the hostages were being held in the communal sleeping quarters situated at both ends of the building's rear. Reaching one of these rooms would be difficult enough, let alone reaching both simultaneously. She had decided to work out a plan that evening. It might not be put into practice, but she could ask for the English experts' opinion of it when they arrived. And once the terrorists had flown away she could examine the lodge, and compare the reality to the plans. It would be an interesting exercise.

All she had to do first was get rid of Mr 'Call me Simon' Kennedy.

'Do you want to be dropped at your hotel?' she asked, as they walked across to the car.

'Oh, yes, I suppose so. Sure you won't change your mind about dinner?' he asked, with what she supposed was intended as a winning smile.

'Sorry, no,' she said, wondering why she found him such a turn-off. He was good-looking, probably clever. She had no reason to think he was unkind.

She felt his gaze on her thighs as she changed gear.

That was it, she thought. The man had no sense of her reality as another person. He had no idea that she noticed his stares, much less that she found them offensive. He probably knew she was a sentient being, but only because he could imagine her writhing in pleasure at his touch. She shuddered.

'Gets cool in the evenings, doesn't it?' he said conversationally.

She spent the next ten minutes concentrating on wending her way through the rush-hour traffic. At the Hotel Samarkand he climbed reluctantly out of the car.

'Your office at seven-thirty?' he reiterated.

'Right.'

'It would be easier if you stayed the night and drove me,' he said.

She smiled at him. 'Try tying an alarm clock to your cock,' she suggested, and pulled away in the car.

It probably wasn't what Zhakidov had meant by maximum co-operation, but at least she hadn't arrested the bastard for sexual harassment.

Back at the NSS offices the Operations Room had no messages from Muratov in Tashkent, but Nurhan found one from Marat on her desk. He was behind his own desk upstairs.

'What have you done with the Englishman?' he asked.

'Less than he deserved.'

'Uh-huh. Well, I need your say-so on an arrest warrant.'

'Whose?'

'One of Nasruddin's cousins. He's in a cell downstairs.'

'What has he done?'

'Nothing, as far as I can tell. But now he knows about the hijack, so I figure we can't afford to let him out until it's all over.'

'I suppose you had a good reason for telling him?'

'I had to give information to get some.'

'And what did you get?'

'The names of the two other Trumpet of God leaders. Talib Khamidov and Akbar Makhamov. Khamidov is another cousin, by the way.'

She grimaced. 'Nice family. Where did you get the first cousin's name from?'

'Our English friends. Do you fancy a drink?'

'What about these men – Khamidov and . . .'

'Makhamov. I've got the uniforms at work trying to find addresses, but with orders only to observe. I assume discretion is still more important than digging for new information, given that the deal is going through tomorrow?'

She agreed, feeling impressed.

'So how about the drink?' he asked.

'A short one.'

They walked downstairs together, and he waited while she countersigned the unfortunate Shahdov in for the night. Out on the pavement the streetlights were glowing against the fast-dimming sky. 'Where to?' she asked.

'I know a café not far from here,' he said. 'We can walk.'

He led the way, zig-zagging through several blocks of the old Russian section to the edge of the Uzbek town. Halfway down a small dark side-street the barely lit façade of a small family restaurant suddenly appeared. The front room was empty save for two old men playing draughts, but the terrace at the back, which looked across the stony bed of a stream, was more populated.

Most of the clientele seemed to know Marat. 'Do you want to eat?' he asked her.

She suddenly realized she felt hungry. They ordered shashliks, and she asked for a glass of red wine. He settled for Coca-Cola.

'Have you stopped drinking?' she asked bluntly.

'It looks like it,' he said. 'Feels like it too.'

'Any particular reason? For the timing I mean.'

He grimaced. 'I think I finally realized one life was over, and it didn't seem like a very good habit to carry over into the next one.' He gave her a faint smile. 'Who knows? Maybe

I'm punishing my wife. She spent years complaining about my drinking, so what better way to pay her back than pack it in the moment I'm living somewhere else.'

'Do you want her back?' Nurhan asked.

'No. We'd run our course and a bit more besides. I guess I'd like to have a better feeling about it all. That's the trouble when it all goes sour – the sourness eats up the past as well as the present.'

'I know what you mean,' she said, just as the food arrived. It tasted as good as it looked. 'How long has this place been here?' she asked him.

'Only a couple of months. I found it by accident one night.'

She took another mouthful, thinking that he wasn't what she had expected. Most men weren't, but usually it was more of a disappointment than a nice surprise. And he wasn't that bad looking, she thought. Maybe a bit overweight, but . . .

She pulled on the mental brakes. The man was a married alcoholic, for God's sake, and she was hardly the mothering kind. They were two colleagues sharing a meal in the middle of a joint operation. A good meal.

When the owner came to offer coffee she declined. 'I've got things to do,' she claimed. 'No, you stay,' she told Marat, 'I can find my own way back.'

And she did, occupying her mind with the tactics of a direct assault on the hunting lodge. Some sort of diversion at the front, she thought, while a dozen men abseiled down the sheer slope behind the lodge and mounted simultaneous assaults on the two side doors. They would need sledgehammers.

Back at the office she checked that no message had arrived from Muratov, and then called him. He told her that the printing presses were rolling out The Trumpet of God's programme, and that the four Islamic extremists were in a holding cell at Tashkent airport. They would be flown down to Samarkand the following morning.

Nurhan then spoke to Sergeant Abalov, who told her there had been no significant developments. The hostages and their takers were still in the lodge. Everything seemed to be going according to plan.

Which reminded her. She told Abalov to call her on the radio if anything remotely out of the ordinary occurred, and took the architectural plans of the lodge home with her. Once there, she spread them out on the only table, took a notepad and pen and started jotting down a timetable for an assault. One diversion tactic that occurred to her was for a telephone conversation to be in progress at the time.

That started her thinking about the wisdom of leaving the phone line open in the first place. She had mentioned her doubts to Zhakidov earlier that day, but his response had been to ask how else they were going to communicate with the terrorists. Which sounded like common sense. The line was being tapped, of course, so there was no possibility of the terrorists using it to organize anything without the NSS knowing.

She walked out on to her veranda, and leaned on the balcony rail overlooking the still far from sleepy street, thinking that if the government thought they could come to some sort of compromise with the new Islamists then they were making a big mistake. There was no room for compromise between male gods and a society based, theoretically at least, on equal rights for women.

To pretend otherwise, she thought, staring at the slim cream crescent which had just cleared the rim of the southern mountains, was – in the words of the old Uzbek proverb – to throw seeds at the moon.

11

After consuming a pint and a Cornish pasty in one of Ilkley's ungentrified pubs, Dave Medwin drove back across the moors towards Bradford. It had turned into a beautiful day, with fluffy white clouds floating serenely across the blue sky.

He wasn't looking forward to interviewing the sister. Her family seemed to have suffered enough without all this. The whole business was like a wound that refused to heal.

Maybe if they had caught the bastard responsible it would have been different. Maybe not. He would be in his early thirties by this time, probably a father infecting his kids with the virus of hatred.

Medwin swerved to avoid an oncoming car that was straddling the centre of the road, and only just restrained himself from turning in pursuit and throwing the book at the bastard. But there seemed to be enough anger going around without him adding to it.

It was shortly after two-thirty when he reached the sister's house, a well-kept semi in a neat suburban street. Medwin sat in the car for a moment drinking in the air of contented conformism, and wondered for the thousandth time how he could both envy and despise the same thing.

He recognized the face of the woman who answered his knock from the photograph he had seen in Martin's flat. 'Sheila Salih?' he asked formally.

'Yes,' she said doubtfully. 'I am Sheila Majid now.'

Medwin showed her his ID, and asked if he could talk to her inside.

'What about?' she asked.

'Your brother Martin.'

'Has something happened to him?'

'He's in good health,' Medwin said noncommittally.

A shadow fell across her face, and she stepped aside to let him in. 'It's not very tidy,' she said.

It wasn't. The first downstairs room looked like a tornado had passed through, or maybe just a bunch of children. The second was festooned with adult mess – papers, mostly. It had that 'lived in', family look, Medwin thought.

She offered him a seat at the kitchen table, and sat down opposite him. Over her shoulder he could see a riotous garden sloping down towards an abandoned railway line.

'What has Martin done?' she asked.

He came straight to the point. 'It looks as though he has been involved in hijacking a bus full of tourists in Central Asia.'

She stared at him in disbelief for a moment, then sighed and looked down at the table.

He waited for her to say something, to ask for details.

'You know what happened to our mother?' she said at last.

'Yes.'

'The man was never caught,' she said, echoing Medwin's thoughts on the drive over. 'Not that catching him would have brought Mum back, but it would have been something,

171

like a line drawn underneath it . . . you know what I mean? Like some sort of place to start again.' She looked straight at him, her dark eyes dulled by resignation. 'As it was, well, we all carry it. David has always buried himself in business, and . . . well, I suppose I bury myself in my family. Martin found religion, but he was the youngest. And I thought . . .' Her voice faded away, as if she was listening to another one inside her head. 'He was there,' she said at last. 'He opened the door.' She smiled faintly. 'We thought that he was coming out of it – building up his business.' Her eyes widened. 'Oh, but he couldn't have been planning . . . what exactly has happened?' she asked.

Medwin told her most of what he knew, omitting only Sarah Holcroft's presence in the tourist party. 'The more we know about Martin, the better chance there is that the authorities out there can resolve things peacefully,' he said.

'Why?' she asked, as if it had suddenly occurred to her that this conversation constituted a betrayal of her brother.

'In negotiations like this it's important that people don't misunderstand each other,' he explained. 'For everyone's sake.'

She absorbed this, and seemed to find it made sense. But she didn't see what she could tell him. 'He's an honest man,' she said. 'If he says something, he means it.'

Medwin forbore from pointing out that the hostages had good reason to doubt such an assessment of Nasruddin's character. 'Is your brother a desperate man?' he asked, thinking as he did so what a ridiculous question it was. 'Do you think he wants martyrdom?'

She shook her head. 'I don't know. Part of him, maybe. But . . . you should see him with the children. He loves them so much. Especially Meyra.' She shook her head.

'Do you think he could kill someone?'

Her eyes widened again, but only for a second. 'I don't know,' she said quietly.

In Samarkand, Kennedy was still chortling over Nurhan's farewell remark as he came down the hotel stairs in search of a belated dinner. He held no grudges over either the fact or the manner of her rejection, having long since accepted that some women found him attractive and some did not. Since he had yet to discover a better way of ascertaining which was which than simply asking, he took it for granted that every now and then a woman would say no. Luckily there had always been enough who said yes to provide him with ample compensation. Spotting the blonde woman from breakfast across the dining-room, he immediately began to wonder which category she fell into.

Annabel Silcott had been waiting almost two hours for him to appear, and the second of two coffees was only beginning its work of cancelling out the bottle of Georgian wine she had worked her way through. Still, here he was, and as far as she could work out no one else was likely to unravel the mystery of the missing tourists for her. There was nothing in the papers here, and nothing in the papers at home either, as she had verified at great length and expense by calling up an old and not very bright school friend. An offer of more money had failed to elicit more information from the receptionist. Kennedy was her last chance.

She waved an invitation for him to join her. He needed no second bidding. As in the morning, he was convinced he had seen her somewhere before, but couldn't remember when or where.

'Simon,' she said, having bolstered her shaky memory of his name by checking with the receptionist.

'Er, hi,' he said.

'Don't be embarrassed,' she said. 'We only met for a few seconds in Tashkent – at the Brunanskys', remember? I'm Annabel Chambers.'

So that was where. Though he still couldn't remember ever having spoken to her.

'You're with the embassy, right?'

He nodded.

'And I'm with UNERO,' she reminded him. 'The United Nations Equal Rights Organization. I'm here on a fact-finding tour, almost literally. Not so much gathering statistics as gathering the different statistical bases which different countries use, so that we can start making useful comparisons.' She smiled. 'Sorry, you probably don't need to know all this.'

'Not at all.' Kennedy smiled. 'UNERO does a great job.'

This was news to Annabel, who had spent part of the last two hours inventing it. Having once ruled out the possibility of approaching Kennedy in a journalistic role, she had decided that a little subtlety would be required. She had chosen to bank on him being one of those chauvinists who couldn't resist the chance to make a play for a feminist. And he was young enough and good-looking enough to spend a night with, if that seemed worthwhile or necessary.

His dinner arrived, and she accepted his offer of more wine. They talked about travel in general, Central Asia in particular, what a hole England was becoming, why Phil Collins was better off without Genesis, the problems of the New World Order. He was kind of sweet, she decided. Not someone you'd want to spend your life with, but fun for a few hours.

'What are you doing in Samarkand?' she asked, about an hour into their relationship.

'Just checking out a few trade possibilities. Nothing interesting. Do you fancy another drink upstairs? I've got some whisky in my room.'

'I've already had enough,' she said suggestively, 'but I'll come and watch you drink.'

They went up in the lift, somehow slipped an arm round each other in the corridor, and were twining tongues the moment his door was closed behind them. Feeling his cock swelling against her belly she undid his belt, pulled down the zip and lifted it free of his boxer shorts.

Kneeling down she ran her tongue lightly up the back, and then abruptly took it into her mouth. For a minute or more she had him moaning with pleasure, only ceasing the tongue massage when she suddenly felt him swelling even more.

'Oh, don't stop,' he said breathlessly. Janice wasn't half as good at this.

'If I don't stop, you won't have anything left to give,' she murmured, standing up and turning her back on him. 'The zip,' she said.

The dress fell to the floor, swiftly followed by her bra and panties. She lay back on the bed, arms above her head and legs bent. 'It's your turn, now.'

He kissed her breasts and stomach before obliging, using his own tongue on her clitoris with rather more delicacy than she had expected.

Soon she was stopping him, and asking if he had . . .

He pulled a condom out of nowhere like a conjuror with his rabbit, slipped it on with more ease than any other man she had ever known, and then lay on his back for her to climb astride him. As she eased herself to and fro with mounting pleasure, a voice in the back of her mind reminded her that this was just a bonus. She was here for a story.

They came together, just like in the manuals, and lay side by side in silence for a few moments. 'That was good,' he said, with a self-satisfied smile.

'Mmmm,' she agreed, managing to keep the surprise out of her voice. It was a long time since she had enjoyed sex anything like as much.

'We must do it again sometime. Like in the next half an hour.'

She snuggled closer. 'OK. But you have to tell me a story in the meantime. Have you seen any excitement since you came here?'

'No, not really.'

She decided to take the plunge. 'What about the disappearing tourists?' she asked casually.

He stiffened. 'What disappearing tourists?'

'Don't you know? Maybe it's not true, then. There's a rumour going round the town that some foreign tourists have simply gone missing or something. I must admit, when I saw you this morning – knowing you were from the embassy – I thought that must be why you were in Samarkand . . .'

He sighed and then smiled. 'I don't suppose it matters if you know,' he said. After all, the deal had been struck, and the hostages would be free by noon. 'A bunch of tourists were hijacked yesterday, but it's all been sorted out. The Uzbek government agreed to the demands and they're being released in the morning.'

'Who were they? Where are they? What were the demands?'

He told her.

'Lucky for the hostages it wasn't the British government in charge,' she said.

He grunted, muttered 'maybe', and hoisted himself up on one side. 'I'm ready,' he murmured, cupping one breast in his hand and leaning down to kiss the other.

176

Her body felt ready too, but her mind was not so easy to put on hold this time around. The grunt and the sardonic 'maybe' seemed to hint at deeper concealments, though what they might be she couldn't begin to imagine. Later, Annabel told herself, letting him in and crossing her legs behind his back.

This time they took a longer and slower route to the same lovely destination. Afterwards she lay there thinking how amazing it was that she could have such perfect sex with someone she didn't care a jot about. Amazing and somehow sad, she decided, because it meant that true love was just what she had always feared it was – a convenient lie.

She was about to share this revelation with her bed partner when he began to snore.

Instead she turned her mind to what he had confided to her. That grunt had been so . . . so definite. She should search the room, she decided. He wasn't going to wake up, and in any case what could he do if he caught her?

As it happened she didn't need to search very far. His jacket was lying on the floor on her side of the bed, and she managed to reach it without falling out. There was a notebook in the inside pocket, and just about enough light coming in through the window to examine it by. Half expecting to see 'Simon Kennedy, Secret Agent' written inside the front cover, she opened it up.

The first thing she found was a list of CDs, presumably ones he wanted to buy. The second was a list of armaments, together with numbers followed by question marks. Looking through it, the notebook seemed a dizzying mixture of the mundane and the stuff of which espionage thrillers were made. Had he really jotted down possible arms sales in a Ryman notebook? She supposed he had, and could think of no real reason why not. It just seemed ludicrous.

She reached the last used page. On it, the letters NSS had been written, followed by an address and Samarkand phone number, and underneath this the name Nurhan Ismatulayeva in capital letters. The word 'superwoman' had been doodled to one side.

Beneath this was what looked like an out-of-town phone number.

Lastly, he had written 'Tashkent arrive 0630, Samarkand around 0800.'

Annabel slid out from under the sheet, walked round the bed to where she had dropped her bag, and extracted a pen. With one eye on the sleeping Kennedy she copied out the address, phone numbers and times into her own notebook. She then retraced her steps, replaced his notebook and walked across to the open window. Outside on the balcony she leaned against the balustrade and looked out across the darkened city towards the silhouetted line of mountains. Maybe the tourists were out there somewhere, she thought.

For some reason she suddenly felt the need to fight back tears. It had to be that time of the month, she thought.

In one of the finished guest rooms Nasruddin Salih lay in the gloom on the double bed, fingers intertwined behind his head, staring at the faintly lit ceiling. He was thinking about the others, how they had all come together, how a plot born one evening of an idle conversation beneath a cherry tree had grown, so effortlessly and logically, into events which would change the lives of so many people.

Talib had been on one of his rare visits to the house of his uncle in the northern outskirts of Samarkand, and Nasruddin, staying with these far-flung members of his family while he organized the arrangements for his agency's planned tour programme, had met him for the first time. He had heard a lot about him, of course. Talib had disappeared on active duty in Afghanistan, and for several years no more had been heard of him. Then the break-up of the Soviet Union had made it possible for many Uzbek deserters to return home, and he had been one of them. He brought with him the wife and children he had acquired in Peshawar, and a stern new faith which made many in his extended family uncomfortable.

Nasruddin was not one of them. Though their lives up to that point could hardly have been more different, each had grasped hold of a purified Islam to pull them through when all else had failed. Almost from the first moment both knew that, whatever their differences in upbringing or culture or tastes, they were brothers of the soul.

The day of that first meeting had been important for another reason: Muhammad Khotali – whom both men had come to greatly admire over the preceding months – had finally been arrested by the government authorities. Nasruddin, Talib and Akbar Makhamov, who was there as a friend of Nasruddin's cousin's family, had discussed the case as the sun went down, and wondered out loud what they could do about it.

Akbar had an answer ready for them – direct action. He had spent several years in Iran as a religious student, and during that time had taken a basic training course in the use of weaponry and explosives. There was no point in trying to work within the system, he said – you could not expect justice from men who had no fear of God.

The three men had discussed possibilities, at first tentatively, and then with increasing seriousness. At one point in that evening's conversation they had all looked at each other, as if

179

each man needed to be reassured that the other two were as serious as he was.

The preparations had taken nearly two years, but not because of any intervening difficulties. Everything had fallen into place with unerring certainty. Akbar had provided ideas, money and a meeting place, Talib the contacts necessary for buying weapons and the four other members of the unit. Nasruddin had offered up the victims.

It had all dovetailed so beautifully, he thought, lying there on the bed. As if it was meant to work. As if God knew that their hearts were pure and their aim true.

Bourne drove the two CRW instructors to Brize Norton, and from there a chopper took them south-east to RAF Northolt, where another car was ready to ferry them across the last few miles. At Heathrow a young man from Airport Security took them through a maze of empty corridors to a room overlooking the runways. They just had time to watch a Virgin Airbus lumber up and away before the door opened to admit a tall, dark-haired man in a navy pinstripe suit.

'Hanson,' he announced. 'Foreign Office,' he lied blithely. 'I'm here to fill in any gaps in your knowledge that you think need filling.'

Brierley and Stoneham took the invitation at face value, and pumped the MI6 chief for details of the hostage situation. He didn't seem to know much more than Bourne had, but promised that they would be fully briefed the moment they reached Tashkent by a member of the embassy staff. They would of course be liaising directly with the local security forces in Samarkand.

'Who are they?' Brierley wanted to know. 'Police or army?'

'A bit of both, really. Strictly speaking it's the old state KGB with a new name – the National Security Service they call themselves now, the NSS. Their Anti-Terrorist Unit are running the operation. With a woman in charge, I'm told.' His voice expressed mild disapproval.

Stoneham, remembering Rosa Klebb in *From Russia with Love*, was inclined to agree.

'I have a list of the hostages,' Hanson told them, reaching into his briefcase, 'with whatever information we've been able to gather about each of them.' He passed it over to Brierley. 'You'll notice that Sarah Holcroft's name has been changed to Sheila Hancock . . .'

'The actress?' Stoneham asked.

Hanson looked blank.

'The actress Sheila Hancock,' Stoneham repeated.

'I was unaware there was anyone famous by that name,' Hanson admitted. 'Is she very well known?'

'No, not very.'

'Well, in that case . . . the name was changed in case this list fell into the wrong hands, of course.'

'Meaning whose?'

'In the final resort, anybody's.'

'But surely the Uzbek authorities must have a record of visitors in their country?'

Hanson spreads his hands. 'Maybe not. I must admit to finding it hard to believe that no one has put two and two together, but . . .'

'Let's hope there's not a branch of the Sheila Hancock Fan Club in Uzbekistan,' Stoneham murmured.

'Indeed. You'll also find information on the terrorist leader – at least we assume he's the leader. That investigation is still ongoing, so you can expect updates while you are in Uzbekistan. Any other questions?'

Brierley could think of none.

'As far as Her Majesty's Government is concerned,' Hanson said carefully, 'your primary mission is exactly what we have agreed with the Uzbek President – a matter of sharing the expertise your regiment has gathered over the years in dealing with these situations. There is however a secondary mission here, as I'm sure you have already realized. If the hijackers become aware of Miss Holcroft's identity then they will presumably begin pressing their demands on us rather than the Uzbeks. In that instance the safety of Miss Holcroft will become a matter of national interest, and it may become necessary for you to take a more active part in the proceedings, perhaps even to the extent of acting without the sanction of your hosts.' He looked at the two SAS men, as if willing them to accept this in silence.

'Are you telling us that we should see the other hostages as second-class citizens?' Stoneham asked abruptly.

'No. Only that the hijackers will consider Miss Holcroft a first-class bargaining counter.'

Brierley and Stoneham exchanged glances. Suddenly it had all got a bit complicated.

It was nearly eight when Barney Davies got home. As usual the darkened house depressed him, and he went around turning on lights before pouring himself a whisky and making the choice between several equally uninviting microwave meals. Once the food was heating he put on a Miles Davis album and sat back to enjoy his drink.

Miles had hardly broken sweat when the thought occurred to Davies that he should ring Alan Holcroft. He didn't like the man, but he did know what it was like to worry about one's kids. And it would be hard to find a more worrying situation than having one taken hostage.

He dialled the first of the numbers he had been given, announced himself, and was told the Foreign Minister had gone home. He dialled the other number and the phone had hardly started ringing when Holcroft picked it up.

'I just thought I'd let you know that our men are on their way,' Davies said. 'They'll be in Samarkand around two a.m. our time, breakfast time there.'

'Thank you, I appreciate it,' Holcroft said.

He sounded terrible, Davies thought. 'There's no more news?'

'No. They should be freed sometime tomorrow morning – at around five a.m. GMT.'

'I hope it all goes OK,' Davies said.

'Thank you.' Holcroft put down the phone and stood beside it for a moment.

'News?' his wife asked anxiously from the doorway.

He shook his head.

'Are you sure we shouldn't be going out there?' she asked.

'It would look strange. Might even jog someone's memory and get Sarah recognized.'

She nodded, as much in resignation as agreement. Both of them stood there in silence, unknowingly sharing the same questions.

How was it possible to care this much about a daughter they had often wished would simply disappear from their lives? And what did such a level of self-deception say about who they were, both as parents and as human beings?

12

Uzbekistan Airways' Wednesday evening flight to Tashkent left Heathrow on time, and was soon travelling east at thirty thousand feet above the north European plain. Brierley and Stoneham had boarded the aircraft before any of the regular passengers, having avoided the usual trek through passport control and the X-ray machines. Their lethally loaded bergens had been stowed separately in the luggage bay.

The plane had turned out to be only half full. There was one tour group of academic-looking Brits, but most of the other passengers looked like they were on their way home, suitably loaded with duty-free purchases from the no longer forbidden West.

After dinner each SAS man grabbed a row of four seats and laid himself out horizontally. Rob Brierley tried his usual remedy for sleep, visualizing the waves sweeping in over the pebbles of the Brighton beach he had lived by as a boy. But he was pumping too much adrenalin, and instead of slipping into unconsciousness he found himself thinking about his late father.

Gerald Brierley had spent his entire adult life commuting to a solicitor's office in London. Day after day throughout his childhood Rob had watched him leave in the morning and return in the evening, and on three or four occasions he had seen his father's face reflect a lack of fulfilment in life that could hardly have been sadder. It was to avoid such a fate that Rob, against both his parents' wishes, had joined the army.

It was one of the three decisions he had never regretted. The others had been to try for the SAS and to stay single.

In the seats behind him, Terry Stoneham was also having trouble getting to sleep. It wasn't the possibility of action ahead which was keeping him awake, but the troubling direction his life seemed to be taking. Lately he had come to realize how happy his life had always been, and how rare such uncomplicated happiness was. He had taken for granted what most people never had – a really happy childhood, good friends, an enjoyable job. Getting married to Jane and starting a family had been more of the same happiness, right up to the moment when she had told him about the boyfriend. The thought of them doing it together had been almost unbearable in itself, and he still didn't know how he had managed not to hit her, even though she was five months pregnant with his child. But the gradually dawning fear that maybe he had been equally blind in all sorts of other ways was even harder to take. His faith in himself had been shaken. Still was.

It was good to be getting away from it all for a few days. He tried switching his problems off, and started mulling over the penalties inflicted on his football team. It was all too fucking predictable, the way the game was run. Such a beautiful game, run by such ugly people. He started imagining himself on the pitch at White Hart Lane, the last minutes against Arsenal in a championship decider, Anderton on the ball, a deep cross, Sheringham nodding it back, and there was Stoneham smashing an unbelievable scissors kick past Seaman into the top corner . . .

There was light in the sky when he woke up, and his mouth was dry enough to tame a swamp. His grandad had always produced this phrase when he had a hangover, to the general mystification of all present. Stoneham leaned forward over the seat in front and found Brierley looking up at him. 'Another twenty minutes,' the older man said. 'I won't ask if you slept well – I could hear you doing it.'

'Gentlemen,' a steward said behind them, almost in a stage whisper. 'We'll disembark you immediately we land.'

He was as good as his word. A few seconds after the rear wheels of the Airbus hit the runway the steward was back, and ushering them past passengers who seemed uncertain whether or not they ought to feel indignant. The moment the plane stopped the door was opened, and a mobile stairway pushed towards it. On the tarmac two uniformed men and a redhead in dark glasses and white dress were waiting for them.

'Janice Wood,' she said, shaking each man by the hand. 'I'm the embassy secretary. 'These are the local NSS,' she explained. 'They don't speak English,' she added, as more hands were shaken. 'They're just here to make sure you don't do anything naughty between getting off one plane and getting on the other. It's OK to ignore them.'

The two SAS men's bergens were trundling down the mobile luggage chute. Once they had been reclaimed the three Britons were put in the back of a jeep-like vehicle, with one of the NSS officers chauffeuring them several hundred metres across the tarmac to where a small propeller plane was already warming up.

Janice told the NSS men 'two minutes' in Russian, and turned to the SAS men. 'There are no new developments,' she informed them. 'The released prisoners are supposed to reach the hijackers at eleven, and then the whole ensemble will fly on into Tajikistan, where the hostages are supposed to be released. Simon Kennedy will meet your plane in Samarkand, and he'll probably have the NSS operational commander with him. Her name is Nurhan Ismatulayeva, and she's the head of the Anti-Terrorist Unit. According to Kennedy she's a bit full of herself, but that probably just means she rejected him. OK?'

Stoneham smiled. Brierley didn't. 'What about the hostage situation?' he asked. 'What exactly has been done?'

'What do you mean?'

'Have they established that the leader can deliver what he says he can? Has the situation on the ground been contained? Have all the means of access been controlled? That sort of thing.'

'Sorry,' she said. 'No one's told me any of that. Simon will know.'

The NSS man was beckoning. The SAS men manoeuvred themselves and the bergens aboard the six-seater and strapped themselves in. The pilot, who looked about eighteen, took one look round at them, grinned inanely, and set the plane in motion. Within minutes Tashkent was spread out beneath them in the early-morning light. It looked more modern than either had expected.

'Where are you off to so early in the morning?' Diq Sayriddin's wife asked, as she watched him pull up his trousers and button his shirt. 'Business,' he said curtly, noticing how her nipples peeked over the rim of the sheet.

187

'What business?' she asked suspiciously, sitting up so abruptly that her large breasts wobbled violently.

'My own,' he said, turning away. Maybe he should insist she wore something in bed, he thought, or at least remember to put something on after he had satisfied his carnal desires.

Sayriddin made his way out through the house, past a disdainful stare from his father's wife, and into the street, where he turned left in the direction of the Bibi Khanum mosque. In the old market-place in front of the ruined mosque he found the kiosk already open, and several men sitting on the nearby seats reading their newspapers.

There was no excited discussion going on, and Sayriddin's heart sank – the government must have refused to print the manifesto. He bought a copy of *Voice of the People* nevertheless, found a place to sit that was as far from his fellow-readers as possible, and started thumbing through the thin pages.

And suddenly there it was – a full page of small type. Looking up to make sure no one was watching him, he extracted his own copy of the manifesto from his jacket pocket and started comparing the two.

They were the same. Exactly the same. He looked up to see if there were any signs of surprise among the other readers, and noticed two of them talking excitedly about something. It had to be the manifesto. This was the beginning, Sayriddin thought, and he was here to witness it. And he was a part of what was making it all possible.

He walked back past the kiosk and up Tashkent Street towards the public phone which Nasruddin had stipulated he use for both calls. This time he intended to obey – there was every chance they were tapping the line, and he didn't want this call traced back to the carpet shop.

At the phone he stopped and looked around before putting the money in. There were a few people on their way to work, but little traffic as yet, and no one seemed to be watching him. He inserted the coins, dialled the number and waited.

'Yes?' the familiar voice said.

'It's me,' Sayriddin said. 'It's in the newspaper. All of it. Word for word. A whole page.'

Nasruddin hung up, leaving Sayriddin with more than a slight sense of anticlimax, and turned to tell Talib and Akbar the good news.

Talib allowed himself one of his rare smiles. 'If all else fails then at least we have told the people,' he said.

'It will not fail,' Akbar said excitedly. 'We have won. Why would they print our words if they mean to renege on the deal? They have simply surrendered, that is all. They are weaker than we thought. We should have asked for more.'

The flight south, mostly across grey-brown desert, took little more than an hour, and it was not quite eight when the two SAS men had their first view of Samarkand's blue domes. Once more there was a reception committee of three, and it wasn't hard to pick out which of the men was English. Simon Kennedy, to both Brierley and Stoneham, looked like an identikit public school product, from the wave of hair dropping over one eyebrow to the boyish grin.

The woman, Stoneham thought, looked like she had just sat down on something pointed. The other man had the slightest of ironic smiles, but otherwise looked vaguely bored.

Which was not far from the truth. Marat's interest in the art of dealing with hostage situations was a purely practical one, and since the only such situation available would soon be history, he would rather have been getting on with tracking down the identities of all the hostage-takers. But Nurhan had asked him to accompany her, mostly, he suspected, to avoid having to cope alone with her breast-fixated Englishman. She had told him about Kennedy's staring, and Marat had been curious to observe the phenomenon in action. But so far Kennedy seemed to be ignoring her, lost in some reverie of his own.

Nurhan watched the new arrivals step down from the plane with a mixture of apprehension, irritation and curiosity. They certainly didn't look like their fellow-countryman, though exactly where the difference lay was hard to pinpoint. Maybe it was just that they had other things on their mind than sex.

'Tell them we are going first to my office,' she instructed Kennedy.

'We both speak Russian,' Brierley interjected. 'Though not perfectly,' he added.

She smiled at them, and Stoneham instantly changed his mind about her. 'Good,' she said. 'But it is a foreign language for me, also. So we are even.'

She introduced herself and Marat, and led them across to a large black car. The bergens fitted into the roomy boot, and the three Englishmen shared the back seat. Nurhan drove.

'Have you been here before?' she asked as they swung on to a four-lane highway.

'No,' both replied at once.

'Well, once the situation is cleared up you must see the sights. And I would like to talk with you about the business we are both in, if there is time.'

'Of course,' Brierley said. It all sounded thoroughly wrapped up, he thought. Which, no doubt, he should find a cause for rejoicing. But that was like expecting firemen to wish there were never any fires – fine in theory, but anyone with expertise could hardly help wanting the chance to demonstrate it in practice.

Through the window he noticed what looked like a field full of levelled ruins, and beyond that a sloping line of buildings, some with blue domes.

'That's the Shah-i-Zinda,' Marat explained. 'They are mausoleums from the time of Tamerlane.'

Once more the male hostages were led out through the lodge to the improvised exercise yard. This was the third time they had been brought out, and the fourth would hopefully be the last. The scenery was stunning, but then the view from Colditz had probably been impressive too.

Docherty had to admit that, as jails went, this had been a pretty luxurious one. The beds were comfortable, the food, though restricted to soup, bread and tea, had been both tasty and nutritious. A new set of clothes would have been great, but the guards always seemed prepared to bring more water. It was how an Englishman would do a hijacking, Docherty decided – politely, courteously, as if it wasn't really happening. But then of course Nasruddin was an Englishman, and he seemed to be in charge.

The other male hostages seemed to be bearing up well. Though the general upbeat cheerfulness couldn't quite conceal the underlying anxiety, everyone was trying, even Ogley. The previous evening had been a long one, despite the draughts tournament. Imran Zahid had won with ease.

This morning there had been a general reluctance to talk, as if each man was busy gathering the strength to cope with potential disappointment. Even now, all eight of them were shuffling around the space in front of the lodge in silence.

In a couple of hours, Docherty thought, things would change. Either it would be all smiles, or the situation would start to deteriorate. The hostages, after all, would not be the only disappointed ones if the deal fell through. Their captors would have to start making tough decisions.

Docherty looked down the valley, thinking that there had to be men out there now, watching them through binoculars or telescopic sights. Someone out there would be working on a plan of how to storm the lodge, and Docherty didn't envy him. The hijackers had chosen well – the site would be a bastard to approach unobserved. It would have to be after dark, but even then . . . There had been a new moon the night before, and a clear sky. Anyone trying to scale the cliff behind the lodge would be a sitting target to anyone at the front. Snipers would have to take the guards out first with silenced rifles.

And then the hostages would have to do whatever needed doing to keep them alive. That might be to hug the floor, or it might be to try to disarm whoever came to kill them. There was no way of knowing until the time came.

He needed some sort of weapon, no matter how crude. On the next circuit he went down on one knee, and as he pretended to tie his shoe managed to pocket a smooth, round stone. It wasn't much, but Docherty hadn't lasted twenty years in the SAS without working out that the difference between life and death was often measured in inches. And when it came down to it, aiming a gun had to be easier if stones weren't flying past your head.

The two SAS men were a very different proposition from Kennedy, Nurhan thought, as she sipped her black coffee and watched them work their way steadily through breakfast. There was a sense of self-containment about them both, almost

192

a glow of self-assurance. It might be all front, of course, and she would probably never know the truth of the matter, but they certainly gave an impression of men who knew exactly who they were and what they were doing.

Sitting across from her, Terry Stoneham was thinking that the SAS had taken him to some pretty weird places, and that the old KGB canteen in Samarkand had to qualify as one of the weirdest. The room itself was unremarkable – they could have been in England but for the slowly whirring fans over-head and the unfortunate lack of Weetabix but the combination of cruelties which it represented had to be unique. Breakfast courtesy of Tamerlane and Stalin!

He had to admit that Major Ismatulayeva didn't look much like Rosa Klebb, but there was no way of knowing whether she had a retractable poison blade concealed in the toecap of her shoe.

'So shall I fill you in on what's been happening?' Simon Kennedy asked in English.

'I think the Major is probably the best person to bring us up to date,' Brierley said diplomatically in Russian. He had taken an instant aversion to the MI6 man, and wasn't making much of an effort to disguise the fact.

Nurhan smiled and did as Brierley asked, tracing the crisis through from the first telephone message to the present, and, to the Englishman's surprise, openly expressing anger at her government's capitulation to the terrorists' demands. Of course, he realized, she probably didn't know how much pressure London had exerted on Tashkent. From her point of view, the government's reaction must have seemed nothing short of spineless.

'How were communications established at the beginning? I mean, who contacted who, and how?'

She told him about the first call from someone in Samarkand.

'I wonder why,' he asked himself out loud.

'To keep us guessing,' Marat volunteered.

'Did it?' Stoneham asked.

'Oh yes. It was about sixteen hours before we found them.'

'Interesting,' Brierley murmured. They must have known that they would be found, and that staying undetected, even for sixteen hours, would not make a great deal of difference. Nasruddin Salih – assuming he was the terrorist leader – was obviously a man who took any slight edge that the situation offered. Brierley thought about the new information from Bradford which the woman had passed on to them in Tashkent. A map-drawer. Precision. Care. 'The telephone line,' he asked, 'is it still open? To the rest of the system, I mean.'

'Yes, it is,' Nurhan said. 'They said they needed independent confirmation that their programme had been printed in the newspaper. We offered to deliver . . .'

'But they realized you could have doctored a copy.'

'Exactly. So one of their supporters phoned them this morning, from a public phone in the city.'

'It might be wise to cut it off now.'

'I suggested it, but my boss decided that it wasn't worth taking any action which could be considered hostile.'

Brierley nodded. 'Fair enough.'

'So, what do you think?' Kennedy asked them, with the air of someone who had just consulted a fortune-teller.

Brierley smiled. 'Not a lot, yet. There are obviously two separate problems in situations like this – how to conduct the negotiation and how to rescue the hostages when the negotiations break down. In this instance there haven't really been any negotiations to conduct – not yet anyway. And to evaluate the rescue option we need an on-site inspection.'

'When you're finished, the helicopter's in the car park behind the building,' Nurhan told him.

Brierley and Stoneham both gulped down the rest of their tea and got to their feet. 'Lead on,' Brierley said.

She did. As the pilot started up the engine and the three Englishmen climbed aboard, she shared a few words with Marat, who raised a hand in farewell and walked back into the building. Both Brierley and Stoneham found themselves wishing that it was Kennedy they were leaving behind.

The flight took less than half an hour, but packed a lot of scenery into the available time. Views of the city gave way to wider vistas of the green Zerafshan valley, and these to desert before the land crumpled and climbed beneath them into a wilderness of mountains.

The helicopter landed in a flat clearing about the size of a tennis court. Two lorries stood to one side, and several young soldiers were sitting in the shade their awnings offered. A dirt road wound up from the valley below, skirted the clearing and climbed out of sight around a protruding ridge some hundred metres further up.

'Some of my unit,' Nurhan explained, gesturing towards the lorry. 'They're on an eight-hours-on four-hours-off duty cycle.'

They looked fit enough, Brierley thought.

Nurhan led the SAS men up the steep path towards one of the observation points, talking into her walkie-talkie in Uzbek as she did so. Sergeant Abalov met them, and they all squatted in a circle as he brought her up to date. She translated into Russian for the SAS men. Both the men and the women hostages had been allowed their half hour of exercise, the latter having been taken back in not much more than twenty minutes before. Nothing unusual had occurred – the two terrorists standing sentry on the road were still there, and were relieved, one at a time, every three hours. The other five remained indoors, except at exercise time, when one would stand guard in front of the lodge.

The observation point was fifty metres further on. Abalov led the way, with Nurhan and the two SAS men following the Uzbek down a rocky gully. At its end the path ducked through a narrow gap between two huge boulders, and a few metres further on came to an abrupt halt behind what looked like a pile of flat rocks some local giant had arranged in a spare moment. Between the second and third from the ground a natural slit some three inches high and four feet wide presented a fine view of the valley's upper reaches.

Some two kilometres away Brierley could see the long, low building, its back up against the cliff wall at the valley's head. Looking through the binoculars, he could make out more details of the structure itself, but nothing of what might be going on inside. They would have to get a good deal nearer than this, Brierley thought. He turned his attention to the intervening space below, which offered a veritable labyrinth of cross-cutting ridges, crevasses and jumbled rocks. There was plenty of cover, he thought, but it was all a long way below the altitude of the lodge. To get near enough for a proper eyeful they would have to practically push their noses up against the front windows.

As Stoneham took his turn with the binoculars, Brierley looked at Nurhan's copy of the architectural drawings and asked her about the building. She told him its history in a tone which suggested she would rather not entertain questions.

It occurred to Brierley for the first time that someone like this – an ex-KGB, Uzbek, apparently intelligent woman – might be having an interesting time making sense of where her loyalties lay in post-Soviet Uzbekistan.

13

After Kennedy had left the room, presumably to meet whoever was arriving at 'around 0800', Annabel Silcott had started going through the rest of his belongings. She found nothing, which at least went a little way to restoring her faith in British Intelligence. Back in her own room she ran as deep a bath as the hotel's plumbing would allow and lay in the water wondering what to do next. Basically, she only had two things to work with: the address with the phone number and the phone number without the address. First she would have to find out who or what the NSS was. It sounded vaguely educational.

She was rummaging through her suitcase, trying to decide what to put on over her underwear, when she suddenly remembered that in Kennedy's story the tour party had been hijacked in the middle of a day trip. So where was their luggage? Still somewhere in the hotel, was the first answer that came to mind.

She put on baggy black trousers and a black T-shirt and went downstairs, hoping against hope that the same receptionist would be on duty. He was, albeit surrounded by an incoming tour group. After extracting all the cash from her money belt in the toilet, she browsed in the souvenir shop in the lobby until the new party had all been dealt with, then walked over and came straight to the point. 'I'll give you a hundred dollars to let me see the missing tourists' luggage,' she said.

He wasn't slow on the uptake. He turned, picked a key off the rack, and placed it on the counter. '*Two* hundred in dollar bills,' he said. 'And if the police ask I shall say you must have stolen the key.'

She counted out four of her five fifty-dollar bills and took the key. He pocketed the notes and said: 'Second floor.'

She walked up and found the room without difficulty. On the outside it looked like any other of the twelve doors leading off the corridor, but the room inside looked more like a left luggage office. Belongings had been gathered in neat piles, and atop each one sat a passport. Annabel went through the names one by one, and then the photographs inside. Inside the one bearing the name Sarah Jones she found the face of Sarah Holcroft.

When the women were let out for their half hour's exercise Isabel found Sarah walking by her side. This wasn't a great surprise – she had the feeling that the young woman had been wanting to talk to her for some time, and there were certainly no chances of a private conversation in their room.

For a few minutes they talked about their situation, and Isabel, struck by how level-headed Sarah seemed, realized that she too had been half expecting the degenerate airhead that the tabloids had presented to the world. Being Isabel, she took the bull by the horns, and asked Sarah if the newspapers had made it *all* up.

'I'm afraid not,' was the rueful answer. 'I did a lot of stupid things, and I didn't make much effort to do them in private.

In fact' – she smiled – 'I probably did them in public on purpose. But on the other hand, if I had slept with as many men as the papers said, I would never have been off my back.' She laughed, but there was a brittle edge to it. 'I've slept with about fifty men,' she suddenly confided. 'Do you think that's a lot?'

Yes, Isabel wanted to say, but who was she to judge? She and her friends might have been revolutionaries but they had also been pretty puritanical with it. There had been none of that 'free love' so popular in the northern hemisphere's sixties. Sarah had probably been sexually active for about eight years, so fifty lovers equalled about one every couple of months. Put that way . . .

'No,' she said, 'but it doesn't sound much like a recipe for happiness either.'

'It isn't, but I guess happiness wasn't what I was looking for then. I don't know. Did you read the orgy story last year?'

Isabel admitted she had.

'That was partly true. It was a party, and we all got very high, and I ended up in bed with two men. That wasn't a recipe for happiness either, but it was fun. And it didn't do anyone any harm. The press . . . I mean, it's all double standards. Men are always fantasizing about going to bed with more than one woman.' She sighed. 'But you're right – it's fun but it gets pretty empty after a while.'

This wasn't a stupid woman, Isabel thought. A damaged one perhaps, but not beyond repair. 'So what are you going to do with the rest of your life?' she asked.

'Something positive. I've given up drugs, and I've decided to be more choosy when it comes to men. You know, I think I was afraid to say no before, as if somehow I didn't have the right to. Does that sound crazy?'

'No, it doesn't. It sounds like you had a really low opinion of yourself.'

'I did. I still do, but maybe not so much, and I have found something I really want to do. You know, in London there's all sorts of fabric shops these days – Chinese, Indian, Turkish, Latin-American, hundreds of them, all specializing in one culture. Well, I had the idea for a shop selling fabrics from all around the world, just the best from each place, you know.'

'Sounds great.'

'But that's not all. I want to get local co-operatives to supply the shop, so that the women who actually make them share in the profits. I don't want it to be just a money-making thing – we have enough of that in my family already. But that's where Brenda and I were the other day in Tashkent, when the rest of you were at the History Museum – we went to see these people whose names I'd been given. And they were really interested.'

Her eyes were shining now, and she was looking at Isabel with a need for reassurance which was almost heart-breaking.

'It sounds fantastic,' Isabel said.

After watching the helicopter drift away across the old city Marat had climbed into his car and driven out to the airport. The plane from Tashkent had arrived half an hour earlier, and the four released prisoners were being held in an ordinary office in the airport's administration building.

It was almost half-past ten. Marat gave the order for them to be taken to the transport helicopter which was waiting on the tarmac nearby, and watched as they filed out of the building, blinking in the sunlight. Muhammad Khotali was the second in line, a tall man in traditional clerical garb, with deep-set eyes under bushy black eyebrows. Marat had seen him in person only once, through a one-way window at the post-arrest interrogation, some two years before. He had been reluctantly impressed at the time, without really knowing why. There was something about those eyes, the intelligence that filled them and the honesty they seemed to promise, even when the mouth was spouting Stone Age nonsense. The man had charisma, all right. In dangerous quantities.

Marat followed the four men across to the helicopter, and watched them received into its cavernous belly. Uzbekistan's new flag had recently been painted on the machine's sides, but the two pilots were both Russian. Marat recognized the senior of the two from his time in Afghanistan.

'Hey, Marat,' the man said with a smile. 'I don't think much of the cargo you've given us.'

Marat grimaced. 'Join the club,' he said drily. 'You're clear about what you have to do?'

'Land outside the lodge, pick up the bad guys and their hostages and take them where they want to go.'

'That's about it.'

'So I can't just drop these four out at six hundred metres?'

Marat sighed. 'Not this trip.' He looked at his watch. 'You'd better get going. We don't want them getting nervous.'

'If you'll step out of the way . . .'

Marat did so. As the giant helicopter strained its way into the air, he called Nurhan on the radio link to say it was on its way. Then he stood watching it dwindle into the south-eastern sky, before walking back across the tarmac towards his car. Tonight they would have to play host to the SAS men, he thought, but maybe tomorrow she would have dinner with him again.

Isabel could remember that last morning in Córdoba with the glass manufacturer. The deal had been struck, but he had grown more terrified as the hour agreed for his release had approached. As they left him there, still blindfolded, for the authorities to find, he had been sobbing with fright.

Now she understood why. The anticipation of release was a good feeling, a safe feeling, but the actuality represented a plunge back into the unknown.

It was almost a quarter to eleven, and it was hard not to simply lie there listening for an approaching helicopter. Instead, she heard the distant ringing of a telephone. That puzzled her for a moment, but she supposed there had to be some means of contact between the hijackers and the authorities, and searching her memory she could see the line of telephone poles which led away down the mountain road.

'Yes?' a male voice asked.

'Hello, who is that?' Annabel asked.

'Who are you?' Nasruddin answered in English. He shrugged at Talib to show that he didn't know who it was.

She found his accent both strange and familiar. 'My name is Silcott. I'm a journalist. If you are who I think you are I would like an interview . . .'

'I think you have a wrong number,' Nasruddin said. It sounded ridiculous, but it was the first of several things that came into his mind. The second was that talking to a journalist would constitute a breach of their agreement with Muratov. The third was to wonder whether that mattered.

'Surely you can only benefit from publicity,' Annabel insisted. His answering in English had been the giveaway. These had to be the people.

Nasruddin didn't offer a reply, mainly because he couldn't decide on what it should be.

'Are you in contact with the British government?' she asked, taking his silence as assent.

203

'No,' he said automatically.

'No?' she echoed, astonished. Why would the kidnappers of the Foreign Minister's daughter not be in contact with the British government?

'You are holding Sarah Holcroft?' she asked.

Nasruddin almost dropped the phone. He had known all along that Sarah Jones's face was familiar, and now he knew why.

'Are you intending to ask a ransom?' Annabel asked. The man at the other end sounded educated enough, but he didn't seem to have much idea of what he was doing.

Nasruddin put the phone down, and instinctively took it off the hook. The motion reminded him of that evening years before, when the phone calls had poured in after his mother's death, half of them offering sympathy, half expressing regret that the whole family hadn't burned with her.

'What is it?' Talib asked.

'It's . . .' Nasruddin's mind was racing ahead. This changed everything. 'The women hostages, the younger blonde girl,' he said. 'You remember her?'

Talib nodded.

'She is the daughter of the British Foreign Minister . . .'

Talib looked astonished. 'But how?'

'She's travelling under a different name. The girl's famous in Britain, or at least she used to be.'

'Why didn't you recognize her?'

'I don't know. I did think I'd seen her face before but . . . well, she has a reputation for drugs and promiscuity, and this girl didn't seem like that.' Nasruddin ran a hand through his hair. 'I still find it hard to believe.'

'It explains a lot,' Talib said.

'What do you mean?'

'Why they have been so accommodating. The British have been leaning on our government.'

Nasruddin thought about it. 'Or bribing them,' he suggested.

'Probably both. The question is, what do we do with this new knowledge?'

'Yes.'

The two men looked at each other, each knowing what the other was thinking. It was Talib who voiced it. 'We can ask for anything,' he said.

It was four minutes to eleven when Nurhan and the two SAS men saw the helicopter, and almost two minutes later before they heard the asthmatic scrape of its rotor blades echoing up the valley. The craft flew almost directly in front of them, before climbing to a hovering position above the improvised landing site in front of the lodge. Then slowly it settled to the ground.

The watchers waited for the hostages to be led out.

One minute passed, and another, and suddenly the door opened and what looked like a group of four males was hurried across the space and into the helicopter. The watchers' eyes returned to the door, expecting the next batch, but before anyone else could emerge the craft was lifting off and climbing rapidly into the sky.

'What the fuck?' Stoneham said quietly.

'What indeed,' Brierley agreed, just as a call came in on Nurhan's radio. They watched her eyes narrow and her lips purse as she listened, and knew the news wasn't good.

'That was my boss,' she explained. 'The bastards have reneged on the deal. They're releasing the four Muslim hostages, but not the others. Apparently they've found out that one of the women is the daughter of the British Foreign Minister. I take it you already knew that.'

'Yes, but . . .'

'It's all right,' she said. 'It doesn't take a genius to work out why your government didn't want anyone to know.'

'Did they say anything else?' Brierley asked.

'No. Only that they'll present a new set of demands some-time later.'

'They probably still can't believe their luck,' Stoneham said.

'Probably. Anyway, we're back to square one,' Brierley said. 'And while we're waiting for Chummy and his friends to work out what they want, I think we might as well start making some plans. Under your authority, of course, Major.'

'Of course,' she agreed drily. 'Exactly what do you have in mind?'

Bakhtar Muratov's conversation with Nasruddin had been not much longer than Nurhan's précis suggested. The terrorist leader had begun by announcing he was cancelling the pris-oners-for-hostages exchange. He had been deceived, he said, as to the true identity of one of their captives. Nevertheless he would release four of them, along with the 'illegally imprisoned' four Islamic leaders.

When Muratov had expressed ignorance as to the decep-tion, Nasruddin had not believed him. 'If you did not know the girl was the British Foreign Minister's daughter, then why did you accept our demands so easily?' he asked scornfully.

Because we were bribed to do so, Muratov thought, but didn't say so out loud. No wonder the British government had been so keen to abandon its own principles.

Nasruddin had moved on to practicalities. 'Our new demands will be addressed to both the Uzbek and British governments,' he said. 'I will talk to both you and the British Ambassador on this line at six o'clock this evening.'

And that had been that. Bakalev was not going to be pleased, Muratov thought, as he strolled the short distance that separated his flat from the President's office.

He was right. Bakalev's face grew harder and harder as Muratov told him what had happened, until the NSS boss had visions of it cracking under the stress. In actuality, the President uttered one explosive 'fuck!' and slumped back down into his Swedish desk chair.

There followed several moments of uncomfortable silence.

'How did they find out?' Bakalev asked eventually.

'We don't know.'

'Fuck,' the President said again, more quietly this time. 'So we print their ludicrous programme . . . Have you got any reports yet on how it was received?'

'Not yet.'

'I want to see them as soon as you get them.' He slumped even further into the seat, and massaged his chin. 'It certainly explains why the British were so generous,' he said sarcastically. 'A ransom for a princess,' he muttered.

Muratov said nothing.

'You say they're busy dreaming up new demands. What else can they ask for? How many more zealots do we have in prison?'

'Maybe two hundred. But none worth feeding. We can give them all away without losing any sleep.'

'OK,' Bakalev agreed. 'What else?'

Muratov shrugged. 'Money. More manifestos. A TV show. Your resignation . . .'

Bakalev grunted. 'When I quit it'll be because I want to.' He looked at Muratov. 'And anyway, I think we've offered these bastards more than enough already.'

'The English may offer us more.'

'It wouldn't be worth it. There's a limit to how much damage you can cover up with money.'

He was probably right, Muratov thought. Any more concessions and it would be hard to avoid getting stuck with a fatal reputation for weakness. 'They'll have demands on themselves to think about,' he said. 'And I can't see them being able to concede very much given their stated policy on terrorism.'

'You mean, up until now they could let us do all the conceding?'

'Of course. But now it may well be different. If the new demands can be met in private, then that's one thing. But if they're the sort which involves publicity then they'll have to live up to their own principles . . .'

'Are the terrorists still saying they don't want publicity?' Bakalev interjected.

'They didn't say one way or the other. They may not have made up their minds yet. It's hard to say . . .'

'Cut them off,' Bakalev decided abruptly. 'Tell them the line's down, or someone acted without authority. Just keep a two-way line open between us and them. Whatever. And get hold of the British Ambassador. Be nice to him. I don't want the British to think we're being anything less than completely co-operative. Give their two military experts a free hand. If it becomes necessary for us to go in, I want the British in there with us, whether they like it or not. If there's a fuck-up they can take the blame, at least as far as the world is concerned. Maybe we can even get them to believe it.'

'It might put the trade deal in jeopardy.'

'I know, but that's too bad. I still want it, but not if it's going to cost me the country.'

* * *

208

Back at the NSS HQ Marat found a message on his desk. He left the building again and drove a few hundred metres down Tamerlane Prospekt to the telephone exchange. In a small basement room he found the two-man unit whose job it was to monitor the hijackers' phone line.

'Listen to this, boss,' one of the men said, and flicked a switch on the reel-to-reel tape recorder.

'Yes?' asked a voice, which Marat instantly recognized as the terrorist leader's.

'Hello, who is that?' an unfamiliar woman's voice asked in English.

'Who are you?' Nasruddin Salih answered in the same language.

'My name is Silcott. I'm a journalist . . .'

Marat listened to the rest of the conversation, noting the shock in Nasruddin's voice when he learnt of the female hostage's real identity. Then he phoned the NSS operations room and asked them to check the journalist's name against the hotel register.

She had been staying at the Hotel Samarkand for two nights.

He was there five minutes later, asking the receptionist if she was in. The man looked vaguely worried by the question, but his answer was definite enough. She had gone out.

'Any idea where?'

'No. Maybe she went to meet the Englishman,' he added, half-consciously trying to divert attention away from himself.

'Which Englishman?' Marat asked patiently.

'Mr Kennedy.' The receptionist managed a leer. 'They got quite friendly last night,' he offered by way of explanation.

Great, Marat thought. The man really was as big a fool as he looked. And since he was up in the mountains with

209

Nurhan the journalist could hardly be with him. So where the fuck was she? And who else was she busy telling?

After putting down the phone Annabel Silcott had been momentarily appalled by what she had done. But there was no way to take it back, and no use in crying over spilt secrets. And in any case, the whole business was ridiculous. She should never have been able to pick up a phone and ring a terrorist group holding hostages – the authorities needed their heads examining for letting something like that happen.

She sat down on a convenient bench, and watched the morning traffic go by. It all seemed so ordinary, so mundane.

What was she to do? This was the biggest story that had ever come her way, and there must be some way for her to make use of it. But how? She could ring the story in to any of the British dailies on the phone right in front of her, but that wouldn't do much for her reputation. Samarkand would instantly fill up with competing journalists from all over the place, and she would be just one more of them, dutifully taking down whatever the official spokesman chose to tell them.

There had to be some way of keeping the story to herself. Maybe she should wait, keep in touch with what was happening through Kennedy. If the authorities managed to keep the lid on right up to the end, then that would be the time for her to produce her investigative masterwork. Blow the whole thing wide open without risking any lives.

That was the way to go. Feeling pleased with herself, and even vaguely proud of letting her better nature win out over the demands of instant gratification, she walked briskly back to the hotel, hoping that Kennedy had returned.

She was crossing the lobby when a man blocked her way. 'You will come with me,' Marat said, showing her his ID.

'But . . .'

'You are under arrest.'

To say it had been a disappointment was definitely an under-statement, Docherty thought to himself. They had been informed in writing by Nasruddin of an unspecified deceit on the part of the authorities, and The Trumpet of God's consequent decision to release only the four Muslim prisoners. The four Zahids had been understandably relieved, but also unmistakably embarrassed by their good fortune. Ali said he would pray for them, and Nawaz promised to bombard the British government with demands for action. The two teen-agers earnestly shook hands with those they were leaving behind, and Javid offered to leave them his *Wisden*.

That had been nearly three hours ago, Docherty thought, looking at his watch. For most of that time he, Mike Copley, Sam Jennings and Charles Ogley had been immersed in their own gloomy thoughts. Somehow, there didn't seem much worth saying.

It was the not knowing that was hardest. Not knowing what was happening out there, not only as regards their own situa-tion, but in the world at large. Docherty had never been addicted to news, and in fact enjoyed few things more than isolating himself in some beautiful spot – the Hebrides came to mind, or Chiapas in Mexico – and just letting time flow by. By choice, that was. What a difference it made when someone did the choosing for you. Then being cut off began to seem . . . well, like the prison it was. You were trapped inside yourself, and being human was about making contact with others . . .

Anything could be happening out there. Another Chernobyl, a cure for AIDS. Celtic might have signed a player who lived on the same planet as McStay.

His reverie was interrupted by the swelling drone of a helicopter. Judging from the noise it was the same one. A big transport chopper. A 'Hip' probably, if he remembered his NATO code-names correctly.

'They suddenly realized they left us behind,' Copley said, but the joke was in the words rather than his tone.

All four of them were probably hoping the same thing, Docherty thought – that any moment now the door would open and someone would tell them that it was all over, and that they were on their way home.

But no footsteps sounded, and no one came for them. The sound of the rotors died, ushering back the silence.

Some three kilometres from the lodge Nurhan and the three Englishmen extricated themselves from the convenient area of shade they had discovered beneath a north-facing overhang and walked back down the path towards the checkpoint on the approach road. On the helicopter's return a few minutes earlier one of the two pilots had been taken out and pointed in their general direction.

They arrived at the checkpoint just as he loomed into view round the bend, walking briskly towards them.

His news proved neither better nor worse than expected. He and his co-pilot had dropped off their passengers on the other side of the Tajik border, and then one of the hijackers had flown the helicopter back. 'He watched us all the way on the outward flight,' the pilot said, 'and then took the controls himself on the return leg. He had obviously flown helicopters before, but probably nothing as big as an Mi-8.'

'That means they're mobile,' Brierley observed. 'We should think about destroying that helicopter,' he added.

'They're keeping my co-pilot on board.'

212

'Fuck.'

Shortly afterwards Muratov came through with confirmation of the co-pilot's whereabouts courtesy of Nasruddin himself. The NSS boss also OK'd the after-dark reconnaissance for which Nurhan had requested permission.

'So how many?' she asked the SAS men.

'Just the two of us,' Brierley said, surprised. 'More than that would only add to the noise.'

'That makes sense,' she agreed. 'But this is a joint operation, so one of the two will be me.'

Brierley and Stoneham looked at each other. 'We've worked together before,' Brierley said. 'I don't want . . .'

'You don't want to wonder out loud what a liability a woman might be,' she said, 'but you're thinking it. Well, maybe I won't live up to your standards. Maybe you won't match up to mine. But this is my operation. Either I go with one of you two, or I go with one of my own men. I'd rather it was one of you two,' she added diplomatically, feeling a pang of disloyalty as she did so.

Brierley and Stoneham shared another look. 'I'll toss you for it, boss,' Stoneham said.

'Forget it,' Brierley said. 'Privilege of rank.'

'Shit,' Stoneham said.

'When do you think would be the optimum time?' Nurhan asked, wondering if she was taking her instructions to be nice too far. 'Around ten o'clock? There were still some lights burning at that time last night.'

'Earlier,' Brierley suggested. 'They won't be expecting anything soon after dark. And if it looks good we could even give the politicos the option of going in before dawn.'

They agreed on eight o'clock, and settled down to wait. Over the next few hours they were interrupted only once, by a radio message in Uzbek which first made Nurhan angry and then amused. But despite questioning looks from the three Englishmen she kept the news about Silcott and Kennedy to herself. Muratov was apparently *en route* from Tashkent to a new operational HQ in the Samarkand NSS building, and bringing the British Ambassador with him. The latter would no doubt be dealing with Kennedy in person.

Around four o'clock the call came through to say Pearson-Jones had arrived. He wanted to see Kennedy immediately, and requested that Brierley accompany the MI6 man back into town. Having been thrust into the role of negotiating for the British government, the Ambassador thought it wise to avail himself of the expert adviser who had been sent from England. A crash course was duly expected over dinner that evening.

'Looks like I'll have to fill in for you on the easy job then, boss,' Stoneham observed casually.

'Yes, I suppose you will, you little fucker,' Brierley admitted, without a great deal of grace.

14

Sabir put the glass of tea down on the polished surface of the long table, and Nasruddin absent-mindedly moved it on to one of the place-mats which depicted Soviet beauty spots. Noticing what he had done, he smiled wryly to himself. It was obviously OK to hijack a bus-load of tourists, but not to leave a ring on Bakalev's table.

'Where is Talib?' Akbar asked, almost angrily.

'He'll be here in a minute.' The Tajik was obviously feeling the tension, and Nasruddin could understand why. He felt nervous and uncertain himself, unsure of his own judgement. One part of his mind – perhaps the most rational part – was telling him that they had accomplished everything they had intended, and that now was the time to cut and run. Another part, which often seemed no less reasonable, was pointing out how much more they could extract from the situation now that Sarah Holcroft's identity was known to them. A third, almost incoherent, voice was crying out that here at last was his chance to make the bastards pay for everything.

All three voices were his, Nasruddin thought, just as Talib entered the room. He watched his cousin sit down opposite Akbar, carefully put two heaped spoonfuls of sugar into his tea and stir. Even doing something as ordinary as this, there was a stillness, a centredness, about his cousin which Nasruddin continued to find impressive. Sometimes he wondered why Talib deferred to him, what such a man could find to respect in a man like himself. Cleverness was the only thing that ever came to mind.

Well, they certainly needed clarity of thought now. Nasruddin set out to prove himself worthy.

'We are here to assess the options open to us,' he said formally, 'and to choose between them. But first I think we should discuss what response we should make to their action in cutting our access to the outside world. If any.'

'We could demand its reinstatement,' Akbar said.

'Only by threatening to kill a hostage,' Nasruddin argued. 'And I think they might call our bluff.'

'Would it be a bluff?'

'I don't know,' Nasruddin admitted. 'It seems to me that killing a hostage for such an unimportant reason would be seen as a sign of weakness.'

'It would,' Talib agreed. 'Especially if we have no need of such access. And that will depend on which of the possible paths we take from this place.'

'Then let us discuss that,' Nasruddin said, looking first at Talib, then at Akbar.

The latter spoke first. 'God has given us this woman,' he said, 'and we must use the gift wisely.'

'How?' Nasruddin asked brusquely.

Akbar was not disconcerted. 'We are agreed that the British must have bribed the regime to accept our demands?'

The other two nodded.

'That shows how far they are prepared to go to save this woman,' Akbar continued. 'I think we must find out how much they are prepared to pay us.'

216

There was a short silence, which Talib broke. 'No,' he said slowly, and looked straight at Akbar. 'I agree that God has blessed us with a gift, but not to use in this way.' He turned to include Nasruddin. 'What more do we need that they can give us? Our leader is free,' he said, his mind going back to their short exchange of words in the helicopter, the awe he had felt in Muhammad Khotali's presence. 'But not enough of the people will hear of his release. The papers and the television will not report it, and they will not print the speeches he will make in exile. The regime will not allow his books to be published, or his cassettes to be sold in our markets. He will be a leader and a guide to those who know him and love him, but these will be few' – Talib smiled at them both – 'unless we bring him to them.'

'How do we do that?' Akbar wanted to know.

'It is simple. We turn this hostage-taking into a public seminar. In the name of the Imam we demand all those things which we know to be right, both from the British and the godless regime in Tashkent. It will not matter that such demands cannot be met – for a week or more we will fill the air with truth and light. I do not believe that Bakalev and his cronies can survive such an onslaught.'

The other two looked at him, the eyes burning in their sockets above the hooked nose.

'It is good,' Akbar said.

'And after the week?' Nasruddin asked. 'Won't a public defeat undermine what we have achieved?'

'Martyrdom is never a defeat,' Akbar said.

'I am ready to die,' Talib agreed, 'but while God has work for me here on earth I am also ready to live. After a week we can accept a compromise, release the hostages in the cause of mercy, and accept safe passage across the border, where the Imam will be waiting to welcome us. And our people will be talking only of things that matter once more, not wallowing in the corruption of the West.'

'I am for it,' Akbar said. His eyes were also shining at the prospect.

Nasruddin understood why. Though his rational self found flaws in Talib's programme, they seemed almost insignificant when compared with the potential harvest of souls. 'What are our demands to be?' he asked.

The appointment by telephone with Tashkent was still almost an hour away when Sir Christopher Hanson was admitted to the Prime Minister's Downing Street study. He found the PM working his way through the pile of briefings that had been prepared with the afternoon's education debate in mind, and not too unhappy to be interrupted. If the new matter in hand had been anything else, Hanson reckoned, he would probably have thrown the briefings in the air and let out a wild whoop.

Or maybe not. This Prime Minister was not noted for his spontaneity. In fact, Hanson couldn't remember a single PM who had been, except perhaps for Harold Wilson, and he'd only used it as a means of keeping other people off balance.

'There's no fresh information,' Hanson said. 'The lid is still on, at least for the moment.'

The PM ran a hand through his sparse hair. 'But for how much longer?' he asked rhetorically. 'And now that we're in the firing line, what are the Uzbeks going to do? Can we rely on them to carry on being discreet?'

On their continued discretion, Hanson mentally corrected him. The PM's way with words tended to falter under stress. 'There doesn't seem to be any profit to them in going public,' the Intelligence chief replied.

'Well, that's something, I suppose.' The PM scratched his head this time. 'But the moment it goes public we have to play it by the book,' he said. 'Her book,' he added as an afterthought.

Hanson nodded.

'Terrorism cannot be seen to pay,' the PM said, as if he was trying to convince himself. Or perhaps he was just rehearsing for the TV cameras.

'How is Alan Holcroft going to take it?' Hanson asked.

'God knows. How would you?' The PM looked at his watch. 'He'll be here any minute. Perhaps I should have excluded him – it seems almost cruel to ask a man to share in decisions which could kill his daughter.'

'But just as cruel to shut him out of a say in such decisions.'

'I know.'

Almost on cue, there was a rap on the door, followed swiftly by the appearance of the Foreign Minister. 'Any news?' he asked at once.

'No,' Hanson said. In one way Holcroft's face looked the same as ever, but in some subtle way it also seemed to have collapsed. There were now two faces visible, Hanson decided: it was as if the human face was pressing up against the inside of the official mask.

The PM waited until the Foreign Minister was seated, and then told him what he had just told Hanson, that in the event of the hijack becoming public knowledge it would not be possible to deviate from official government policy.

'I realize that,' Holcroft said tightly. He had just left an hysterical wife at home, and, had he but known it, every instinct in his body was urging him to go down on his knees and beg. But he had survived a lifetime in politics by severing the connections between brain and soul, and now all he could hear was the beating of blood in his temples and the mad racing of his heart.

The three men sat there waiting for the call.

It came through punctually, at 1400 hours GMT, and the laborious business of holding a conversation through translators began once more.

President Bakalev seemed determined from the outset to placate those whom he was addressing. There was no mention of the British having concealed Sarah Holcroft's identity from him, or of the fact that it had been a British journalist who had let the cat out of the bag. Instead there were expressions of gratitude for the men who had been sent, and confident predictions that the business could still be contained and resolved outside the spotlight of publicity. They would all know more in the morning when the terrorists passed on their new demands, but in the meantime joint planning was under way in case decisive action proved necessary. He sincerely hoped that such co-operation between the two countries would continue, though of course in less harrowing circumstances.

The PM kept his own remarks to a minimum. After the call was over he let out a deep breath and shared a look of resignation with the other two. All they could do was wait.

They had been given no exercise that afternoon, and no reason why not. Perhaps the presence of the helicopter outside had something to do with it, but Isabel couldn't see why. It seemed more likely that the terrorists were feeling less generous since the breakdown of their deal with the authorities.

The women had been given a pretty good idea of what the alleged deceit had been. Twice that morning, eyes had appeared in the door hatch, and scanned the room before settling on the face of Sarah Holcroft. If they hadn't known before, they knew now.

Isabel put herself in the hijackers' position, something she found alarmingly easy to do. With their new knowledge they would make new demands, and these would be either accepted or rejected. If it was the latter, then the hijackers faced their moment of truth – could they kill someone in cold blood?

Of course, they might have killed someone already. She had always thought that if something happened to Docherty or the children she would know it, but maybe she was just fooling herself. Francisco had been dead for days before she found out for certain.

'We ought to do something,' Brenda Walker said, her face suddenly looming over the rim of Isabel's upper bunk. 'Play a game or something.'

She was right, Isabel thought. They were all drifting off on their own. Like paper boats on a lake. She remembered a moment in the previous week, and her daughter catching her in mid-reverie. 'You're staring at *nothing*, Mama,' Marie had said.

'Good beer?' James Pearson-Jones asked.

He and Brierley were sitting on the balcony adjoining the former's recently taken room at the Hotel Samarkand, watching the last embers of the sunset fade in the western sky. The Ambassador was nursing his second G&T, and Brierley was into his second bottle of a surprisingly fine beer.

'Not bad at all,' the SAS man said.

'Probably German in origin,' Pearson-Jones said. 'During the First World War there were several camps for German POWs in this area. Then there was the revolution in Moscow, and Russia pulled out of the war, and of course all the POWs had to be released. Only problem was, they couldn't get home. Russia was in chaos, with civil war and famine breaking out all over, so the Germans had to wait several years before they could leave. In the meantime, being Germans, several of them started breweries.'

'Interesting,' Brierley observed politely. And he supposed it was, though considerably less so than reconnaissance jaunts with beautiful majors. That bastard Stoneham! Still, at least he hadn't been sent back to London with his tail between his legs, like that idiot Kennedy. 'What's happened to the woman journalist?' he asked.

'She's still locked up,' Pearson-Jones said. He grunted. 'If I had my way they'd throw away the key.'

'Her and the rest of the media,' Brierley said sourly.

'All right, let's run through it once more,' the Ambassador said, perhaps sensing something of Brierley's mood. 'I'll go over the points, and you can correct me if I'm wrong.'

'Right,' Brierley agreed, with more enthusiasm than he felt.

'Negotiating points,' Pearson-Jones began, holding up a fist to raise fingers from. 'One, try to keep the enemy in detail-coping mode. Overload him with decisions that don't really matter.'

One finger shot up. 'Two, always ask open-ended questions, ones that can't be answered just yes or no. Three, use their own rhetoric against them when possible. So if they keep going on about God, stress what a nice guy God was, and maybe they should try a bit harder to live up to him.' He smiled at Brierley, who smiled back.

'But?'

'But four, avoid ideological confrontation. In fact don't talk about God or sex or politics if you're afraid you might enrage the enemy by doing so. This is a thin line, isn't it?'

'Very. What's five?'

'Play down the importance of the hostages. Let the enemy know that they are not the *only* factor you are taking into consideration. There are limits as to how far you can or will go to save their lives.' A thumb joined the four raised fingers. 'Christ, this is depressing.'

'I know. Six?'

'Try and divide the hostages into groups, so that you can ask for their release bit by bit. The children first, for example. And then the women.'

'One more.'

Pearson-Jones searched the sky. 'Don't tell me . . . I know, avoid completely negative responses. Even if he says he wants a night with the Queen tell him you'll see what you can do.'

Brierley grinned. 'You can tell him it's unlikely she'll be in the mood, but don't slam the door entirely. Now the three general points.'

The fingers came back down again. 'Right. One, if they set deadlines try and talk through them . . .' He stopped. 'Who are we trying to get off the hook by doing that – them or us?'

'Both.'

'Hmmm, I see. Right. Two, make sure that their access to the outside world is as much under our control as possible. Pity that wasn't done two days ago. But it is under our control now, isn't it?'

'Not completely. They could be talking to supporters by radio.'

'Yes, I suppose they could. Oh. Three, manipulate their environment . . . I'm still not clear about this.'

'You don't really need to be. It's just that in the past people have found that shutting off water, electricity, things like that, can wear down the terrorists' morale. One hostage-taker in the States actually surrendered rather than crap in front of his hostages, after the authorities cut off access to the toilet they were all using.'

Pearson-Jones sipped at his G&T. 'Sounds a bit like a two-edged sword,' he observed. 'Surely there's just as much chance of provoking a violent reaction.'

'Good point. You do have to play that one by ear.'

Pearson-Jones beamed, like a little schoolboy with a gold star.

Brierley looked at his watch. Stoneham and the Major would probably be on their way by now.

A hand on his shoulder woke Stoneham from his few hours of catch-up sleep. For a few seconds the strange surroundings disoriented him, but then he remembered he was in one of the locals' lorries. He stretched and groaned at the stiffness, and lay where he was for a few more moments, remembering the thoughts which had been spinning around in his head for what seemed like eternity as he tried to get to sleep. Bloody Jane! Even five thousand miles away she was still ruining his day. He had to talk to her, really talk to her, find out what had gone wrong.

He couldn't do that halfway up a mountain in the middle of Asia.

Work, he told himself. Concentrate on the here and now.

He edged himself the short distance to the open back of the vehicle, and found Major Ismatulayeva there waiting for him, dressed in what looked like a black boiler suit, her usually severe face looking softer in the pale light.

Work, he told himself again. 'Time to go?' he asked.

'It soon will be,' Nurhan said. She felt nervous. It was all very well insisting on taking at least an equal part in this operation – national and gender pride demanded no less – but

224

she didn't want to end up making a fool of herself. Five years ago she would have seen no reason to worry, but over the last tumultuous few years the inferiority of just about all things Soviet had become painfully obvious. Specialist training might well turn out to be another case in point. She had done courses with the Spetsnaz special forces which had stretched her to the physical and mental limit, but who knew what these wretched English supermen could do?

'Make-up?' Stoneham asked her. He took a small canvas bag from his bergen, removed a handful of tubes from the bag, set up a mirror, and began spreading a dark cream across his face. 'It's not Helena Rubinstein,' he added.

'I'll use the mirror after you,' she said. 'Let's get some things straight. Like what we want to achieve from this.'

'Who's in which room, accurate ident on weaponry, access points,' Stoneham rattled off. 'Maybe an astrology chart for each terrorist, if we can manage it.' He daubed an artistic streak of lighter cream across the dark background. 'But the one thing we have to know before we go busting in there with a full team is where the hostages are being held. Even if that's the only thing we find out, then this little jaunt will still have been well worth taking. Your turn,' he said, stepping away from the mirror.

Nurhan stepped up to it, smelling the cream before applying it. In the good old Soviet days they had been told to find any dirt that was available. 'We've got another problem,' she said. 'They've turned on the searchlight under the helicopter, and they must have placed a mirror directly underneath it, because the whole area seems flooded with light.'

'Shit,' Stoneham said in English.

She understood the tone. 'Exactly,' she said in Russian. 'There's no way we can go in from behind – the whole rock-face is lit up.'

225

'Wait a minute,' he said. 'If most of the light is being reflected upwards then the ground must be in some sort of shadow, even if it's not actually dark.'

'Maybe,' she agreed. 'There's no way to tell from here.' She turned to face him. 'How do I look?' she asked.

'Like Catwoman in *Batman Two*,' he told her. 'But I don't suppose that's reached Samarkand yet.'

'It has,' she said coldly. 'Now what about signals?'

They decided on a basic selection of hand signals, and agreed that sub-machine-guns, while decidedly useful when it came to a fire-fight, might well get in the way if silent climbing became necessary. They settled for silenced automatics, in his case a Browning High Power, in hers the German SIG-Sauer P226. Both would carry walkie-talkies, for reporting in to Sergeant Abalov if necessary, and for talking to each other if they had occasion to separate.

They walked to the head of the path they intended descending and checked out the ambient light. The new moon had just risen above the mountain in front of them, but the valley below remained deep in shadow. Stoneham didn't think they needed the Passive Night Goggles, but just to be sure he donned them. The world turned greener but no clearer. He took them off again.

She smiled for no reason apparent to Stoneham, displaying white teeth in a blackened face.

'Don't do that too often,' he warned her.

'Do what?'

'Smile. Your teeth can reflect the light,' he explained.

'I'll try not to find anything amusing,' she said drily. 'Are you ready?'

He nodded, and she turned to start down the path. It looked no more than two hundred metres in a straight line to the

226

bottom of the valley, but it was more like four by the winding path. By the time they were halfway down it seemed to Stoneham as if the rest of the world had been left behind: there were only the jagged rocks silhouetted against the star-strewn sky and a silence which was eerily complete. He felt his senses shifting into some sort of overdrive, and the familiar, almost glee-like intoxication with pure danger.

And even in the gloom he could see that she had a nicer bum than Rob Brierley.

He smiled to himself, saw Jane in his mind's eye, and felt a sudden wave of sadness wash over him. It wasn't a painful sadness though; it felt almost like an acceptance of the fact that she was gone.

They reached the bottom of the valley, where a thin swathe of dry pebbles marked the rainy season stream-bed. They could no longer see the lodge – only the aura of light which shone in the air above it. Nor could they be seen, except in the unlikely event that the terrorists had thermal-imaging equipment. Stoneham was guessing that the trick with the searchlight offered evidence that they did not.

Nurhan led off again, keeping as close to the winding stream-bed as the terrain allowed. The ground under their feet was sometimes bare rock, sometimes sandy soil with clumps of scrub-like vegetation. Visibility was often reduced by the rocks which tumbled down on either side, and which the stream-bed squeezed its twisting way between. Progress of any sort, let alone the silent progress required, was often difficult, and as they slowly climbed the valley each became more conscious of the road above and to their right, and the sentries whom they knew were watching it.

Every now and then they would stop and listen. On the first two occasions they could hear nothing but the faintest of breezes brushing against stone; on the third they heard distant voices floating down from at least fifteen metres above them. They couldn't make out any of the words, though it seemed to Nurhan that the language was Farsi.

They continued, finding that they needed to exercise ever-greater care not to dislodge loose stones on the steepening slope. The hunting lodge was only about two hundred metres away, but still visible only as a balloon of light beyond the rim of the shelf on which it sat. The last stretch was more of a climb than a walk, but at least they could tackle it in almost total darkness. As they neared the top Nurhan had the sudden memory of stepping out from the wings and on to the lighted stage for a school ballet performance.

She moved her eyes over the edge, and was almost blinded by the light. It took several seconds to make out the front of the lodge, the steep wall of rock behind the building and the shallower slopes on either side – all bathed in the reflected glow. In the foreground the bulbous shape of the transport helicopter stood in stark silhouette.

Nurhan beckoned Stoneham forward to join her, thinking what a brilliant idea it had been to mirror the searchlight. Not perfect though: the Englishman had been right – the ground wasn't in darkness, but with everything else so brightly lit a distant watcher would have a hard time picking out any movement across it. And there certainly didn't seem to be any close watchers in attendance.

Stoneham had reached the same conclusions. He raised his eyebrows at Nurhan, who hesitated for only a second before nodding her agreement. He carefully dragged his body over the rim and started moving, ever so slowly on his stomach, across the open ground towards the side of the house. She followed, thinking that someone was bound to spot them, and after ten of the thirty metres wanted to ask Stoneham if he could try speeding things up a little. She couldn't remember ever feeling more vulnerable; it was, she imagined, rather the way an ant must feel in the middle of a pavement.

But no shouts of alarm, no deadly bursts of gunfire, erupted in their direction. After what seemed hours, but was in fact slightly less than eight minutes, they reached the corner of the lodge and passed into deeper shadow. There they slowly got to their feet.

If they had only brought another four men, Nurhan thought, they could have ended this tonight. But then again, it might have been harder to get six soldiers here undetected than two. And they still didn't know where the hostages were.

But so far it had been easy, she told herself, just as the sound of footsteps inside the lodge spun both their heads round. The side door was only a few metres away, and the footsteps seemed to be heading their way. Stoneham gestured with his head and ran swiftly towards and past the door, with Nurhan at his heels. As the door opened outwards both of them pulled the silenced automatics from their belt holsters, sucked in breath and held it.

The door closed again to reveal a man walking away, an AK47 held loosely in his right hand. He disappeared around the corner of the house, chewing a hunk of bread.

Stoneham signalled for her to stay put and padded after the man. When he reached the corner of the lodge he stopped and slowly edged an eye around it. A minute later he was back beside her, drawing a diagram in the sandy soil with the end of his knife. A rectangle marked the lodge, a cross superimposed on a circle the transport helicopter, a thumb-mark the man who had just come out. He had taken up position covering the space they had just crossed, and was effectively blocking their way home.

Maybe that was his normal post, Nurhan thought, as Stoneham erased his drawing. In which case they had been extremely lucky to get this far.

But they had, and there was no point in wasting the trip. She started off towards the back of the lodge, turning another corner to find a long, narrow gap, about two metres wide, between the rock-face and the building. About four metres down they came to a window that had been thoroughly boarded up, with adjoining wooden planks nailed into the outside frame. Only the thinnest strips of light could be seen between them.

No noise was coming from the room beyond. They waited for about three minutes, hearing nothing, and were about to give up when a woman's voice suddenly broke the silence. It was faint, as if heard through more than one room. 'The water's almost gone,' it sounded like to Stoneham.

'This must be the toilet they're using,' he whispered.

'Should we try to talk to them?' she whispered back.

He shook his head. For one thing, they would need to almost shout to make themselves heard. For another, there was no way of being certain the hostages didn't have terrorist company. 'It's too risky,' he murmured.

She nodded, having reached much the same conclusion, and led off again down the back of the lodge, ducking to pass beneath several unbarred windows. At the far end they found another one lit and barred. Here male voices were dimly audible in two accents – American and Glaswegian. Docherty was still alive!

Stoneham gave Nurhan a thumbs up. They had got the info they most needed.

Now they had to get it home.

They slipped gingerly past the end door and approached the front corner of the lodge. Once more Stoneham put his eye round the edge of the building. The bread-eater was sitting about fifteen metres away, in a patch of shadow cast by the tour bus, his attention apparently fixed on the valley beyond. Their way in offered no way out.

They waited five minutes, and another five, hoping for some change in the situation. Taking the terrorist out with their silenced automatics would be easy enough, but the consequences of doing so were likely to rebound on others. There had to be a better than even chance that the other terrorists would take their revenge on one or more of the hostages.

The minutes ticked by. At this rate, she thought, they would still be here when the sun came up. There was no way up the rock-face behind the lodge, and crossing the slope in front of them would place them in plain view of the watcher. And there was always the chance that one or more terrorists would emerge from the door just behind them, trapping them between guns. Nurhan felt the beads of sweat running down her back.

Suddenly a door banged. The one at the front of the lodge. Two men exchanged a few words in Farsi, and then, just as Stoneham was about to risk another look, a man crossed their line of sight, headed out on to the road, an SMG draped over his shoulder. A minute later he disappeared from sight around the first bend, and Stoneham edged forward to check out the bread-eater.

He was no longer in his original position, and Stoneham searched the shadows for him in vain. Had he heard the front door shut again as the man walked away up the road, or was that just wishful thinking?

'I think he's gone,' he whispered to Nurhan. 'And we probably won't get a better chance.'

'Right,' she said. Anything was better than more waiting.

He checked the situation once more. 'We'll just run, OK?'

'OK.'

The syllables were hardly out of her mouth and he was gone. She sprung into motion, following his spurt across the open space, swerving past the bus, under the Mi-8's tail rotor, expecting any moment to feel bullets crashing into her body, or at the very least to hear cries of discovery. The Englishman vaulted over the rim of the steep slope leading down to the valley, and Nurhan followed, leaping into dark nothingness, and landing almost on top of him. They both lay there, breathing heavily, listening for any other sounds.

A door banged quietly, and then nothing. The man had come back out, Stoneham guessed. This had been their lucky night.

She made a downward gesture, and they started working their way laboriously down the slope. An hour later they were back at the main observation point, where Sergeant Abalov had witnessed their race across the front of the lodge. Hot tea was waiting for them.

'We need some sort of diversion at the front,' Stoneham said, examining the plan of the lodge with the help of a torch, 'and two teams ready to knock down those side doors. Unless the guards are in with the hostages – which seems unlikely – we should have no trouble getting them all out alive.'

'And how do we get the teams there?' she asked.

'Down the rock-face at the back.'

Nurhan smiled to herself. She had reached the same conclusions as the man from the famous SAS.

Nasruddin lay on the bed unable to sleep, his mind whirring. Tomorrow they would be famous, he thought. Even if Bakalev managed to censor the Uzbek papers, still the world's press would carry The Trumpet of God into homes across the planet. There would be pictures on television, recitals of their demands, and people would begin to wonder why it was that men had to do such things for truth to be heard.

He supposed his sister and brother would read the news in their morning papers, his brother on his way to work at the Wakefield business he ran, his sister at the breakfast table after the kids had gone to school. He knew that they would not understand why, but he hoped that somewhere, deep down in their hearts, they would accept that he was following the dictates of his own.

Though sometimes it was hard to share his grief, he knew that they too had lost a mother to the flames, a father to a broken heart.

He shook off the memories, and embraced the future once more. Their demands would set the whole world talking, and Britain in particular. Islam had been abused for so long in his adopted country, but the tide was turning, had perhaps already turned.

'"But they shall know the Truth,"' he murmured to himself, '"before long they shall know it . . . the Trumpet shall be sounded."'

15

The four male hostages were all woken by the rap of the hatch sliding back on the door. 'You leave in five minutes,' a voice said, and slid the hatch shut once more.

It was five forty-five and still dark outside. The men scrambled into sitting positions and stared at each other. Where were they going? The room they had occupied for the past sixty hours suddenly seemed more like home than it had before. 'Better get ready,' Docherty said, thinking it was almost amusing that they had been given five minutes' notice. The phrase 'gentlemen terrorists' came to mind, like an echo of the 'gentlemen crooks' who had peopled the thirties thrillers he had read and loved as a boy.

The four men had time to dress, have a piss and gather together their few belongings before the door swung open to reveal the familiar armed figure gesturing them out. Docherty smiled at him and led the way along the corridor which led to the outside world. Another terrorist was momentarily silhouetted in the front doorway, but stepped aside to usher them through. The large transport helicopter they had heard the day before was perched on the flat shelf in front of the building, its rotor blades reaching out across the void beyond, a bright light directly beneath its belly. The side doors were open.

As they walked towards them a man in uniform was brought out and led off on a diagonal path towards the ill-fated tour bus. He glanced across at the hostages but said nothing.

Approaching the helicopter, Docherty noticed a definite lightening of the sky above the mountain crest. The sun would soon be up. For the moment though it was still decidedly cool, and the dark interior of the chopper at least offered shelter from the wind.

The door slammed shut behind them, and the four men sat down on the floor, backs against the inside walls, and waited fearfully for the sound of rotors starting up.

Silence continued to reign, and as the minutes went by their hopes began to rise. Then the doors swung open again, and the face of Alice Jennings appeared in the space.

'Well, give me a hand,' she said.

Copley and Docherty helped her aboard, their eyes hungrily seeking out their own wives as they did so. Sharon Copley collapsed into her husband's arms with almost a sob of relief, and Isabel buried her head in Docherty's shoulder, murmuring '*A Dios gracias.*'

'How are you doing?' he asked, lifting her chin with a finger and looking into her eyes.

'OK, I guess.'

He shook his head. 'Some tour, this.'

Stoneham and Brierley were woken by one of Nurhan's men with a message to join her immediately at the observation point. They scrambled out of the lorry into the pre-dawn air and fumbled with the laces on their rubber-soled boots. 'It's probably just me she wants,' Stoneham mused. 'It was the

235

recon. She spent the night trying to forget me, and found she couldn't.'

'No one could,' Brierley agreed.

They made their way swiftly up the winding path, down the gully to the OP, and squeezed in alongside Sergeant Abalov and Nurhan. The first thing they noticed was the sound of the helicopter rotors turning; the second was the glow of the dawn above the mountain behind the lodge.

'The hostages are on board,' Nurhan told them. 'The women were brought out about ten minutes ago; the men five minutes before that.'

'What about the terrorists?' Brierley began to ask her, but at that moment two things happened. First, the whirr of the rotors abruptly went up a gear, and the Mi-8 lifted itself ponderously into the air. Second, Nurhan had to take an incoming radio call from Muratov.

'They're on their way to Samarkand,' she told the two SAS men as the helicopter glided past them on its way down the valley. 'They called Muratov to demand that the sky over the city be cleared of traffic.'

'Where in Samarkand?' Brierley asked.

'They didn't say.'

In the crisis room on the second floor of the NSS HQ, Bakhtar Muratov and James Pearson-Jones were both slumped in their seats, as if KO'd by the latest message from the hijackers. Marat got up, left the room and walked down the corridor to his own office. Samarkand, he murmured to himself, as if it were a word he'd never heard before. They would be here in half an hour, or even less. But where?

Think, he ordered himself. There had to be a reason for leaving their mountain fortress. Had cutting their phone contact with the outside world forced them to make the move? Was it publicity they wanted? Were they headed for one of the tourist spots?

His mind flicked through the possibilities. Being an atheist, he wasn't too sure how Muslims felt about using holy ground for political purposes, but he couldn't imagine them risking the destruction of mosques and *madrasahs*. In any case, the Registan didn't seem a promising place to sustain a siege. Nor did the Bibi Khanum mosque. There were no suitable spaces for a landing anywhere near the Shah-i-Zinda. Which left the Ulug Bek observatory and the Gur Emir, Tamerlane's mausoleum . . .

Marat recalled something Nasruddin's cousin had said during one of their interrogation sessions, about how much Nasruddin had loved the story of the inauspicious tomb-opening in 1941. And then he remembered suggesting Tamerlane's mausoleum himself, during the dawn conversation with Nurhan in Shakhrisabz.

He looked at his watch. Fifteen minutes had already gone by. There would be no time for concealing troops or anything like that, so what . . .?

He spun on one heel and raced out of the office, taking the wide stairway down to the ground floor three steps at a time. Still running, he headed down a corridor which led to the operations room where the surveillance equipment was stored.

'Bugs,' he told the officer in charge breathlessly.

'How many do you want?'

'Just a few. But quickly.'

The man gave him a strange look and disappeared into a maze of cabinets. The seconds ticked by.

The duty officer ambled back. 'These do?' he asked.

Marat took one look, grabbed the small box of listening devices, and stuffed them roughly into his jacket pocket as he headed back down the corridor. On his way through the front doors he slowed sufficiently to examine his watch again. He had between ten and fifteen minutes, depending on how fast they were flying the damned machine.

The Gur Emir was three minutes away by car, but even at this early hour the traffic was already building and his car was a block away in the wrong direction. He decided he could get there on foot in under ten.

Marat started running, cutting across the wide boulevard and down the first side-street which ran in the general direction of the distant blue dome. It had to be less than two kilometres away, he thought, and tried to remember how long it had been since he had run anything like that distance.

The first few hundred metres seemed surprisingly easy, and Marat was congratulating himself on being in such good shape when his breath began to grow laboured and his calf and thigh muscles started showing signs of seizing up. He pushed himself across another street, dimly aware that a passing motorist was throwing abuse in his direction, and promised himself a second visit to the NSS gym. He thanked his lucky stars he had stopped smoking.

The dome grew slowly nearer, disappeared from view, and then, just as his legs were telling him that they could go no further, suddenly appeared only a hundred metres or so away, at the end of a cul-de-sac. He jogged towards it, clambered over the ornate stone wall which surrounded the complex, and almost stumbled through a side gate into the courtyard.

His watch told him he had run out of time. His mind tried to work out where to place the devices. Put yourself in Nasruddin Salih's place, Marat told himself. Where would you put the hostages? Where would you make your HQ? There were only two obvious sites for the latter. Marat started striding towards the administrative office and felt his left thigh seize up with cramp. He rubbed it a couple of times and hobbled on, trying to ignore the pain.

The door was locked but one of the small windows had been left on a latch, slightly ajar. He reached his hand through with the self-adhesive bug and managed to clamp it above the internal window frame. There was no way of knowing how visible it was from inside the room.

The main chamber of the mausoleum was next, and here he fixed a bug beneath the rim of Tamerlane's cenotaph. The old man would have approved, Marat thought, and limped back outside.

In the eastern sky a large dot was growing even larger. Marat scurried as best he could down the courtyard and across the stretch of grass in front of the mausoleum. With the drone of the helicopter now loud in his ears, he expended what felt like his final reserves of energy in almost falling over the wall, and managed to drag himself upright behind a convenient tree.

The helicopter came down out of the still-lightening sky, and settled on the barely adequate expanse of grass in front of the Gur Emir. Chunar, who had been selected to bear word of the operation to their supporters in the city, hurried towards the rear of the complex and disappeared into the adjoining maze of streets, several days' worth of communiqués stuffed inside his jacket pocket.

Talib, meanwhile, had left two men guarding the hostages, ordered another to carry their supplies into the building, and gone off himself in search of the site's caretaker. While the latter was nervously explaining which key was which on the jangling chain at his belt, Nasruddin and Akbar walked through into the courtyard. Above them the ribbed cantaloup dome seemed to almost float above the octagonal mausoleum. Nasruddin felt a sudden pang of unfocused regret.

'Come, we must hurry,' Talib said, arriving at his shoulder.

The three men walked swiftly across to the door of the administrative office, which Talib opened with the appropriate key. Nasruddin went straight for the telephone, taking the list of news-agency numbers from his pocket as he did so.

Meanwhile the hostages had been ordered out of the helicopter at gunpoint, and ushered in through the towering gateway. Several of them recognized where they were, having walked down to view the outside of the building on the evening of their arrival four days earlier. This time they had their guide with them, Docherty thought wryly.

Across the courtyard they filed, and into the octagonal chamber where the world's largest slab of jade served as Tamerlane's cenotaph. The actual graves were in the crypt below, where tourists were not allowed to go.

Hostages were. The ten men and women were ordered down a stone stairway into the company of Tamerlane's bones, with only each other and a single electric light-bulb to keep them company.

President Bakalev was woken by the bedside phone, and instantly knew something had gone wrong. He grabbed for the receiver, scattering pills and almost knocking over the glass of water. His wife groaned and turned over.

Muratov's report exceeded the President's most pessimistic expectations. The zealots had taken over Tamerlane's mausoleum! In the middle of Samarkand! How the hell could they keep a siege in the centre of the country's second city quiet?

They couldn't, as Muratov soon made clear. The first couple of foreign journalists had already been on the phone to the local government press office.

'Don't give them anything,' was Bakalev's instinctual response.

'We'll have to give them *something*,' Muratov said.

'Just the basics then – a bunch of armed madmen have taken some hostages and occupied the Gur Emir. Stress what an insult this is – profaning the tomb of the Father of Uzbekistan.'

'Understood,' Muratov said drily.

Another question occurred to Bakalev. 'How the hell did foreign journalists get wind of this?' he asked belligerently.

Muratov had hoped to avoid that one. 'The terrorists had about half an hour's use of the phone in the Gur Emir's administrative office before anyone thought to cut it off,' he said.

Bakalev looked at his bedroom ceiling and then closed his eyes. 'They no longer have access to the outside world?'

'No. Only a direct line to us.'

'Well, that's something.' Maybe the situation could still be contained, at least for a while.

'And we have listening devices in the Gur Emir,' Muratov added. He had been saving this good news until last.

'Have you heard anything?' Bakalev asked sharply.

'Not yet – we've only just set up the reception equipment.'

'Anything else I should know?'

'I don't think so. We should be hearing their new demands soon.'

'I can hardly wait.'

In London it was almost two in the morning, but Sir Christopher Hanson had only been sleeping a short while when the call from Pearson-Jones in Samarkand was patched through to him. He listened, with a sinking sensation in his

241

stomach, to the same news with which Muratov had woken President Bakalev.

After replacing the receiver he lay back for a moment, before abruptly swinging his legs over the side of the bed and sitting up. This was going to be one of those nights, he thought. When the demands were released he would have to wake up the Prime Minister. And probably Alan Holcroft, though he didn't suppose the Foreign Minister was finding it easy to sleep these days.

He put on his dressing-gown, walked across to the window, and looked out through the gap between the curtains. A light rain was falling on the Kensington street and a couple were walking, almost dancing, arm in arm along the opposite pavement. They stopped to look in a skip and then walked happily on, oblivious to the rain, to ageing men watching them from windows, to terrorists in fabled Samarkand.

Lucky buggers, Hanson thought.

'I think it's time to tell them we mean business,' Talib said, letting himself into the Gur Emir's office. 'There's about two hundred soldiers out there, and one of them may take it into his head to be a hero.'

Nasruddin nodded, and read one last time through the list of demands they had decided on the previous evening. Then he picked up the phone and waited for the enemy to answer.

'Yes?' Muratov said, almost immediately.

'*Assalamu alaikam*, Colonel,' Nasruddin said cheerfully. He had come to enjoy these conversations, he thought. He didn't think he wanted to know why.

'Is the British Ambassador there with you?'

'I am,' Pearson-Jones said tightly.

'The first thing I must tell you both,' Nasruddin began, 'is that the hostages are being held in the crypt below the mausoleum chamber, and that if any attempt is made to rescue them – or if any action whatsoever is taken against us – then one of our men is stationed by the doorway, ready to throw a grenade down the stairs.' He allowed a slight pause before asking: 'Is that clear?'

'Very,' Muratov said quietly.

'We shall consider the stone wall that surrounds the site the border between our respective territories,' Nasruddin said. 'Any attempt on your part to cross that line will be considered the opening move of a rescue attempt, and we shall take the appropriate action. Understood?'

'Yes.'

'It is written that "Whoever fights for the cause of God, whether he dies or triumphs, We shall richly reward him".' Nasruddin allowed himself a theatrical pause before adding: 'So you see, we have nothing to lose here on earth.'

'If you say so.'

'I do. I shall now read the list of our demands.'

He cleared his throat.

'One, we demand the immediate release of all political prisoners in Uzbekistan. I have a list here of two hundred and seven men and women, which can be handed to one of your men at the gate.

'Two, we demand an extension of the current British blasphemy laws to cover Islam and other major religions.

'Three, we demand the cancellation of the trade deal about to be signed between the governments of Uzbekistan and Britain. The people of Uzbekistan will not be sold into a world of empty pleasures and materialism.

'Four, we demand payment by the British government of 500 million dollars to the Islamic Green Cross as reparation for its part in the massacre of half a million Iraqi citizens during the Gulf War.

'Those are the demands. In addition, we are prepared to exchange the hostage Sarah Holcroft for the British author Salman Rushdie.

'Copies of this communiqué will be circulated throughout this city and Tashkent during the rest of the day.'

Oh shit, Muratov thought.

'We expect a clear response by this time tomorrow,' Nasruddin concluded. 'Do you have any questions?'

Not really, Muratov thought. These were not demands that anyone with a shred of intelligence would expect to be conceded. The bastard hadn't even give them a real deadline – he just wanted a 'clear response'. No, this was a media circus in the making, a week or more of publicity for the fucking Trumpet of God.

'Mr Salih,' Pearson-Jones was saying, 'I will convey your demands in good faith to my government in London. I can even sympathize with some of them, though not of course with your methods. I am assuming you intend to release all the hostages if and when your demands are met. Might I suggest that you show good faith by releasing the two oldest hostages, both of whom must be in some danger from such a stressful situation.'

'You can suggest it,' Nasruddin said, 'but there will be no release of any hostages until all our demands are met in full. I assure you Mr and Mrs Jennings are in good health.'

There was silence at both ends of the line.

Nasruddin put down the phone and looked at Talib and Akbar. 'So far so good,' he said.

'Did they sound surprised?' Akbar asked.

'Not really. Neither of them said anything until the British Ambassador tried to start bargaining. They are already playing for time.'

Talib grunted. 'Of course. We know our demands are not going to be met. But time is not on their side. The question is: do they believe we will kill the hostages if they try anything?'

'And what if they don't?' Nasruddin said. 'They cannot take the chance that we are bluffing.'

'They will try to find out whether we are or not. Probably not today, but tomorrow, or the day after. One of their soldiers might stray accidentally across the wall, or they'll cut the phone line again, or the electricity. They'll keep pushing. They won't break our rules too blatantly but they'll try to bend them.'

'We have already decided what to do in that situation,' Akbar said. 'We must make it hard for them to find an excuse.'

'And we can always choose to ignore any minor transgressions,' Nasruddin interjected. He sat back in the chair, hands behind his head. 'And in any case,' he said with a smile, 'they'll be too busy dealing with the public outcry at their own actions. Tomorrow our second communiqué will be released, and everyone will find out how the Uzbek government was promised English gold in exchange for the Imam, and how the British government was willing to abandon all its principles just because the daughter of a minister was involved.'

'That is all very well,' Talib said, 'but there still may come a moment when we are forced to choose between killing a hostage or surrendering the initiative. If they are not going to meet our demands, they will probably have to try something else.'

'We shall just have to be vigilant,' Akbar said. 'What else can we do?'

After listening in with the others to the terrorists' conversation, Muratov left the operations van and walked the kilometre or so back to his temporary office in the NSS building. They had been given a day to formulate a 'clear response' to the demands, and Muratov was in no great hurry to hear Bakalev's appreciation of the situation. Or lack of it.

What he wasn't ready for was the violence of the President's temper. 'If this is allowed to go on for days,' Bakalev half shouted, 'there's no way we can keep it quiet. We shall end up looking indecisive, stupid, opportunistic, inept . . . you name it. Even if we manage to kill all the bastards the damage will have been done.'

'So what do you want us to do?' Muratov asked, finding a gap in the tirade.

'God knows. What I'd *like* is for you to find a way of ending this before tomorrow morning. If the whole business lasts less than twenty-four hours then it'll be forgotten just as quickly. The world press won't have time to descend on us. CNN won't have time to get their cameras here.'

Muratov examined the back of his own hand. 'And the hostages?' he asked.

'It'll look better if they're rescued,' Bakalev said. 'Or at least some of them. But first we need a good reason for going in, even if we have to invent one.'

'I'll see what I can do,' Muratov said.

'Good,' Bakalev said, and hung up.

Muratov sat at the desk for several minutes, leaning back in the chair, hands behind his head, eyes shut. Then suddenly they opened, and his lips twisted into a cynical smile. He picked up the phone again, and asked the operations room to put him through to the mobile incident room. 'I want copies of all the listening tapes sent over here,' he told Nurhan.

'So we start from scratch,' Stoneham had said, once the van doors had closed behind Muratov and Pearson-Jones. 'Tell us what's over there. What's the place called for a start?'

'The Gur Emir,' Nurhan said. 'It means Grave of the King. Tamerlane is buried in the crypt with his son Ulug Bek and about six others.' She passed across the floor plan which the Ancient Monuments department had sent over. 'The crypt is under the octagonal chamber, and there's only one entrance.'

'Great,' Brierley said sarcastically.

As the two Englishmen examined the diagram Nurhan went through a mental checklist. Two battalions of regular troops were holding the perimeter, and it had been made clear to their commanders that no one was to even lean on the stone wall, much less cross it. Men from her own unit were currently seeking out the best available vantage-points in the area surrounding the mausoleum complex. These would be used for general observation, but also be available for the half-dozen snipers who had been placed on standby. Two more members of her unit were sitting at the other end of the van with headphones on, listening to and recording the terrorists' conversation.

That had been a brilliant idea of Marat's, she thought, and wondered where he had got to. He had been in the van five minutes earlier.

She stretched her arms in the air. There was no more she could do, other than make contingency plans for a last-resort assault. And that, she guessed, would be days away – now that the terrorists were contained the bargaining would start in earnest. There would be no point in putting the hostages' lives at risk through action, unless it became apparent that they were more at risk through inaction.

There was even the building to consider. The ministries of both tourism and ancient monuments had already expressed their concern at what gunfire might do to the green alabaster tiling and blue-gold geometric panels. Blowing in the latticed windows was out of the question.

And who knew what Tamerlane would think of it all? The words 'If I am roused from my grave the earth will tremble' were allegedly written on the underside of his tombstone, and the last time anyone had tried to take a peek had been 21 June 1941. The Germans had invaded the Soviet Union the following day. A grenade exploding in his crypt might cause an earthquake. Or a nuclear war somewhere.

Her brain was addled, Nurhan thought, and for good reason – the past seventy-two hours had been decidedly light on sleep. She yawned, just as Marat reappeared with four steaming glasses of tea balanced in a cardboard box.

'And he remembered the sugar,' Stoneham said happily.

Brierley took his glass and placed it on the floor beside the floor plan. 'I think it's time we got to work,' he said.

16

Morning turned to afternoon, and the temperature kept rising as the sun started on its downward track. In the NSS building a retired sixty-eight-year-old Russian by the name of Alexander Kustamov was working on the tapes Muratov had given him, a nostalgic smile fixed almost permanently on his face. Two storeys above, Muratov was finishing a liquid lunch, and feeling a little sorry for himself. This was not why he had joined the Communist Party all those years ago.

In London the Prime Minister was watching Sir Christopher Hanson eat an early take-away breakfast of croissants and coffee, and trying in vain to prepare himself mentally for the days that lay ahead. The prospect of an extended hostage crisis, with Her Majesty's Government a distant and largely impotent bystander, was bad enough in itself. The news that the hijackers intended publicizing Britain's attempt to buy them off for Sarah Holcroft's sake was nothing short of catastrophic. The newspapers, the opposition, the goddam BBC – they would all have a field day. Except that it would go on for weeks. His chances of surviving it all were virtually nonexistent.

In the mobile incident room in Akhunbabaeva Street Brierley and Marat were trying to work out the likely location of the six terrorists they suspected were inside the Gur Emir. It had been seven, but the appearance of fly-posters around the city announcing the terrorists' demands suggested that at least one of the original seven had flown the coop immediately after their early-morning arrival.

Brierley and Marat didn't have much solid information to go on – the layout of the mausoleum complex made visual sightings hard to come by, and the thick walls of its construction had defeated the thermal image intensifiers. Basically, the two men were building their suppositions on educated guesswork, the little information offered by the two listening devices, and common sense.

Their partners of the last couple of days had both been given a few hours to catch up on their sleep, Nurhan at home, Stoneham in the British Ambassador's suite at the Hotel Samarkand. Both had gone out like lights the moment their heads hit the pillow.

In the mausoleum crypt the ten hostages were slowly adjusting to the sudden turn of events. All four couples were still feeling the relief of reunion, but the drastic down-turn in their living conditions, and the definite feeling that the stakes had been dramatically raised, made for an increase in stress levels which each individual expressed in his or her own way. There wasn't much talking as the afternoon wore on, and the little that there was was mostly confined between partners. Neither the knowledge of what lay above them, nor the tombs which filled their prison, were conducive to optimism.

The doctored tape was brought to Muratov's temporary office in the NSS building soon after three in the afternoon. He sent down for a cassette recorder and sat there wondering about the ethics of what they were about to do. There weren't any, he decided. The situation in Central Asia had gone beyond ethics: now it was a simple choice between Us and Them, between a difficult future and a swift regression to the Middle Ages. These men had to be defeated, and quickly. If that defeat also involved the death of the British hostages it was unfortunate, but not much more.

The recorder arrived. He inserted the tape, listened to the footfalls of the courier recede down the stairs, and pressed the play button.

It began with the voice of the man named Nasruddin, whom Muratov assumed to be the terrorists' leader. 'And what if they are just playing for time?' he asked.

'We have already decided what to do in that situation,' another man said. The voice was deeper, the accent probably that of a Tajik.

'Of course,' a third, rougher voice said. 'If our demands are not met by the day after tomorrow we will kill the hostages.'

'What else can we do?' the second voice agreed.

That was all there was. Muratov played it through again. It was an excellent piece of work – even though he was listening for the joins he couldn't tell where they were.

Of course it was too short, but he supposed this was only the centrepiece. More could be added to pad it out.

It wouldn't stand proper testing, but that didn't matter. There would be no court of law involved, only the press. After a couple of people had heard it then the tape could get conveniently lost or destroyed. Or even stolen by Islamic zealots in an attempt to save the reputations of the dead terrorists.

He reached for the phone.

It rang three times before the President answered it himself, sounding decidedly sleepy. Muratov explained what had been done, and then played the tape to Bakalev over the phone.

'It's brilliant,' was the President's response.

Muratov said nothing. He wanted instructions, not a blind Presidential eye.

'What's the situation like in the city?' Bakalev asked instead.

Muratov told him about the fly-posters which had begun to appear all over the old city. 'And there's a big crowd around the area we cordoned off,' he added.

'An angry crowd?'

'Not particularly. I'd say it was one of those crowds which doesn't really know its own mind yet. It could turn nasty, could turn into a street party.'

There was another pause, and Muratov could almost hear the wheels going round in Bakalev's mind. The revelations due out the next day, the sense of a populace slowly focusing its anger, the chance to end it all.

'Order your people in,' Bakalev said.

'This moment?'

'Use your discretion. But before dawn tomorrow. I will talk to the British Prime Minister, and tell him we have no choice. And send me a copy of the full tape the moment it's finished. With any luck we won't need to use it.'

Muratov listened to the click of disconnection, and turned off the recording instrument attached to his phone. He wondered how Major Ismatulayeva would like her new orders.

'Good morning, Mr President,' the Prime Minister responded dully. In London it was shortly after eleven in the morning, one of his teeth had just started aching, and another call from the President of Uzbekistan was the last thing he felt in need of. He wished he'd never heard of the damn place.

'Mr Prime Minister, we have received information which suggests that the hostages are in imminent danger. Of course,

I would not take such a crucial decision without consulting you, but from what we now know I feel certain that decisive action must be taken within the next twelve hours. Such action will involve an element of risk for the hostages, but we feel that doing nothing involves a much greater risk.'

'What is the nature of this information, Mr President?' the PM asked, hope rising in his throat. Could this be the miracle he had been praying for?

'As you probably know from your people here, the terrorists are under audio-surveillance. We have a tape of them saying that they intend to kill at least some of the hostages tomorrow if their demands are not met.'

There has to be a God, the PM thought. The matter was being taken out of his hands, and the blame for any subsequent disaster would stick to someone else.

'The experience of your men will help to minimize the risk,' Bakalev was saying.

This brought the PM back to earth, but only for a moment. He couldn't be held responsible for the proficiency of the SAS, and in any case the SAS themselves could hardly be blamed for any failure if they were operating under overall Uzbek control. They were all off the hook. 'I understand, Mr President,' he said. 'If, in your judgement, immediate action represents our best hope of saving lives, then we must take such action.'

'I am glad we see eye to eye,' Bakalev said. 'I would be grateful if you could immediately inform your people in Samarkand of your decision. I will inform mine. Let us hope for a happy outcome.'

'I agree, and thank you.' The PM put the phone down and, conscious of Hanson's eyes on him, managed to repress a smile of triumph. 'They want to go in,' he said shortly.

'Why? When?'

'Within the next twelve hours. As to why – they have found out that the terrorists intend killing hostages from tomorrow.'

'Found out? How?' Hanson asked suspiciously.

'Audio-surveillance. They have a tape.'

I bet they do, Hanson thought. He hadn't spent most of his life fighting the KGB without knowing what they were capable of. And MI6 had manufactured a few fake tapes of its own down the years.

'I think my toothache's gone,' the PM said suddenly.

Hanson looked at him. There were only two groups of people, he realized, who had ever had an interest in prolonging this business – the hijackers and the hostages. And both were expendable.

The name Simon Kennedy flickered across Hanson's mind, and he found himself hoping that the SAS had sent better men to Uzbekistan than he had.

Muratov and Pearson-Jones arrived at the mobile incident room together, shortly after four-thirty in the afternoon. They found Nurhan, Marat and the two Englishmen considering the aftermath of a simulated rescue bid, with black, blue and red pieces of folded card representing the hijackers, hostages and rescuers. None of the black pieces were still upright, but neither were four of the blue ones.

'Comrades,' Muratov began, inadvertently slipping into historic usage, 'our governments have taken a decision. You will mount a rescue operation tonight.'

Eight eyes opened wide with surprise. Nurhan was the first to react vocally. 'What!? Why? I don't understand. Every expert in the world agrees that such situations should be played long.' She looked at Muratov, more bewildered than angry.

'Those are your orders, Major,' Muratov said lightly. 'The whys are in the political realm.'

That was not what she wanted to hear. 'If you think . . .' she began.

Brierley cut her off in the same language. 'These are British lives at stake,' he told Pearson-Jones. 'Does London really support this?'

'Yes,' Pearson-Jones said quietly, not looking Brierley in the eye. 'It has been decided that a speedy end to the crisis will be in everyone's interest.'

Brierley indicated the fallen blue figures on the table. 'I don't think the hostages would agree with you,' he said coldly.

'If you want to help them,' Pearson-Jones said in English, 'then I suggest you stop worrying about why and start thinking about how.'

Brierley waved an arm angrily, but said nothing more.

Nurhan wasn't finished. 'If I'm to lead my men into a situation like this then I think an explanation is in order,' she said quietly.

'I can't give you one,' Muratov told her. 'It's not in my control.' He was wondering how she and Marat would react if and when the faked tape had to be used. Angrily at first, no doubt. But she would understand the need. They were all on the same side in the end.

She bowed her head. If someone had to lead her unit in, then she would rather it was her.

'Who dares wins,' Stoneham muttered.

'I've been in some strange places in my time,' Docherty observed, 'but this really takes the biscuit.'

He had an arm round Isabel's shoulder as they sat against one of the tombs in the dimly lit crypt. It was decidedly cool now, though not at all damp. The other eight hostages were scattered round the room, like children playing hide-and-seek in a graveyard.

He wondered if anyone was coming to find them.

Across the crypt someone was softly crying – Sharon Copley, it sounded like. Docherty could just about hear the murmur of her husband's voice as he tried to comfort her.

'I could do with a pint of Guinness,' Isabel said softly.

'Aye. With spring-onion-flavoured crisps. Outside on a summer evening. That pub we found on Mull that was miles from anywhere.'

'Where Marie threw the dart into the German tourist's leg.'

'That's the one.'

She looked up at him with a smile. 'I want you to know how much I love you,' she said.

It was rapidly growing dark now, and the dome of the Gur Emir was a deepening silhouette against the western sky. Brierley and Stoneham stood looking at it from the other side of Akhunbabaeva Street, imagining the ten hostages gathered in the crypt below ground level.

'If we could only find some way to give them advance warning,' Brierley murmured. 'It obviously can't be visual, so it has to be sound of some sort . . .'

'Eleven gunshots,' Stoneham suggested, not very seriously.

'Brilliant. First off, they'd have no reason for counting them, or at least not until it was too late. Second, they'd have no reason to think it was a message at all, let alone one aimed at them. Third, even if all that's pure pessimism on my part, and they're all happily counting up to eleven and saying, "Hey, that means there's a rescue coming in at eleven o'clock tonight", what makes you think the hijackers wouldn't have come to exactly the same conclusion?'

Stoneham grinned at him. 'No one can rubbish an idea like you can,' he said with mock admiration.

'Well, think of a better one. It has to be something they'll know is aimed at them.'

'And something they will recognize but the hijackers won't.'

'Right,' Brierley agreed, 'so what separates them?'

'They're foreigners,' Stoneham said, only half in jest. 'Different cultural references. I bet none of the hijackers would know who Arthur Daley was . . .'

'Or recognize the *Coronation Street* theme music,' Brierley mused.

'Except for Salih,' Stoneham reminded him. 'In most ways he's as British as we are.'

'Shit, yes.'

The two men stood in silence for a few moments, watching the orange sky turn yellow-green behind the mausoleum.

'I've got an idea,' Stoneham said eventually.

'I hope it's better than the last one.'

Stoneham ignored that. 'You ever see the film *Rio Bravo*?' he asked.

'Probably.'

'Well, John Wayne and Dean Martin and the others are holed up in this town with a prisoner, and the prisoner's brother has the town surrounded, and there's this slow Mexican music playing in the distance and John Wayne says it's getting on his nerves and why haven't they heard from the chief bad guy. And Ricky Nelson looks up at him and says something like "He's talking to us now." Turns out the music is some sort of death march, which means no quarter will be given when the time comes.'

'You think we should try scaring this bunch to death?'

'No, you idiot. I'm saying we should use music. That's culture-specific, isn't it?'

'Not really. You can hear Michael Jackson anywhere.'

'Make it even more specific then. How old is Docherty? What sort of music does he like?'

'He's about forty-five. If he likes rock, then it would probably be the sixties stuff he grew up with . . .'

'That would be perfect. Salih is almost twenty years younger, so the chances are he wouldn't recognize it.'

'Sounds good. But what sort of song has the word "eleven" in it?'

'God knows. But . . .' Stoneham's face lit up. 'I've got it. Remember the song "In the Midnight Hour"?' He sung the first line softly – '"Gonna wait till the midnight hour . . ." We can put the op back an hour.'

'Maybe,' Brierley agreed, grinning in spite of himself. 'But what if Docherty's an opera freak and Salih's got a huge collection of American soul records back in Bradford. And how the hell do we find a copy of the record in Samarkand, or are you planning to sing it at the top of your voice?'

'Don't quibble,' Stoneham said. 'These are all mountable obstacles, as my grandad used to say whenever my grandma let him watch *Charlie's Angels*.'

It was early in the afternoon when the call came through to Dave Medwin. He heard the request, and asked for an explanation, but none was forthcoming. Salih's sister was the best bet, he decided, and reached for the phone.

'Is there any more news?' she asked, after he'd identified himself.

'Not that I know of,' he told her.

'Then what . . .'

'This may sound like a daft question,' Medwin said, 'but can you tell me what Martin's musical tastes are? And were.'

In Hereford, meanwhile, Barney Davies was phoning round the men who had seen serious service with Docherty. He eventually got what he wanted from Razor Wilkinson.

The Londoner's old Platoon Commander was apparently more than a little partial to Motown. 'You know what Scots are like – if they don't have a strong beat they lose concentration when they're dancing, and they fall over,' Razor told the Regimental CO, before it occurred to him that the original request for information was somewhat unusual. He found it even more upsetting when Barney Davies refused to tell him anything more.

In London, MI6 had dispatched a secretary to Denmark Street in a taxi, and her fifteen-minute search through several shops finally turned up sheet music for both 'In the Midnight Hour' and – another Stoneham contribution – Gladys Knight & The Pips' 'Midnight Train to Georgia'. These were then faxed via the British Embassy in Tashkent to the NSS building in Samarkand, where a young Uzbek music student was waiting with his tenor saxophone.

Darkness had fallen in the world outside, but to those entombed in the crypt the coming of night showed only on their watches. The single bare light-bulb gave off its meagre glow, aided and abetted by the light filtering down through the open doorway at the top of the steps.

The atmosphere was better than it had been a couple of hours earlier, offering new confirmation of the old adage that, given enough time, it was possible to get used to just about anything. All ten of them had played the alphabet film game, and had followed it up with a biographical Twenty Questions. Alice Jennings had survived her twenty as Amelia Earhart, but Mike Copley's Tamerlane had just fallen at the third. It was in the middle of Brenda Walker's 'dead, female and not English' that Sharon Copley first noticed the sound of distant music.

Once she had picked it up, the others strained to do the same. Some could, some couldn't – it was very faint. Docherty suggested they move around the crypt in search of the best reception, and they all did so, feeling rather silly, like adults playing a children's game.

But it worked. For some strange reason the acoustics were best in the unlikeliest of positions – deep inside the alcove behind the stone steps. It was a single instrument that was being played, a brass instrument of some sort. And the tune was one that Docherty, both Copleys and Elizabeth Ogley recognized immediately: 'In the Midnight Hour'.

Only Docherty and Sharon Copley recognized the succeeding 'Midnight Train to Georgia'.

'Midnight,' the Scot said softly, excitement in his voice. The other nine faces all looked his way, as if they were waiting for his instructions. In the yellow light each face seemed to reflect a different blend of fears, hopes and anxieties.

The saxophonist now seemed to be improvising, and for a few moments Docherty wondered if it was only an enormous coincidence. But then the player reprised the opening line of 'Midnight Hour', before striking out on his own once more.

'Gonna wait till the midnight hour . . .' It was no coincidence. There was a bunch of lunatics from Hereford out there.

Upstairs, all the doors in the octagonal chamber were closed, and the music was only slightly more audible. Nasruddin, sitting in one of the cushions they had brought in from the adjoining chambers of the *madrasah*, thought at first it might be a signal of some sort, and got to his feet to listen more closely.

Minutes went by and nothing happened, except that the musician seemed increasingly uncertain of what he was playing. It had to be a music student who lived in one of the houses behind the Gur Emir, Nasruddin decided, busy practising vaguely familiar Western tunes on his Western instrument. He probably wanted a job in one of the hotel bands, and dreamed of appearing on one of the new pop music TV shows.

He had liked such music once himself, Nasruddin thought. The Jam, the Clash, Talking Heads. He remembered getting his mother to listen to the Sex Pistols' 'God Save the Queen'. She had been outraged.

He leaned up against the enormous jade slab which marked the spot above Tamerlane's grave in the crypt below, and looked up at the ceiling, which seemed to sparkle like faint silver stars in the dim light. This is paradise, he thought, as seen from death's entrance door.

The other five men were also in the chamber – Shukrat and Akbar standing sentry by the north and south doors respectively, while Sabir and Farkhot slept on beds of cushions by the wall between the north and east doors. Across the chamber from them, Talib was squatting beside the top of the steps which led down to the crypt, AK47 in one hand, grenade in the other, an open Koran between his knees. Nasruddin didn't see how Talib could read in such light, but then his cousin seemed to know most of the suras by heart in any case.

In the mobile incident room, once the plan of assault had been agreed, the evening seemed to crawl by. It had been argued by Brierley, and somewhat reluctantly conceded by Nurhan, that using the entire Anti-Terrorist Unit would be counter-productive. There were only a limited number of entrances to the mausoleum, and it would be easier to reach them in silence with five men than twenty. For much the same reason, it had been decided that, with the exception of the sector including their point of ingress, the cordon of regular troops deployed around the mausoleum complex would be given no advance information of the rescue bid. The Unit's two sniper posts would be in constant touch with the assault party in case the need for covering fire arose, but most of those in the vicinity would only know something was happening when the first shots rang out.

The figure of five had originally been suggested by Nurhan, mainly on the grounds that the members of her unit should at least outnumber Englishmen when it came to operations in Samarkand. She got her ways as regards the number, but Marat's insistence on being one of the five – 'I'm head of the Tourist Protection Unit, and if this isn't tourist protection then I don't know what is' – meant that only Sergeant Abalov could be included from the Unit.

The composition of the team once settled, the one woman and four men had gone over the plan twice. Once certain they knew what was expected of themselves and each other, they had driven the incident room around the other side of the complex and settled down to wait, mostly in silence, for the appointed hour to arrive. Brierley's thoughts were only of the operation to come, but Stoneham couldn't keep images of Jane and his unnamed son from occupying his mind. Nurhan occasionally caught Marat looking at her, and wondered whether she would risk going out with him. He was finding that daydreaming about making love to her was one of the better ways of coping without a drink.

At eleven-fifteen they started on their final preparations, and at exactly eleven-thirty they filed out of the mobile incident room and into the street. It was a clear night, with the stars dazzling in the sky above, and a yellow crescent moon only recently emerged from behind the mountains. The two SAS men were carrying Heckler & Koch MP5SD sub-machine-guns, the three Uzbeks Kalashnikov AK74s, the upgraded version of the AK47. The two MP5s had aiming point projectors fixed above the barrels, the three Soviet weapons a more primitive but equally effective torch.

The two SAS men were carrying spare magazines for the MP5s in pouches on their left hips, and one spare magazine for the holstered High Powers on their right wrists. Brierley also carried the Remington 870 shotgun, Abalov the rope ladder. All five of them were wearing body armour and communications helmets, and carrying stun grenades, CS gas grenades and gas respirators.

At eleven-forty they reached the low stone wall which had been declared inviolate by the terrorists, and halted for something like five minutes, scanning the moonlit ground in front of them with both the naked eye and nightscopes. Nothing was moving. The terrorists, as expected, were all inside the complex walls.

Brierley led the way across the wall, closely followed by Nurhan, and the five of them walked swiftly across the short, yellowed grass towards the four-metre wall which surrounded the courtyard. Stoneham got down on his haunches for Brierley to climb aboard his shoulders, then straightened himself out to lift the senior man up the wall. With his eyes only an inch or so beneath the top, Brierley took a deep breath and heaved himself up on to the top of the wall. A few bits of stonework fell down the far face and landed with a pattering sound on the stonework below.

Brierley didn't move for a full minute, his ears straining for any sound in the courtyard below. There was none, and he slowly moved himself into a position from which he could verify with his eyes what his ears had already told him, that nothing was moving in the courtyard beneath him but the branches of the trees away to his right. Slightly to his left, some twenty metres away, the south door to the mausoleum chamber was closed.

So far so good.

He beckoned for Nurhan to join him. Stoneham did the honours once more, and Brierley helped her up on to the wall beside him. Abalov then sent one end of the ten-metre rope ladder spinning up towards them, rather like a fisherman casting his tackle. Brierley lowered half the ladder down the inner face of the wall, checked that Abalov and Stoneham were ready to take his weight, and swiftly descended to the ground. Nurhan followed him. The two of them held the ladder for Stoneham to climb up the other side, and then Marat and Abalov took the strain as he climbed down into the courtyard.

Brierley looked at his watch, and raised four fingers to show the others it was four minutes to midnight. While Marat and Abalov worked their way around to the entrances which opened off the corridors from the north and east doors, the other three squatted down in the shadows beneath the wall and put on their respirators. They looked, Stoneham thought, like Dr Who's Cybermen.

At exactly one minute to midnight they rose together, Brierley and Nurhan heading for the east door, while Stoneham, still wishing he had a more active role, made for the side door which constituted the terrorists' last possible escape hatch. As they walked stealthily across the courtyard the sound of loud talking, even shouting, could be heard from inside the mausoleum chamber.

Nasruddin heard it too. He had only left the octagonal chamber a few minutes before, having passed through the north door and into the adjoining administrative office in search of a pencil to copy down a particularly beautiful line from the Koran's 'Night Journey' sura. He walked back through, and found everything as normal.

'They wanted more water,' Talib explained from his position at the top of the steps. 'Akbar has gone down.'

Nasruddin nodded and checked his watch. It was midnight. He looked up suddenly, his mind racing with the words 'Gonna wait till the midnight hour . . .' That was the song.

It had been a signal.

Ten metres away, on the other side of the south door, Nurhan stood to one side, wondering what the Ancient Monuments people would say if they could see what Brierley was aiming the Remington at.

The gun boomed once, twice, and the hingeless door tottered for a second before Brierley shoved it aside. He and Nurhan flattened themselves against the edges of the frame, hurling stun and CS gas grenades through the opening as they did so. A dazzling light flashed out across the courtyard as the thunder sounded.

In the crypt the first blast of the shotgun jerked Akbar's head around, and Docherty launched himself across the three-metre space between them, hitting the Tajik with the concentrated force of an American linebacker in full motion. The AK47 went off, scattering bullets across the ceiling, and then flew out of the terrorist's hand as he hit the floor. Docherty landed on Akbar's chest with a force which probably broke several ribs, and a horrible wheezing noise erupted from the man's throat.

Nurhan and Brierley had stepped through the doorway, the siting-lights on their SMGs searching for targets. A man came into view directly across the chamber, coughing and spluttering. Two concentrated bursts slammed him against the far door.

On the wall to the right one man was halfway to his feet, another trying to bury himself in his hands. Both died instantly, their blood splattered across the onyx marble panels which lined the wall behind them.

Nurhan's torch beam moved right, just in time to catch a door closing behind someone. Brierley's moved left, and the lighted red dot from his aiming point projector alighted on a man's face. He pulled the trigger just as the face dropped from sight down the steps leading to the crypt.

Docherty looked up to see Talib bumping his way down the first few steps, took in the grenade in the terrorist's hand, the eyes that still seemed to burn in the bloody shattered face, and lunged for Akbar's AK47. As the Scot turned, his fingers reaching for the unfamiliar trigger, Talib, his broken face a study in demented concentration, drew the pin from the grenade, and stared around in triumph. Docherty fired, ripping the man's chest apart, and with a last loud sigh Talib crumpled forward on the steps, the hand that still held the grenade crushed beneath him.

A few seconds later it exploded, showering the crypt with a martyr's flesh.

Nasruddin had instinctively pulled the door shut behind him as he stepped back into the passageway. It was over, he thought, and that was cause for sadness, but somehow he felt a sense of relief.

He stood in the corridor for only a second, and then calmly opened the door of the chamber opposite the administrative office. He walked across it, and waited for a moment by the door leading out into the courtyard. The only sounds he could hear were coming from the corridor he had left behind.

Nasruddin pulled back the bolts and opened the door on to the night.

A man in a helmet was silhouetted against the stars, as he had been all those years before.

Nasruddin had no weapon, but it would have made no difference if he had. His limbs were frozen in the shock of recognition, and his finger on a trigger would have needed a thousand times the time it took for Stoneham's MP5 to blow his life away.